THOMAS SI

Blackened

First published by Independently published 2020

First edition

ISBN: 9798581801697

Cover art by Ian Robson at Suit Suit Studio

This book was professionally typeset on Reedsy.
Find out more at reedsy.com

Dedicated to you
2020 has been some ride

Prologue

The forest whispered a name, the name was Poveglia. It was a warning, a caution to those who dared approach the island. Placed by history in the Venetian lagoon, its history spoken in hushed tones. The real evils that man had committed there quickly gave birth to fear and superstition as its truth became myth.

A violent gust whistled through the trees and made its way to the asylum. It was never christened with an official name. The locals on the neighbouring islands preferred to ignore its existence. It was a blight on their community. A foreboding stain of depravity that only served as a reminder that their undesirables could be locked up but not forgotten. Yet there it sat. Looming and menacing. Its bell tower pierced the skyline: a black silhouette against dark clouds that smothered the moon.

The asylum had contained three hundred and forty-five patients at the height of its use. By that November night in 1947, it was home to a hundred and four. Sixteen of them were locked up in the prison building, assessed as being so dangerous they could never function in society. They were the boogeymen who lived in stories told to frighten children. The rest of the patients were classed low risk and were housed in the main building. Posing little danger, they were allowed to socialise with each other. Those who would unlikely recover from experimental procedures were deemed the lowest risk of all.

The gale rattled the front doors of the asylum. Nurse Rossi startled at the disruption. She looked up from her desk to see if the disturbance troubled any of the patients. Caged in their ward, they slept soundly. As did the orderly that was meant to be watching them. They may have posed little risk, yet the authorities took no chances when it came to lights out. For as much their own safety as that of the staff.

Rossi was weary of the weather, concerned that her boat back to Venice would be cancelled. She had only worked on Poveglia for three months. Unlike her colleagues, she was yet to be accustomed to its presence. A presence even the most experienced staff could not ignore. They were more than happy to leave the island at the end of their shift.

Rossi was smart and logical. The asylum was only a building. Buildings had history, but they did not have any desire. They possessed neither the ability nor capacity for ill will. Its inhabitants, however, were men. Men with wants and thoughts, the flair for violence - even those who wished her good day. There hadn't been an incident in her time there, but she knew the stories. The rumours that twisted with the facts. How a male orderly had his throat ripped out by a patient who sunk his teeth in without provocation. Or how a female nurse was accidentally locked in the prison cells one night, her remains never found.

Urban legends, like most stories, had an element of truth. Poveglia was no different and although Rossi feared little of that which went bump in the night, she had nothing but respect for the dangers that lurked within those walls. Even though she was safe- as safe as could be - she never took her security for granted. Perhaps it was the essence of the asylum itself that kept her alert. For that, she was at least thankful.

The wind was ferocious and showed no sign of letting up. Rossi looked at her watch. 10:30 p.m. Half an hour of her shift remained and forty-five minutes before the boat left. She was the last person on duty scheduled to leave the island. Only the orderlies were required to work the nights, no nurses were needed, not since Dr Paolo agreed to cover those shifts. The man was an enigma. He practically lived on Poveglia, after he arrived on the island in 1933, some say the last time he left it was in 1945. Rossi was intimidated by him, both professionally and personally. His work on psychology and the biology of the brain was without peer. Yet, he was a controversial figure in the medical community. A name that was spoken in hushed whispers. His dedication to his work on Poveglia fuelled many rumours. Rossi chose not to dwell on such tales, yet there was something about the doctor that made her shiver. She found him highly intelligent with a cold charm. A charm that made her feel uneasy whenever he spoke. Thankfully she had little interactions with him. It was for the best.

As she let the thought slip from her mind, there he was. His short, thin stature didn't make him any less imposing. He walked with an authority that commanded respect, or fear, dependent on the circumstances. Rossi felt both. She was surprised to see him and was unsure as to why he had come to speak to her. She hoped it was nothing important. Nothing pressing that couldn't wait until morning.

As he approached her desk, Paolo's gaze shifted to the orderly in his chair. A hulking man whose name he couldn't remember. He cleared his throat loudly - the man, Costa, woke with a snort. As his eyes slowly focused on Paolo, distress rushed through him. He leapt out of his chair, almost tripping as he rose.

"Apologies Dr Paolo," he said. "I must have nodded off for a second." Costa towered over the smaller man physically but cowered at his superiority.

Dr Paolo didn't respond, not verbally anyway. His eyes drilled into the orderly. A silent warning that was heeded. He turned his attention back to Rossi, his features softer and warmer.

"Good evening Nurse," he said. I wasn't expecting to find you still here at this time."

"Good evening Doctor," she replied. "I've still half an hour of my shift, and plenty to keep me occupied until then."

"Yes, I'm sure you do. Our nurses are unsung heroes, that's what I always say. No one would ever find you neglecting your duties." He gave a sideways glance to Costa, who stood with eyes still lowered in shame.

Rossi smiled nervously. She liked Costa, found him friendly, if a little work-shy. Still, she daren't side against Paolo. Her own eyes lowered as she shifted her attention back to the files in front of her. Her concentration had abandoned her.

Paolo's gaze turned to the main door. The wind whistled through any cracks in the frame it could find. "It's a bad storm, nurse..." he looked at her name tag. "Rossi. Why don't you get your belongings and make sure you get on that boat? You're the only one they'll be waiting on at this time and I wager the captain will be anxious to set off."

Paolo smiled, and Rossi felt a chill crawl down her spine. Afraid this was some sort of test, she had to at least show a semblance of loyalty to her work.

"Are you sure?" she asked, her voice hopeful that the original offer would not be withdrawn.

"Of course," he replied. "I'm more than confident that our narcoleptic friend and I are more than capable of covering your thirty minutes. Also, I won't tell anyone if you don't." He raised a finger to his lips, his eyes narrowed with devious glee.

The storm continued to build in the heavens, the clouds stirred as they prepared to unleash their fury upon Poveglia. Nurse Rossi was thankful for the small reprieve.

"Thank you, Doctor," she said. "I'll see you tomorrow perhaps." Perhaps not, she hoped, but she was thankful for getting away. She gathered her things and clasped a hand on the main door. She turned to wave as Dr Paolo stood at her station. He waved back as Costa stood to attention at his post.

She opened the door and was surprised at the stillness that greeted her. It didn't last. As she left the building, a ferocious gust slammed the door shut behind her. Rossi jumped in fright, her handbag almost slipped from her. The path to the waterfront walkway was poorly lit, but she could see it. The rain fell slightly but the sky teased it would worsen. Rossi increased her pace, hoping to get on the boat before it did.

When she got to the waterfront, the sky fulfilled its promise and unleashed a torrent of rain. The wind slowed its attack slightly before rhythmically beating Rossi. She lowered her gaze to shield her eyes. The walk to the dock wasn't far, as long as she could see the path she didn't fear falling into the lagoon. The wind rocked her, but she retained her balance with her goal in mind: the craving for the shelter of home was enough motivation to brave the storm.

She elevated her gaze to see the wooden dock. The rain

stung her face as her eyes adjusted to the blackness. They widened in horror. The dock was empty. The boat was gone. It must have left early. The captain must have panicked at the weather. But he wouldn't leave her, right? He wouldn't leave knowing he'd be abandoning her? Knowing he was confining her to a night at the asylum? He wouldn't, he just wouldn't.

But he had. The boat was gone and Rossi was trapped. Trapped on the forsaken island with only one place to go. One place to shelter. She cursed the captain and all his crew before slowly turning back towards the asylum.

The wind howled as the rain came down, soaking her before she made it back to the front door. She tried the door handle. Locked. Panicking, she banged on the door, her hands stung against the metal as her dull clang went unanswered. Alarm seized her. She couldn't spend all night outside, not in this weather. She pounded the door again, her cries for help carried away by the wind.

Close to defeat, she wracked her brain for any solution. Surely there had to be another way in. Her job only allowed her to work in specific areas of the asylum, however she recalled her first day when she was given a tour of the grounds. Where else could she go, even if just to get some shelter? There was the old bell tower. But that was condemned, she had no idea how safe it was to enter. She filed it under last resort. What else? There was the prison. It scared her too much. With the cuts to funding, she wasn't even sure if it would be manned. She knew Costa had been asked to check in on the patients there from time to time. What about the hospital? Yes, that was it. Patients were rarely admitted there; most procedures could be performed in the main building. It would be quiet. She could find a bed as well as shelter.

Rossi stayed as close as she could to the wall while the storm got stronger. The saltwater from the sea licked at her face as the rain got heavier. As she approached the hospital's door, she summoned up the last of her strength and threw herself at it. The door opened with ease and she crashed through it onto the hard floor. The storm followed her and she felt great relief when she closed the door and shut it out.

The nurse's station was small and empty. The room dark and full of shadows. The dust that gathered was a reminder of the little use the building had seen in recent times. Rossi was just glad to be out of the storm, yet her contentment was short-lived. Her clothes were soaked and the room was cold. An unnatural chill saturated the air that reminded her of her first night shift in the asylum. She was grateful to have found shelter. It didn't mean she felt safe. She had to get out of her wet clothes and warm herself. Hopefully, there'd be a change of clothes in one of the lockers. She could steal some blankets and find a bed. Yes, things weren't too bad after all. She stumbled about in the dark, careful not to trip on any unseen obstacles. She needed some luck on her side. As if a prayer had been answered, a flash of lightning momentarily lit the room allowing her to see a doorway. Her answered prayer came with a price as it also revealed the horror that stood in her way. A figure adorned in black stood in that same doorway, a large hooked nose prominent on its grotesque face. She yelped as she fell backwards, her mind struggling to comprehend what she had just seen. Another flash of lightning lit up the room. The figure was gone.

This is silly, she thought to herself. Her mind played tricks on her, she just had to remain focused. She made her way to the door, carefully. Afraid of tripping, afraid of the unknown.

Afraid of her own imagination. Anxiety crept in as it flirted with the irrational side of her brain. As she entered the corridor, the storm was silenced. The calm should have soothed her. Instead, she missed the familiar noise. Staying close to the wall, she was unable to make out shadows. If she just kept to the wall she'd come across a light switch sooner or later. As she focused on logic, rationality and hope; her mind began to wander and fill the emptiness. The noise formed into a teasing melody. Although faint and unrecognisable, it was unmistakably music. Music meant people, but who was left on the island? Dr Paolo was a known music fan; her colleagues often spoke of hearing records playing from his office. Yet, his office was so far from where Rossi stood. Unless tending to a patient, she couldn't think of why Paolo would bother with visiting, or indeed working, in the hospital but it was a small lifeline for her to cling onto.

She made her way down the dark corridor, the wall was damp and cold, it made her skin crawl. Goosebumps formed and her teeth chattered as she honed her hearing in on the music. It was her only guide, her vision deteriorated with each step into the black. Her fingers clung to the wall, feeling every imperfection in the brickwork. Her nails gently scraped the brick for fear of falling into nothing.

Minutes seemed like hours as the music got gradually louder. Finally, a sliver of light appeared, and Rossi hurriedly ran towards it. As the corridor neared the end, the light got brighter. She turned a corner and saw a double door. Solid with a slight gap where they closed, the source of the light and music lay behind it.

Yet Rossi hesitated. Something deep within her gut screamed at her to flee. Turn back, go no further. Irrational.

Silly. She'd laugh about this one day, she thought. Still, she approached the door with apprehension. The gap, though small, was large enough for her to see into. The music was so profound now she could hear the crackle of the vinyl. Voices. Unintelligible. Hushed. Her eyes scanned the room for what she could see. There he was. Dr Paolo. Dressed for surgery, his back to her. Her eyes followed him over to an operating table. Until she saw it she wasn't even aware that she was peering into the operating theatre. Strapped down on the table and very much conscious lay a man familiar to her. It was one of the patients. His eyes bulged with wonder and with no fear. There was a natural calmness in his face. The man was not afraid, unlike Rossi. She wondered if he should be.

The patient's head was strapped down. Paolo approached him with a methodical walk, whistling the music he listened to. He had a surgical instrument in his hand. Rossi recognised it, it was a leucotome, a tool used for lobotomies. A cold vice tightened on her heart. Yet she did not run. She was scared to take her eyes from Paolo. He made his way to the opposite side of the patient, allowing his uninvited audience a full view of what was to happen. He placed the leucotome down on his tray and picked up something that frightened her more so. A drill.

The rational part of her brain struggled to calm her down. Sure, Dr Paolo was a professional, an expert in his field, he was more than qualified to perform such a procedure. Alone, at night. Paolo placed the drill against the temple of the patient, his hand carefully placed on the handle. And then he began to turn it. The patent's placid demeanour left him and he screamed in agony. Rossi had never seen a lobotomy performed live before but she knew this was not how it was done. The bone fractured as the drill twisted the flesh and ripped open a hole in the skull. Satisfied with this work, Paolo placed the drill upon the tray and picked up the leucotome. The patient's cries echoed the internal screaming that went on deep within Rossi, but she was too scared to make a sound. Whispers swirled around the room, but she had no idea who was voicing them. They were gleeful, encouraging. Aimed at Paolo, they instructed him.

Rossi's breathing became rapid and shallow. She watched Paolo insert the leucotome into the skull when the patient's eyes flickered towards her. He could see her. He could see her and there she stood, cowering. Doing nothing. The voices got louder, filled with ecstasy at Paolo's act. Her eyes looked at the doctor. His shadow was unnatural, misshapen. It grew up the wall and appeared to detach itself from the stone. It was ghastly. An abomination of decency. The whispers suddenly stopped and so did Paolo. The shadow appeared to turn. Towards the door. Towards Rossi. She had no idea what she was looking at but she was certain of one thing. It was looking at her. Having seen enough, she ran.

With little light to guide her way, Rossi threw herself back into the darkness. The music faded until it abruptly stopped. He knew she was there. Tears fell from her face as she ran and ran. She tripped, falling so hard she fractured bones in her arm. She couldn't stop. Not now. Not ever. She had to run and get out of there. To escape. To where? She remembered she was on an island. Escaping the hospital didn't mean escaping Paolo. Costa. If she could get to Costa, he would help her.

She crashed into a corridor wall, screaming in anguish as her fractured bone hit the brick. She paused momentarily, allowing the pain to paralyse her. She summoned all her strength and ran, leaning against the wall for guidance. By luck, she found herself back at the entrance and back outside, in the storm. The weather was more violent than before, the wind-battered her as rain stung her face. Whispered voices carried through the wind. Voices that didn't make sense. She ran towards the trees which provided some shelter from the weather. With no idea where to go, she continued through the trees until she saw a clearing. There it stood, her salvation. The island's small church. She'd never used it herself, but she knew of it, only wishing she had thought of it as a refuge earlier. Mercifully the doors were open. She slammed the door shut and dragged herself down to the altar and hid behind a pew. Feeling safe, she assessed the damage. She ripped a piece of her shirt to make a crude sling for her arm. With one free hand, she gripped it tightly and prayed. She prayed intensely and with such focus, she hadn't noticed that she was not alone.

1

Julia gripped the armrests tightly as the plane made its descent. This was the part she hated the most. Her eyes fixated on the toddler in the seat in front of her. His wide eyes looked at her, he couldn't have been any older than two. The toddler had been quiet for most of the journey. A small mercy for someone that hated flying as it was. His face was calm, his eyes lacked much wonder or concern. How she envied him.

She dreaded the flights. Roughly ten hours in the sky between home, London and Italy with nothing but certain death below. She'd never missed the ground of New York as much as she did at that moment. Soon she'd land and it couldn't come quick enough. Julia looked over at her husband Lawrence, her brand-new husband of one week, three days and seventeen hours to be precise. Married on the 30th of June 2017, many felt he took his time proposing considering how long they'd been dating. Oh, how he slept comfortably, no care for the impending doom that threatened every moment they remained in the steel coffin.

She was tempted to wake him but decided against it. He looked so peaceful and besides, his predictable and incessant attempts to calm her down would've added to her already building anxiety. Flying was a luxury for some, yet an unfortunate necessity for Julia, especially if she ever wanted to see Italy. Yes, the flight was tense for the nervous flyer she was but Italy was approaching and the honeymoon could commence.

The plane continued its descent, smooth and flawless. Julia began to feel at ease. *This pilot is on the ball,* she thought. After hours of being trapped in the air, she figured she could withstand the final minutes.

Then the plane hit the tarmac. She bounced from her seat and the child in front screamed. She looked over at Lawrence who grunted in slight discomfort. The plane hurtled down the runway at a speed she was sure was too fast. Strapped in, she found herself leaning to her right side as the pilot took a corner at a dangerous speed, other passengers voiced their concerns which made her feel worse. It wasn't just her.

As the plane slowed to a stop, Julia could feel her heart pounding against her chest. Lawrence stirred and looked up at her with a childlike innocence she would have found endearing in different circumstances.

"Hello, babe," he said. "You okay?"

Julia couldn't see her own face but she didn't imagine it looked like she was okay.

She turned across the aisle, a young Italian woman with dark hair, sat calm and composed. Noticing the look on Julia's face, she smiled and reached over and placed a comforting hand on her shoulder.

"Welcome to Rome," she said.

2

Kirsty stood face to face with the wall of skulls. Cavernous eye sockets stared back at her. Surrounded by the dead, she remained steadfast in her resolve. Dimly lit bulbs were strewn throughout the spacious corridor. An artificial attempt to create a creepy atmosphere. She never found darkness by itself frightening, she didn't fear that which she could not see. Kirsty wasn't afraid of the dark, and she certainly wasn't afraid now.

There was something oddly inhumane about the skulls, their size and shape appeared almost forged and moulded. She took a sip of water from a bottle and studied one of the skulls more closely. One in particular stood out to her. It was slightly larger than the others and glistened in the warm light. It looked fresh. Her hand was drawn to it, but she didn't touch. Instead, she imitated caressing it as thoughts of Hamlet filled her head.

"Alas, poor dead man," she whispered to herself. "We hardly knew ye."

She was bored. The Catacombs of San Gennaro had impressed her for around ten minutes and now the novelty had worn off. Once she had seen one skull she had seen them all. Thirty minutes into her exploration her mind was made up that there would be nothing more of worth to see.

"What've you found?" Aaron called out. Kirsty turned to see her little brother descend the small staircase that led them deeper into the catacombs. His DSLR camera was clasped in his hand, ready for action.

The catacombs were meant to be more than this. Kirsty noticed a sterility to them that revealed how mundane the tourist attraction was. There was no danger. No risk. No potential.

"Absolutely nothing," she answered.

Aaron was more impressed. He was easily impressed. The catacombs represented history, the ability to travel to a morbid side of Naples. He raised the camera and started recording the skeletal remains that Kirsty stared at.

"This is good, this is very good," he said.

"This is dull," Kirsty said. "I've seen a million skulls already and can't think of how a million more is going to be any more appealing."

Aaron lowered his camera. He took Kirsty's scorn personally as the catacombs were his idea. Their European ghost tour was off to a bad start. Yes, he was aware that the chances of seeing something in the catacombs were highly unlikely, but Aaron thought it could be a fun place to start. It was simple and safe. Emphasis on the latter.

Four tourists approached them with German accents. They looked around in wonder and awe at the gloom. Kirsty wished she could be so content. She craved an experience that would give her goose bumps. One that would make her question her own scepticism. She wouldn't find it here. She didn't expect to and it strengthened her opinion that she wouldn't in any manufactured tourist trap.

Aaron continued to record, oblivious to his sister's concerns. He planned to document a ton of footage then edit it when they got back to England. Edit it into what, he wasn't entirely sure. While planning the trip they spoke about touring the darker side of Europe. Areas where tourists dared tread. The catacombs gave him a chance to test the camera in low light plus they had been on his bucket list.

"If you've filmed enough bones, can we move on?" Kirsty asked. She tried to soften her tone, it was an act she often found difficult. Her abrasive attitude was as natural as breathing.

Aaron sighed as he lowered the camera. "Fine," he conceded. "Lead the way."

The sentence echoed in Kirsty's mind. Yes, she would lead the way. She'd be picking where to go next. She had an idea, a place that was marked on her list as provisional. A little too ambitious for their skills as urban explorers. It would require jumping in the deep end and learning to swim the hard way. The idea alone was exciting.

3

Welcome to Rome, Julia repeated to herself. She looked forward to seeing Rome: The Colosseum, the Vatican. To sit on the Spanish steps and throw coins into the Trevi Fountain. Yes, she had been looking forward to soaking in the warm nights with a glass of wine as she watched the world go by with her husband by her side.

Except she wasn't supposed to be in Rome, not yet. Julia was supposed to be in Venice, instead, she found herself in Leonardo da Vinci airport, waiting for a hire car. The unrepentant Roman sun shone through the metal and steel of the airport, boiling those that dwelt within. Hundreds of holidaymakers, many from the same flight, stood in the queue intermixed with other travellers going about their business. Even those used to the heat found it unbearable. Some had succumbed to the drain it placed upon them and decided to nap on the airport floor. Julia was tempted herself, considering how little sleep she had on the flights.

Lawrence shuffled anxiously on the spot. Sweat dripped from his forehead in an unhealthy manner.

"We are sorry to announce," the captain said on the plane, "that due to technical issues we will have to ground the flight in Rome. The cabin crew will announce further guidance for passengers. Amity Airlines are sorry for the inconvenience."

If being stranded six hours from your designated destination is considered "inconvenient" then so be it. The honeymoon was not off to a good start and yet it seemed so simple on paper. New York to London with a couple of days layover. London to Venice, three nights in the city before flying to Rome for a week, then a direct flight home.

"Why couldn't we have landed at a nearer airport?" Lawrence had asked when the stewardess came around.

"Unfortunately sir, this was the closest available location that could accommodate us," she smiled a bizarre smile that was neither sincere nor ingenuous. A trained smile that had been practised over many flights to ensure passengers felt relaxed. Julia did not welcome her cordiality.

The stewardess handed them both free rental car vouchers with a fuel allowance up to 600 km, which Lawrence initially mistook for miles like it made much difference.

"Can't we just get a flight straight to Venice?" Lawrence asked.

"No, sir," the stewardess replied, her grin firmly stuck in place. "Unfortunately, only one flight departs for Venice from this airport per day and that flight is full. There are trains available however I assure you you'll get to your destination quicker by car. It should take you a little over five hours." Her smile never left her face, yet Julia noticed it was strained.

The situation was far from ideal. They departed the flight at seven that morning. The drive from the airport to Venice could be done in less than six hours according to her map app. A little more than just over five hours. They'd already been in the queue for two hours and it didn't look like they'd be moving anytime soon. Tension pulsed through the air as frustration snowballed from one person to another, threatening to avalanche at any minute. The searing heat only added to the situation.

"Maybe we should just stay here for a night and take that other flight tomorrow," Lawrence said.

"No," Julia said. "I don't want to lose any more time in Venice than we have already."

"At this rate we'll be spending our honeymoon right here," he said.

Julia looked down at the mass of people in front of them. She turned her head to see more behind them. It always made her feel better while standing in a queue to see more people behind her than in front regardless of how long she still had to wait.

"I've slept in worst places," she said. Her mind flashed back fifteen years prior when she was eighteen. She attended a Black Sabbath concert with her friends and missed the bus back home. With no money for a hotel or even a hostel, they ended up staying at the bus station with nothing but a rusted bench for the three of them to huddle together on. She thought of how cold it was and embraced the memory like a lost lover as the heat in the airport intensified.

"Well I haven't," Lawrence said. "And right now, a hotel at the airport is looking better and better. We can take a train into Rome and make a day of it. Get a good sleep and boom, be in Venice right as rain tomorrow."

There was some sense to what Lawrence said. Julia was close to yielding, she just wanted out of the airport. She also had no intention of seeing it again until she was ready to go home. Julia couldn't wait to see Rome but not at the expense of Venice. First world problems.

"Let's give it another hour," she said. "Besides, the road trip could be fun. We'll get to see some of Italy we wouldn't otherwise see." Ever the optimist.

The road trip did appeal to Lawrence's sense of adventure. He hated driving and knew his wife would happily volunteer. That'd give him plenty of opportunity to look out for interesting places that they could stop at, time permitting of course.

"Okay, deal," he said. The idea now firmly planted in his brain, he took out his phone and opened an internet browser, looking for anything off the tourist trail. He narrowed his search to the journey between Rome and Venice. Many hits came back for both cities, though not much in-between. There was one website that caught his eye. One that enticed him to know more. He bookmarked the page, promising himself he'd have a proper look at it later. His curiosity uplifted his mood. He turned to Julia and blew her a kiss. She caught it and placed her hand on her heart. She knew her husband was up to something, she just couldn't think what.

4

Rino looked out at the Venetian lagoon. The blistering blue sky reflected off the calm water. His old fishing boat gently bobbed up and down in a calming rhythm. His work done for the day and his haul taken care of, he'd driven back out to the open water to clear his head. A rugged man in his late sixties, Rino had been a proud fisherman most of his life. He didn't know much else. He was old school. His father before him fished the same waters. His father before him and so on.

But it was a different time from the days of his father and grandfather. It was a different time for Rino, who saw his trade plummet at the expense of an evolving world. Age had caught up with him; the modern world was leaving the old man behind. He lived a comfortable and modest life but his savings didn't amount to much. Rino enjoyed working, but the early morning rises got tougher as his bones creaked louder. A lifetime of hard work had taken its toll, and he found himself tiring more quickly as each year passed.

He loved the sea. He loved the stillness of the water as the sun rose over the mainland. Decades of memories and experiences most could only dream of. He was old. His knees were causing him more problems than he cared for and arthritis had begun to take hold in his wrists. He knew his days on the water were coming to an end, unfortunately he was unable to retire.

His granddaughter, Elena, suggested he host tours of the lagoon. She pitched her idea to him whenever she could.

"Look at all the tourists," she said. "How many of them would pay good money for a genuine authentic cruise of the lagoon?"

The idea made him laugh. He looked at his boat as he recalled her persistent badgering. His vessel, l'ultimo squalo, was a Novi boat. Known for its seaworthiness, durability, and economical operation, it wasn't glamorous by any means. It was also twenty years old and showed the scars of a life well-lived.

"That's part of the charm," Elena would argue. "Your boat is a part of the real Venice. The history."

He laughed at the memory. The idea he was a part of history amused him. Elena was nineteen, to her a near seventy-year-old man must be someone that remembers what the world looked like in black and white.

"Nonno, you've lived on these waters your entire life. The stories you could tell. People would pay generously."

He would've been lying to say the idea didn't stir some curiosity within him. It did seem a less laborious way to make money. It also meant putting up with idiot tourists and inane questions. He'd lived a mostly solitary existence, his working life. Easy money wasn't without a price.

"All I'm asking is for you to think about it. I can even come help out. I could even host it."

Despite the proud legacy of his family, Elena's mother didn't share the same views as the older generation. It was an outlook they learned from his wife, Eleanora, may she rest in peace. The women in Rino's family were forward-thinking, while the men were accused of clinging onto a past that was drowning and would drag them down with it.

Rino felt a death at sea would be romantic. It would be a far more fitting end than being hooked up to machines while strangers watched him breathe his last breath.

"Just think about it."

He did think about it. However, he did not deliberate it. Not seriously. Had he begun to? Maybe. Just maybe it'd be worth trialling. What did he have to lose? His self-respect was high on the list. His pride was important to him. Would it come before a fall?

He dismissed the idea and took a sip of his coffee, black with two sugars. He winced at how cold it was and emptied it over the side. He looked over at Poveglia, the small island that was cloaked in its own history. As much a part of the real Venice as his granddaughter believed he was. To the starboard side, a large fishing vessel came into view. It must've been about 90ft in length, more than three times the length of his own boat. There was no competition. The fight hadn't been fair for a while, and he felt like a relic of a romanticised era.

Maybe Elena was right. Maybe he did have an advantage. He stretched his arms over his head, his wrists cracking unhealthily with each movement. Rino took control of his boat and made his way towards Lido. Perhaps the old sea-dog had some new tricks to learn.

5

The car's air conditioning blasted onto Julia's face as she drove down the E35. The never-ending hell that was the wait for the rental car had ended. Over three agonising hours of waiting in line was a distant memory to her as they made their way towards Venice.

Thankfully the Italians drove on the same side of the road as back home, albeit much more aggressively than she'd have liked. Cars hurtled past her, some angrily blasting their horns at her for having the audacity to do the speed limit.

Lawrence sat in the passenger seat, eyes wide, as he took in the surrounding scenery. Julia was unable to take much of it in, her full concentration on the unknown roads. She was focused on a set goal: get to Venice and begin the honeymoon properly.

"Do you think those women are hookers?" Lawrence asked.

The question bounced around Julia's head like a pinball. She didn't mind driving, she preferred to, especially if Lawrence was the alternative. She loved her husband, but she did not marry him for his driving prowess.

"What?" she replied. Her tone was abrupt. Perhaps even harsh. She didn't feel bad. It was a stupid question that had unnecessarily demanded her attention.

"The women at the side of the road," he said. "What do you think?"

"I think," she said, "that I'm driving 80mph on a road I've never driven on, in a country that I've never been in."

Lawrence shifted awkwardly in his seat. He pulled his phone out and began mindlessly scrolling through his Twitter feed. He was in a sulk. Julia felt guilty.

"I'm sorry," she said. "I didn't mean to be so snappy, I'm just tired."

She reached her right hand across to him and caressed his knee. He deliberated for a few seconds, then reciprocated the affection by clasping her hand.

It had been a long journey and they were still miles away from where they should be. Julia imagined her honeymoon to be a relaxing and stress-free experience. Instead, she found herself stranded miles from her destination, waiting for hours on a rental car she shouldn't have needed and now driving on a road she shouldn't be on to get to where she was supposed to be hours ago.

She could forgive herself for being a little tetchy. It wasn't Lawrence's fault though. It just felt like he was able to enjoy the holiday while she had to do the work. As usual, again, it's how she preferred it. She wasn't a martyr, she just liked to be in control of the situation. It was one of the reasons she hated flying. To relinquish control and be at the mercy of fate. There was little she could do should the pilot decide he's having a bad day.

Lawrence looked out the window and watched the world go by. There wasn't much to look at. Some trees and the occasional building. Nothing exciting. Julia wasn't missing anything.

He saw another woman sit by the road and wondered if they could all be prostitutes. Selling their body to drivers who were looking for a quick fix. It seemed incredibly dangerous to him, but he was looking at it through a New Yorker's gaze. He had no idea of the culture of the land he was in and tried not to judge. If they even were prostitutes. He was fairly confident they were. He thought about suggesting they stop at one to test his theory. Just for fun. He read the room and decided against it. Julia was more likely to drive into an oncoming truck at the suggestion than fulfil some juvenile curiosity.

Lawrence stretched his legs out as much as he could. He looked at his phone to see his signal had cut off. He had planned to look up the route and see if there was anything of note worth seeing. He glanced over at the satnav. Just under four hours to Venice. He was impressed with the time they were making. Still, he was restless. He hated just sitting about. It's why he wasn't a great fan of beach holidays. He liked to explore. See new things and soak in new cultures. As long as he could get a beer as well, that went without saying.

"Do you need me to take over driving for a bit?" he said.

"It's fine honey," she said. "Don't you worry about me." She blew him a kiss from a side-glance, her eyes never leaving the road. The airline had covered the cost of insurance for both of them. Lawrence might have hated driving but he had to volunteer his services. He knew Julia didn't want him to drive. He knew she hated his driving and the idea of him being let loose on a foreign road would have filled her with fear.

He remembered a time they drove back home. It was just outside the city and Lawrence hadn't long had his licence. He was driving without a care in the world when they approached a parked van obstructing his side of the road. Looking at an oncoming car, he knew he had enough space to get through. Julia disagreed and let it be known with an audible gasp as Lawrence narrowly avoided hitting either vehicle.

The episode did little for his confidence and it was one he would often bring up to use as a weapon when the subject of driving came up.

Restless, he began switching radio stations. Most of them played popular songs he recognised, others he assumed to be in Italian. He knew little of the language. His entire vocabulary consisted of *Vorrei una birra?* He figured that this would be enough to satisfy a local waiter and in turn look impressive to Julia. His own ignorance would be content by others' ability to speak his tongue.

The ever-changing radio stations grated on Julia. She fought against the urge to speak in fear it would come out coarse. Mercifully, Lawrence seemed content and settled on a station playing a song she didn't recognise but knew the language was Italian. Unlike her husband, Julia learned some of the basics in preparation for the trip. Far from fluent, she felt it was important to learn some Italian to be polite. Manners meant everything.

Lawrence pulled out his phone again and checked his signal. A bar flickered on the screen, prompting him to refresh his web page. The site he had visited was *The dark side of Bel paese*. The webpage was amateurish. The basic graphics reminded him of his first foray onto the internet when he would use his dad's dial-up modem in a quest to look for the fabled nudity his then classmates spoke of. A black and white picture of an old house was on the front page. It looked stately and rundown, the prototype haunted house that teenagers are warned not to enter before they inevitably do. He clicked on the menu and read the headers. *The Devil's Monk Monastery* caught his eye, partly because it was the only words in English. It told the story of a monk who fell in love with a woman he believed to be a witch. The monk tortured the woman to extract a confession. Instead, she died. Aside from driving him insane, it altered his soul to such a degree that it changed him physically. Many unexplained murders occurred at the local village and the monk was suspected of the vile crimes. Eventually, the King had him hung; however, his ghost reportedly never left the monastery.

The story made Lawrence smile. He loved a good ghost story. He was a massive fan of horror movies. He knew it wasn't plausible, so there was nothing to fear. He'd love to visit the monastery, but Salerno was a little south of where they were heading.

He read the rest of the headings and scanned the locations: Napoli, Milan, Parma, Aoasta, Venice.

Venice. Now, this was more like it. He looked more closely and found a few places in the city that promised goose bumps. A couple looked intriguing: a haunted palace, a cursed house. Both were of interest. He was drawn to one in particular. The website claimed that not only was it the most haunted place in Italy, it was more than just a haunted building. It was an island. The island of Poveglia, the Island of madness and death. He bookmarked it as he lost signal again. Poveglia. Now, that sounded exciting.

6

"This is the golden ticket," said Kirsty. "We've been going about this all wrong. We've been looking to build ourselves up to some sort of grand finale. Instead, we should start *at* the top. Anything else is a bonus."

Aaron raised his eyebrows and took a sip of his beer. If he was to agree to this he'd likely need something stronger.

The bar was filled with a clash of languages as tourists from many cultures spoke. Some generic soft rock song played quietly over the PA. Aaron knew it, but he couldn't place the title or artist. He struggled to focus on it as Kirsty's proposal echoed in his head.

"A haunted island," he said.

"Exactly," said Kirsty. She smiled a smile that reflected how pleased with herself she was. "It's perfect."

Aaron took another sip. His sister was fearless. Aaron himself, not so much. He did, however, own a camera and was proficient in video production.

Three months had passed since Kirsty first suggested they combine urban exploration with ghost hunting. Aaron thought she was joking. She had always had a fascination with urban legends and ghostly tales, but Aaron never imagined she would take it as far as she had.

"With my ideas," she had said, "and your skills. We can produce something pretty special."

He laughed it off but quickly realised she wasn't joking. Kirsty was a dreamer, an admirable trait which some found endearing. Her brother was the opposite. Many thought him unadventurous but he didn't mind. He didn't see it as a bad thing. Playing it safe was not a negative quality.

He certainly had no intention of exploring condemned buildings. Aaron was open-minded to the idea of ghosts and more so to rotting floorboards and rusty nails. He also had an overactive imagination. It may have been easy to dismiss the idea of the supernatural in the daytime, it was difficult to think rationally upon hearing a creak in the middle of the night.

Aaron knew that despite his initial protestations he would eventually yield to his sister, and he did. Her ideas were half-baked and promised jeopardy, yet she was convincing and persistent.

Kirsty had been keen to start right away and had a short list already prepared of where they could cut their teeth. Top of that list was The House of Reston Mather, a local legend that Aaron heard about at school. The house was situated in the village of Provanlea, thirty miles west of London, where they both grew up.

The house was said to be the oldest in England, although that claim was disputable and held by many. It had a long and gruesome history, even if most of the tales were unsubstantiated; the older generations were respectful of the stories and would warn children to stay clear.

Ghost stories. Fables to scare children, Aaron thought, and they had done when he was younger. Once open to the public, it had closed years earlier for renovations only to stay closed due to funding issues. Aaron would question the character of someone that wanted to hang out in such a place. His sister was not excluded from that.

Kirsty insisted that the pair visit it at night. Aaron rolled his eyes at the clichéd thinking of his sister but didn't argue. He made sure the batteries for his DSLR camera were charged while Kirsty invested in a good torch.

"Shouldn't I take a torch as well?" he said.

"You'll be fine," she said. "You've got the night vision on the camera, and we don't want it too well lit. It'll take away from the atmosphere."

The house was fenced off with signs that warned trespassers would be prosecuted. Kirsty felt it was all for show as there were no cameras or security personnel on-site.

"How do you know this?" Aaron had questioned her, unconvinced.

"I just do, now come on."

The house was situated near a quiet road. It sat at the bottom of a hill, obscured by trees. Even if someone drove by, the chances of the two of them being seen were unlikely. They had parked their car about half a mile down the road and walked the rest of the way on foot. The night air was cold, the path before them lit only by a half-moon.

Aaron's concern covered his face. He was more worried at disturbing a delinquent's drinking den than he was of Reston Mather. They approached the steel mesh fence. It wasn't very sturdy and was more of a superficial deterrent than a barrier to keep people out. Kirsty pulled at the edge and was able to make space for them to squeeze through. They made their way through the trees and there it stood. The House of Reston

Mather. Aaron had seen it before, his school class even visited it when he was younger. It never looked as scary back then. It radiated an ominous black warning for them to turn back.

Kirsty explored the front, looking for a way in. The door was padlocked shut, the windows boarded. She went over to a smaller window to her left. The board was loose. She pulled it gently and it slowly prised open.

"That was lucky," Aaron said, although he didn't believe it to be fortunate.

"I had some sources tell me this is the best way in," said Kirsty.

"I'm sorry, what?" Arron's tension rose, and he felt his muscles tighten.

"I checked some forums and some teenagers said that this was how they got in."

Aaron thought back to his fear of delinquents. He didn't fancy being stabbed by some teen, drunk on cheap cider that made them feel invincible.

"Maybe it's not as abandoned as you think it is then."

"Will you shut up? It's fine, now come on. Make sure you're recording all this."

Aaron grabbed the camera that hung from his neck. He almost forgot what they were there for. He turned the camera on and set it to night vision. He looked at his screen to see the world illuminated in green. The board that Kirsty had pried open remained in place and she disappeared into the house. Aaron took a deep sigh and followed her.

He found the entry more difficult than his sister did, which didn't surprise him as he was the one with the camera. The room was in total darkness. Aaron viewed it through his camera. It looked like a sitting room: old and rundown, it couldn't have been part of the renovation project. He noticed graffiti on the walls. It made him shiver. Kirsty turned on her torch, which caused a glare on Aaron's screen. He couldn't see a thing through the camera and changed the setting back. He weighed up the pros and cons of his visibility options. The torch allowed them to see more naturally, although not as well as the night vision. The camera offered more periphery, but it was artificial. It didn't seem real. It also freaked him out more.

"You getting all this?" Kirsty asked.

"Yep," said Aaron. He didn't feel the need to explain his dilemma. "So, what now?"

"Now, little brother. We explore."

Each step Aaron and Kirsty took was amplified by the silence. It tore at him as he anticipated other sounds that didn't come. They made their way to a different room. It was closed off and in complete darkness. Kirsty panned her torch over the walls, revealing nothing innocuous to her. To Aaron, everything was coated with a sinister layer.

His gaze remained fixated in a vacant corner. He knew he was overreacting, and he couldn't do much about it. He took a deep breath and scanned where Kirsty was yet to reach. He let out an audible yelp as two blackened eyes stared back at him. Kirsty swung her light round to illuminate a portrait that hung proudly above the fireplace. His face had a twisted grin, his clothes depicted that of a past century. They both knew the figure, it was Reston Mather himself. A landowner many years ago who legend says drowned his wife and her lover in the local lake before taking his own life. Except only two bodies were ever found and the story goes that Mather still haunted the house, ready to continue his bitter revenge against any lovers that dare trespass. Others say the ghost of Mrs Mather appears to them, pleading for help before she slowly dissipates. A warning. A story. One Kirsty and Aaron both knew well. A cautionary tale for teenagers to promote abstinence and not turn the house into a den of decadence.

Kirsty enjoyed the stories for what they were, but she did not fear bumping into the Mathers or any other tortured spirit that was trapped in the walls. She could tell Aaron was becoming less sure but couldn't help teasing him.

"Here, look at his eyes. Look at them really closely," she said. She slowly walked around the room, her gaze never leaving the portrait.

"What's your point?"

"The eyes. They follow you around the room."

She lit up her face with the torch and laughed.

"You're hilarious."

"I agree, now stop the whiny act. You getting this clear enough?"

It took him a second to realise what she meant then he remembered he was holding a camera. He looked at the screen and saw the portrait was out of focus. He slowly adjusted it and saw the eyes much clearer. Kirsty was right. They pierced him. He wasn't enjoying himself.

Kirsty led the way into the next room and came across a staircase. She remembered it from childhood when her school visited the house. It spiralled slightly with a steep curve near the top, leading into a room that they weren't allowed to visit. *No more teachers,* Kirsty thought. She was the one in charge and if she wanted to she would ascend the stairs and have herself a little peek at what lay behind the door. And she did want to.

"Hey, Aaron. Give me a second pair of eyes over here."

6

Aaron aimed the lens towards the staircase.

Her first step on the wooden stair caused a loud creak that was like nails across a chalkboard. Aaron winced as Kirsty climbed the stairs with trepidation. Each stair let out anguish as Kirsty slowly made her way upwards. As his sister was in danger of disappearing out of sight, he knew he would have to follow her.

A cold sweat ran down Aaron's back while Kirsty remained calm. She got to the top of the stair and placed a hand on the door handle. It was ajar. Slowly, she pushed it open, the door glided with surprising silence. Her light found something she did not expect, something she did not want to see. Suddenly, at that moment, she realised she had made a mistake.

"Aaron," she whispered. "I think it's time to go."

Arron's adrenaline spiked, then he remembered what Kirsty was like. It was probably another joke. He wasn't falling for it this time.

"Hilarious. Look, stop being daft, I'm not in the mood."

"No, listen to me." Her voice quiet and trembling.

She slowly backed away from the door. She made her way down the stairs in silence, forcing Aaron to descend the narrow staircase.

Her pace quickened when she got to the bottom.

"What's the matter?" Aaron said.

His sister didn't respond. Not verbally. Instead, she grabbed his arm and lifted a finger to her lips. They left the house in a hurry. Kirsty refused to speak until they got back to the car.

It wasn't a ghost in the room. It was terrifying and very real. The room had been used as a drug den. She couldn't make out how many people were there, but she could see the rhythmic breathing of at least two adults. The third...the third was a much smaller person and not breathing. Those lifeless doll-like eyes locked onto hers. Reflecting like glass with nothing operating behind them. Not anymore.

Aaron hoped Kirsty was still trying to scare him as she told him what she saw. The pain in her voice was proof she wasn't lying. They reported their findings anonymously to the police. The news story was published three days later. It made page twelve.

Aaron took a gulp of his beer as the bar came back into focus. The incident should have deterred Kirsty. It certainly scarred her in ways she never told him. He wasn't present for the sleepless nights. The night terrors that paralysed her to the bed as those innocent eyes stared at her from the corner of the room.

It didn't deter her. It motivated her. Despite the terror she experienced, it drove her. Kirsty didn't want that experience to be her peak. It was the bar. Nothing she could come across could chill her like that night. No creaks, no bumps, no otherworldly attempts would dissuade her. She had experienced a fear like no other and now she was fearless to what lay ahead.

"So," she said. "Poveglia. Thoughts?"

Aaron finished his beer. Thoughts? Did his thoughts matter? He was always going to agree. Kirsty would persuade him if he put up a fight. He didn't have it in him. Especially when he knew he'd lose.

"I'll think about it. I'll need to look into it more."

"No worries, we can look at it on the plane to Venice. There's a flight early tomorrow morning."

"What happens if there are no seats?"

"Then some poor fool isn't getting on. Luckily for us, I've

already booked ours."

Aaron lifted his empty glass to his lips. Yep. He was going to need something stronger.

7

Rino despised tourists. Their presence infuriated him. They littered his home and polluted the beauty of Venice. They were a perpetual nuisance. The city was a novelty for them. A chance to take a picturesque snap for their social media or whatever. Tourists were nothing to him but fame junkies that wanted the gratification of the achievement of others. He was old and surly, but the surliness didn't just come with his advanced age. He'd been like that most of his adult life.

His home on Giudecca was less of a tourist hot spot, however the last few years saw more and more outsiders treat the island like their own. He contemplated moving somewhere more remote. If he had the money, he'd invest in a houseboat and enjoy a life at sea. That was the dream.

An unlikely one at that. Still, he knew when faced with his own mortality, he would pack enough to last and allow his boat to drift out to open waters. Fate would decide what to do with his remains and the burden would be lifted from his family. Would they understand? His daughter wouldn't. Neither would Eleanora, had she still been alive. Cancer was a cruel and unforgiving affliction that robbed families of their hope and had robbed Rino of his love.

The deaths broke him in ways he wouldn't deal with. Instead, his already hardened shell was galvanised to the point it created a rift in his family. Elena was the only one that had the patience to tolerate him. What the others didn't realise was that he was different with her. She softened him in a way that his own daughter couldn't.

He sat in a Venetian coffee shop that had no view of the water. He couldn't see the lagoon or even a canal. These factors didn't make it popular with the tourists. It suited him perfectly. He sipped at his black coffee, two sugars, and looked upon the photographs on the wall. It depicted the Venice from his youth. It made him nostalgic and his nose wrinkled. He wasn't fond of the feeling. It sat in his gut and turned his stomach as the suffering to return gestated. He was fond of his memories. He just had no desire to focus on a period that would be impossible to relive.

He looked up to see Elena burst through the door. Her rounded face carried the wide smile she usually had, especially when seeing her nonna. She breezed over to where he sat, unaware how close her backpack came to knocking over a cake display on the counter. Elena held many of the same strong ideals that Rino did, but her carefree recklessness was a trait she inherited from her mother.

He stood to greet her, ever the gentleman. She hugged him without speaking, squeezing him so tight it hurt and, for a second, he struggled to breathe. She was getting stronger. He was getting older.

They both sat before either said a word.

"How was your journey?" Rino asked.

"Meh," she said. "Tram was busy and there was something wrong with the air conditioning. Streets were a little quieter than I expected on the way down here though." Elena lived in

Florence where she went to university, but as her term was finished, she was back with her parents in Mestre. Everyone in the family left the Venetian islands sooner or later in life. All except Rino.

"How's university?"

"It's been fine. Community empowerment and qualitative research methods isn't the most compelling of subjects, but Florence is fun."

Rino knew the words she spoke of but had no idea what it was Elena was talking about. He knew she was studying psychology and that was about it.

"More importantly, how are things with you? You sounded a little different on the phone."

Rino sipped at his coffee and thought long and hard about what to say next. He didn't feel nervous often. Little phased him yet the only word he could conjure that would describe the feeling in his stomach was nerves. He was apprehensive to speak, to tell la nipotina that he was ready to have a serious discussion with her about using his boat for tourism. After so long fighting her on it, Rino was about to yield. He took a risk every time he went out on his boat, an action he performed with ease. At that moment he felt like he was ready to jump out of a plane without checking if the parachute was packed.

"I've been thinking," he said at last. "Maybe, and this is a definitive maybe, that...perhaps..."

Elena looked at him quizzically. Was he dying? Was he losing his mind? Had he already lost it? The suspense was killing her and patience had never been her strong point.

"This tourist idea you have-"

"Aha!" she interrupted. "I knew it, I mean I didn't know it. I didn't know that's what you were going to say but I knew you'd been thinking about it, I knew you'd say yes."

"Now, wait," he held up a hand. She sat perfectly still and attentive, struggling to contain her smile. "I haven't said yes to anything. I just want to talk. I want to hear more details about what you're suggesting here. That's all."

Elena let out a little squeal, it was loud enough for one local to turn around and tut.

"Your boat is old, Nonna. It's very old."

"Like me."

"Exactly. It's not manufactured to look pretty for the tourists."

"You're meant to be selling this idea to me, not insulting me."

"I'm going somewhere with it. It's authentic. It's real Venice, like you."

"You've told me all of this before."

"Yet you called me here today to discuss it."

Rino sipped at his coffee. He winced at how considerably it had cooled.

"You really think people would be interested in listening to an old man like me?"

"That's where I'm happy to help. You're a wonderful man, Nonna. Full of wonderful stories. But you're not, how do we say…"

Rino raised his eyebrows, daring his granddaughter to speak.

"You're not the warmest person when it comes to tourists. You tell me some stories about the city and the water, I'll do the rest."

The old man took a deep sigh. He couldn't believe he was contemplating this. It went against his ethics. Yet there he was. The old man. Not getting any younger. Struggling to maintain his trade. He wasn't sure how long he had left in the world. How much longer he had to make money, to leave something of worth to his family. To spend time with them. To spend time with Elena. With this idea, at least he would see her more.

There was a long silence between them before he finally spoke.

"Okay, let's try it. On a trial basis. If I don't like it for whatever reason, my decision is final. And remember it's my boat, so my rules."

"Yes, I know you're not going to regret this. It's going to be so much fun. We'll sail the seas and sell memories."

"How do we get people interested?"

Oh, don't worry about that. I've already got a few people lined up."

8

"And if you need anything else, don't hesitate to ask," Caterina said. Julia looked at their host. A small middle-aged Venetian woman with dark eyes and a warm smile. Julia liked her, she seemed friendly. But all Julia wanted at that point was peace and quiet. The journey to Venice had been testing. She loved her husband but a four-hour car journey across a country you're unfamiliar with will test even the most ardent relationship.

She couldn't blame him for staying quiet and sulking when scolded, albeit it mildly, for distracting her from the roads. What concerned her was when he would go enthusiastically quiet, it was then she knew he was up to something and it turned out she was right.

With a few miles to go, he opened up.

"All I'm saying," he said, while she tried to avoid a crash, "is it could be fun."

Fun. Such a subjective term with its own boundaries. Fun. Fun to Julia was embracing the local culture and enjoying a nice glass of wine with a late dinner by the lagoon. Fun sounded like taking a trip on a gondola and feeling like a proper tourist as they made their way down a canal. Fun was getting to Venice and ditching the car. What Lawrence suggested, was not her idea of fun.

"Visiting some haunted houses doesn't sound like my idea of fun. You know I hate horror movies, why did you think this would appeal to me?"

"Because," he said, then realised he didn't know why. He didn't take into consideration her feelings on it. He had found some spooky sounding places on *The dark side of Bel paese* website that he wanted to check out. The Palazzo Dario was referred to as the most haunted house in the world. Then there was the Casino degli Spiriti where fishermen dare not cast their lines. There were others that he bookmarked. Although none appeared open to the public, he did find some ghost tours who would take them around the sites.

"You like walking tours," he eventually said.

"I like walking tours of things I'm interested in. Come on, you know stuff like that freaks me out."

"You don't even believe in ghosts."

"But I believe in history and bloody scary history designed to give me the creeps isn't how I imagined spending my time in Venice."

He scrolled back up the page to number one on his list. Poveglia. It seemed like a fantasy by comparison. If Julia wasn't interested in walking to these places, what were the chances she would want to take a boat out to one?

He was close to going back into a sulk when a brainwave hit him.

"How about two birds with one stone?"

"What's your pitch?"

"There's an island. Sounds really cool. Has an old asylum on it, supposed to be one of the most haunted places in the world."

"Your pitch is ambitious, I admire that. I'm hoping it's also going somewhere."

"You wanted to take a boat trip anyway. All we'd need to do is find something that sails past the island. I get to see it and take some pics, maybe learn something about it. The whole tour isn't a ghost one. How does that sound?"

"I am not visiting some ghost island."

"We don't, we just go near it. I'm not even sure how near we can get to it, the place is abandoned and condemned by the sounds of it. It's off-limits to the public." The element of danger gave weight to the legend he had read about.

Julia took a long sigh. "I'll think about it," she said. She meant it. She would think about it. Granted, she didn't think about it much between him mentioning it and arriving in Venice. It wasn't high on her list of priorities. Unlike Lawrence who was excited at the idea. He knew that if Julia was thinking about something, there's a good chance it would go in his favour.

They didn't speak about it for the rest of the journey. Julia had all but forgotten about it. The idea she was on vacation didn't really register, all she had wanted to do was get to their apartment and now that she had accomplished that, all she wanted to do was rest.

Lawrence's mind ran at a million miles a minute at the best of times. Venice was Julia's idea. He was looking forward to seeing it, but had been told by a friend that he'd get bored with it quickly. The idea of Poveglia had burrowed into him and he couldn't shake it. He was very aware that he hadn't even heard of it until a few hours prior, yet it had intoxicated him. He had to see it, get close to it. It was a bad itch, and who knows, maybe he was a little too enthusiastic to scratch it. He was tired, which often gave his mood a manic upward swing that even he would admit could be irrational.

It was this self-awareness that prevented him from asking Caterina about it outright. He also knew Julia wouldn't have been pleased. They had made it to Venice, it was a long trip made worse by an unexpected detour to the capital. It was time to just enjoy the moment.

"No thanks," Julia told their host. "I think we're both looking for some rest."

Caterina's huge smile never left her mouth. "Don't worry," she said. "I'm available any time, you just call."

Julia liked her but she couldn't tell where the genuine warmth ended and the politeness of a host began. Caterina backed out of the room and closed the door, leaving the honeymooners in peace. Both their plans for their first night had now been rearranged. Collecting their bearings followed by a wild passionate night as husband and wife had yielded to a quiet night of recharging their batteries.

The apartment was gorgeous with rustic stone walls and a wooden ceiling. A snapshot of the past. The mint green and very modern couch contrasted with the aged aesthetics but it made Julia smile. The family room and kitchen were one, a long room with a large arched window that looked onto the canal. It was exactly like the pictures, and although Julia was pleased, she did feel slightly claustrophobic. The ceiling was lower than she'd like and the dark wood and stone made the room feel smaller. She was also aware that she was tired and it'd likely look different in the morning. She made her way to the bedroom and noticed the same mint green decorating the bedspread. She spread her arms and gently fell onto the mattress, allowing the comfort to shroud her.

Lawrence made his way to the window, less impressed with

the view. Sure, the canal was nice but staring straight onto a brick wall offered no stimulation. He'd have been more annoyed had he paid attention to the booking in the first place. His stomach rumbled and he realised he was hungry. He hadn't eaten much on the car ride other than stopping at a roadside restaurant for a quick sandwich that he demolished in the car. He opened the small fridge and contemplated taking a complimentary bottle of water. He then deliberated making a coffee as he realised he was feeling a little chilly. The aircon was blasting ice into the apartment. At first, it was a welcome embrace from the blistering Italian sun. Then it made him shiver. *And this bear's porridge was too cold,* he chuckled to himself. He looked out the window, wholly unimpressed with what he had seen of Venice so far. The water taxi had taken them almost to their door. He wasn't sure what he was expecting. Something bigger, something from a postcard. His expectations were mired by reality. He hoped Poveglia would live up to the hype at least.

He made his way into the bedroom to discuss a foraging plan with Julia. She was quiet, too quiet for his liking. Her legs hanging off the bed, her eyes were closed as she slept peacefully. He decided he'd give her ten minutes then wake her, she wouldn't thank him for letting her sleep too long. He went back to the couch and connected his phone to the Wi-Fi. Opening up his new favourite website, he soon fell down a rabbit hole of stories on Poveglia. Photographs of the island were blurry and questionable. The articles had clickbait titles that enticed Lawrence. Maybe he would give her thirty minutes. An hour, maximum.

9

Her nap lasted more than she'd intended. She was out for around half an hour when she stirred and realised she was fully clothed on the bed. She went into the sitting room to see Lawrence glued to his phone.

He had been consuming information on that stupid island he was becoming obsessed with. He tried to talk to her about it but she was too tired and hungry.

"Let's go for a walk," she suggested. "And get some dinner. I'm quite hungry."

The setting sun bathed the street in an orange glow. The newlyweds walked hand in hand down the cobble paths, absorbing their surroundings. Julia was so happy to finally arrive in Venice yet she still felt restless. She hated arriving somewhere new so late, she knew she wouldn't fully appreciate the city until she'd had a good sleep.

They found themselves in a tourist trap as they blindly walked the area. Night was approaching but the city was showing no signs of closing. They sat at the first restaurant they passed, ushered in by a waiter whose conduct bordered on harassment. They were too tried and naive to the city to argue and ended up paying a lot more than they'd have liked. Both agreed to be more resolute going forward.

9

They walked for a while after dinner but the wine added to their travel fatigue, and they decided to have an early night. While they both imagined their first night in Venice to be full of passionate lust, they were sleeping by 10:00 p.m.

The next morning a sliver of light managed to creep through the closed curtain. Julia had been awake for a while, but now that the light had made its way into her line of vision, she knew it was time to get up. She checked her phone. 07:05 a.m. It was early, and she felt like she had been asleep for days.

Julia stretched on the bed, a little loudly in the hopes of stirring Lawrence while able to maintain plausible deniability. It didn't work, he was a much deeper sleeper than she. Despite hoping he would wake, she found herself careful not to wake him as she made her way to the kitchen area of the next room. She liked the open-plan studio apartment look yet knew she'd hate to live in a place without a separate kitchen. It was a novelty that would wear off if she got used to it.

She boiled some water in the kettle as she fumbled with the coffee. She made sure to make enough for two should Lawrence wake up. If he didn't, she could wake him with the coffee. A good excuse as any to get him up and out. What to do, she had no idea. There were the obvious tourist attractions she had on her list, but to her Venice itself was the real attraction. The canals, the gondoliers. She got a taste of the city the previous night, now she was ready to absorb it. They already lost half a day due to the travel woes and wanted to get as much out of her time there as she could. And if that meant starting the day with a grumpy hubby, then it was a price she was willing to pay.

She poured the water into the cafetiere and inhaled the fresh smell of the coffee. Before she even tasted it, she knew she was in for a treat. Authentically Italian, it filled her with a buoyancy. She let it brew for a bit before filling two large mugs and taking them into the bedroom. She placed them both by the bedside table at Lawrence's side, hoping the aroma would gently stir him.

"Morning babe," she whispered, feeling the coffee needed a little assistance in waking him. "I've made you some coffee."

He grunted something, never the morning person, and turned to face her.

"What time is it?" he asked.

"Time to get up. I've made you coffee."

He threatened to fall back asleep and her eyes leapt to the window. She thought about opening the shutters and allowing the harsh morning sun to jolt him out of his slumber. Too cruel, but an option all the same. Lawrence sat up, the thin duvet fell and exposed his pale chest, sparse hair covering pecs which lacked definition. He struggled to focus his eyes, not yet fully awake, he thought it was later than it really was. He reached over and touched the coffee cup. It was too hot to drink, so he left it.

"What time is it?" he asked.

"Time to start our honeymoon, my love," Julia said.

That meant it was early. Lawrence squinted as he looked at the time on his phone. He dropped it without ceremony and groaned, rolling back over in a mock attempt at sleep.

"Hey," Julia said. "Don't even think about it. We've lost time to be making up here. I didn't come all the way to Venice to lie in bed."

And I didn't come to Venice to wake up at the crack of dawn. Lawrence thought better of speaking his mind but something slipped out anyway, "What am I a farmer?"

"What?"

"Nothing. I'm not awake. It's the middle of the night. Just one more hour, please."

"No, no and no. You can doze until your coffee cools then you can get that down your neck."

Lawrence thought about how hot the mug was to touch and tried to do the math on how long he reasonably had to lie in.

"I don't want to lose out on any more time," she said. "We were late getting in last night as it was and the drive mixed with the flight and the stress of everything...we didn't really get a chance to enjoy our first night."

"You wanted to drive, I was happy to stay a night in Rome," he said, unaware that he actually did say it out loud. Maybe he thought it?

"Prick."

He got his answer.

"If I didn't drive we'd still be in Rome," Julia continued. "Most likely still at the airport. Most likely miserable, tired and stressed just like we were yesterday. I'm going to go get showered. I'm then going to get dressed. I'm then leaving this apartment to go get breakfast whether you're ready or not. It is up to you if you're going to have your wife wander Venice, on her honeymoon, alone. It's your choice. Make it wisely."

She left the room, taking her own coffee with her. Lawrence rolled onto his back, inadvertently allowing a sliver of sun that made its way through a crack to hit him in the right eye. He picked up his mug and sipped at the scalding hot coffee. *Well done*. Mornings weren't his thing. He didn't do well when his slumber was ambushed. He hadn't meant to be coarse. It was just his morning manner. He had a chance to rectify it, all he had to do was get up. Calling on Herculean strength, he swung his feet from the bed and sat upright. He opened his phone and checked the weather. The number frightened him. He would need the industrial-strength sunscreen to ward off death.

He heard the shower turn on. The hiss of the water left him with a decision to make. Try and steal a few more minutes of sleep. Possibly miss breakfast for it. Risk the wrath of a new bride. It was a no brainer. He got up and made his way towards the bathroom. He opened the door; the steam had already filled the room. Julia had her back to him, unaware he was standing in the doorway. He watched the water fall down her back and drip off of her naked body through the glass door. He felt a stir in his groin and quickly took off his underwear. He slowly walked up and knocked on the door. She turned, slightly startled, surprised to see him, assuming he'd fallen back asleep.

He opened the door and stepped into the shower. He slowly ran his hands up her sides and gently pulled her close to him.

"I'm up," he said.

She smiled. No longer in a rush.

10

Rino took a swig of his coffee and winced. Cold. Useless. He threw the remnants overboard and looked out towards the lagoon. His boat gently bobbed up and down, tethered to the pier. He looked at the boats already on the water. Fellow fisherman, contemporaries and rivals. Men, like himself, that made their living from the sea and continued to do so.

Except he was selling out. He had agreed to take tourists out on his boat. He, Rino, an irascible and difficult man. A remnant of old Venice who had spat on those that polluted his city.

It wasn't just the tourists themselves he had an issue with, it was the trade. The supply and demand cycle the city found itself in angered him. Tourists loved Venice, and Venice needed tourists. Now, he was nothing but a glorified gondolier willing to serenade couples with his vessel for a coin.

He had tried his hand as a gondolier in his twenties. He hated it then, lasting less than a day. His boss had frowned on how Rino dealt with a mouthy customer. An older man, in his forties possibly, visiting from Milan with his much younger fiancé. He had tried to show off by barking orders at Rino and directing the routes he took. The inevitable argument didn't end well as Rino, who swore to the Carabinieri he was defending himself, punched the customer into the canal. The man's fiancé told the police a different story but Rino was local and was admonished after spending a night in the cells. It did end his short-lived career and soon after he joined the Marina Militare.

He made himself a promise that he wouldn't punch anyone into the lagoon. The police may not be as lenient as they once were and his granddaughter would be even less forgiving. It's a promise he really hoped he would keep. At least Elena would be there to act as a filter. Still, if anyone was rude to her, he'd find it difficult not to enforce some manners.

He looked at the blue sky. He could feel rain in the air. The weatherman said differently but Rino was a man of instincts. If he felt something, he knew it to be true. An old sailor and fisherman's sixth sense was something to bet on. He looked over at the island of Poveglia. Venice's most famous urban legend and where he had planned to take his customers. Not to the island, heaven's no. He wasn't a fool. He'd steer around it, and allow Elena to tell some ghost stories.

Yes, not only had she convinced him to prostitute his boat, she had also sold him on making it a ghost tour.

"It's perfect," she said. "People will pay more as there's a theme and all you'll need to do is navigate around the island. Give them a chance to take some pictures. I'll narrate, you can tell me some true stories about what happened there, stuff they won't learn from anywhere else."

That wouldn't be an issue. Rino was old enough to remember when the asylum was still in operation. The island had already formed a gruesome history by then, having been used as a quarantine station for victims of the plague. At school, children would share stories about how the ghosts would torture the patients, making them believe they were insane. Every second classmate knew someone that was locked up in the asylum, each with similar stories that all seemed plausible to an eight-year-old.

By the time the asylum closed, Rino was in his teens and was more interested in chasing girls than ghosts. As a teenager, he had friends that would take their girlfriends to the island in a bid to scare them out of their pants - literally. Not Rino. He respected the girls he courted too much to try and trick them into bed or use any other sort of nefarious plot. He would tell others he was too mature to go hunt for ghosts, but the truth was the island scared him. Even to look at it from afar gave him the chills.

As he got older, his belief in the supernatural faded and the island had become just another part of Venice. He might not have believed in ghosts, but he did respect the history of Poveglia. Many had died there, it shouldn't be a place of celebration. Rumours had it the island was covered in black ash, the remnants of its former inhabitants. To even step on it would be desecrating the dead. It was best left alone.

Rino's memory wasn't what it used to be but he was sure he remembered a story about a doctor that committed suicide shortly before the asylum was closed down. The story grew as it whispered from person to person. Tales of his malevolence and brutal treatment of his patients became legend: the mad doctor who used to scoop the brains from their skulls and drink blood from their veins.

Nonsense. He wasn't even sure if a doctor had even killed himself. He wouldn't be surprised if that was made up as well. Elena was right, he did have stories other tours wouldn't except maybe his weren't as fantastical and therefore not as exciting. Maybe, just maybe, he could embellish the stories a little. Add some flavour to them to make them a little more ghoulish.

He'd leave that to Elena. The less he had to say the better. He was happy to just drive the boat and allow his old face to add some legitimacy to the tour.

Despite his ageing memory, he did recall a particular story his grandmother used to frighten him with when he was very young. How the ghosts of the damned would torture the patients. How those that were sentenced to the island went as sane men and were driven mad by the spirits who could never leave.

As he thought about it, he wondered if the story of the doctor did have some truth to it. Maybe there was an accident one day and the story just grew arms and legs. As a seaman, Rino wasn't a stranger to tall tales. What he would find was there was usually an element of truth somewhere. If you drilled down far enough, there'd be an origin that gave birth to myth.

He laughed as he found himself getting carried away. Maybe he would have some fun on the tour after all. What harm would it do to spin a yarn or two? Perhaps he could scare someone from his boat as opposed to physically eject them. Either way, he looked forward to spending time with Elena, the thought made him warm. He checked the time. 07:30 a.m. He still had a couple of hours before the customers arrived. Elena had done well at drumming up interest in a tour that was yet to exist. She was smart and cunning. He was impressed by her drive and confidence. He had faith in her. The least he could do was give it a shot. What scared him most was that he might like it.

11

The flight was a nightmare. Kirsty had left the plane in a rage while being eternally thankful that she was no longer on it. The plane was full to capacity and she found herself sandwiched between a larger gentleman and a toddler who had an innate talent for noise. Aaron, on the other hand, sat nearer the back, blissfully unaware of the pain his sister endured.

The larger man, on the aisle, had zero spatial awareness while the mother and child to her right tried to break the record for most bathroom breaks on the relatively short flight. When the fresh air of Venice hit her as she disembarked, she knew how prisoners felt that tasted freedom for the first time. She made no apologies for the comparison as she descended the steps, soaking in the space to move for the first time in over an hour.

She waited at the baggage carousel, the toddler's wails still ringing in her ears. Too loudly, like he was still present. She turned. He was. Across from the carousel, the child still bawled, the mother not doing enough for Kirsty to shut him the hell up. She wasn't proud of the thoughts she had. Grim, cruel thoughts to shut the child up. To silence it and stifle the screams. Her eyes locked with his, just for a second, but a second was long enough. The tears made them look glassy, and she was back in the House of Reston Mather. Those lifeless eyes staring at her. Absorbing her. Drinking in her naive curiosity and spitting it back in her face. Despite the sweltering heat, she shivered.

Aaron made his way over, large soundproof headphones shielding him from the horrors of reality. An inoffensive swagger and carefree strut which told her he was oblivious to her pain. She hated him at that moment.

"Decent flight, eh?" he said, no trace of mocking in his voice.

"I hate you," she replied.

He read her lips, bewildered by her venom. He turned his headphones off and the crying anguish of a child too young to understand where he is but old enough to understand that this is how he gets attention pierced his ears. The penny dropped.

"Ah," he said. "I take it..."

"The. Entire. Flight." She didn't go into details regarding her recent trip down memory lane.

"Where were your headphones?"

"In the suitcase."

"Well, that was silly."

Kirsty balled up her fist and punched her brother in the ribs. It wasn't a full swing but was powerful enough to register pain and attract the attention of the larger passenger she had gotten to know. He looked at her with raised eyebrows, clearly feeling they had some sort of kinship despite her best efforts to ignore him the entire time.

She stared back at him with dark eyes. A dare to challenge her. Kirsty won the staring contest.

"Uncalled for," Aaron said.

"Wrong. Now either shut up and don't annoy me or say something that won't make me punch you."

11

Aaron opted for silence, fearing anything he would say would prompt another punch. The heat inside the airport was unbearable. For all the issues Kirsty encountered on the plane, at least the air con worked. The absence of cool air in Marco Polo Airport was doing little for her sustained rage. The name of the airport amused her. She knew Marco Polo to be some sort of explorer, but all the name reminded her of was some children's game Americans would play in TV and film. She didn't know what the rules were and never cared to look them up. A fleeting thought to distract her from her mood.

The baggage claim was reminiscent of a huge bunker. She stood in silence as the welcome alarm of the carousel sounded and the luggage began to circulate. Naturally, her suitcase came off last.

As they exited the airport, the unshielded heat of the sun hit Kirsty with a fresh ferocity. The few clouds that littered the sky were afraid to shield them from the ball of fire. She stretched her neck and got her game face on.

"Right," she commanded. "We have two options here in getting to the city. We take a water bus, which I'm in favour of, or a land bus. Thoughts?"

Aaron toyed with the options in his mind, but he knew his preference. He wasn't a great fan of boats. In fact, he was afraid of the water. The idea of being on a boat filled him with more anxiety than the ghost hunting aspect of the trip. He knew Kirsty knew this. He also knew her well enough to know that his trivial concerns weren't high on her list of priorities. She asked him what he preferred, although he suspected she had decided.

"I'm quite happy with the land bus as you bizarrely called

it," he said.

"In this heat? Are you nuts?"

"Then why bother asking me?"

"Well, I know you don't like boats so I thought I'd be considerate. I also thought you'd think with some sense."

"Look, if you want to get the water boat…bus! Then fine, let's do that. Don't bother asking me in future."

"Well, I'm so sorry for thinking about your feelings once in a while little brother. Next time I'll just go ahead and book it in advance and not tell you."

"You did that with the flights!" He didn't realise how much he'd raised his voice until the sentence finished. Kirsty looked at him with her dark eyes, eyes that methodically betrayed she was carefully considering her next sentence.

With complete calm, she spoke, "I just felt that someone had to take some initiative. Naples wasn't doing anything for me. *Or* you. I thought outside the box. You didn't once object."

"All I fucking said was I'd prefer to take the bus over a boat!"

"Technically, they are both buses."

The sweat dripped from Aaron. It felt a hundred degrees in the airport yet he could distinguish between the heat and the rising anger he was struggling to quell.

"If," Kirsty continued, "if you'd rather get the bus, the one with wheels, we can do. I would just like to highlight that the water bus will be cooler and will get us there a little quicker. That's all I'm going to say. The decision is entirely yours."

He hated that she was right. As much as he hated boats he was about to spend a few days in Venice and travel to a haunted island. What difference would one more boat make? It wasn't the point, he shouldn't have to go on one if he didn't want to if he didn't have to, not when there were other options available to him. He wanted to stick with the bus, the grounded wheeled one he was used to, just to spite her. But, then he knew how the journey would go. The uncomfortable silences, the strained attempts by him to make conversation. His sister was a nightmare, always had been. Always will be. He cursed himself for allowing her to work him up so much.

"Fine," he said. "We'll take the boat. Clearly means more to you than me."

"We don't have to. If you'd really prefer-"

"Don't," he interrupted. "Just don't."

The water bus was smaller than Aaron envisioned. It was lower to the water than he would have liked. The inside cabin was busy and stuffy with not much of the sea breeze making its way in. Kirsty sat happily on the deck, relishing the wind sweep through her long black hair. She imagined herself in an eighties rock video, it made her smile. She felt at peace for the first time since boarding the flight in Naples. The trip promised adventure. She was thankful for the contented feeling that flourished through her.

She peered inside the boat, to look at Aaron. He sat looking slightly cramped with his back to the window, looking glum and anxious. A slight tinge of guilt threatened to ruin her good mood. As miserable as he seemed, she knew she'd be more miserable had they taken the bus. Did that make her selfish? Of course, she couldn't deny that. But did it make her any more selfish than Aaron if he was to expect her to do something she didn't want to?

Regardless, she did feel bad and vowed to make it up to him in Venice. As if he read her mind, he turned and locked eyes with her. She smiled and mouthed, "you okay?"

He nodded, his lips twisted in a half-smile. He held no

resentment towards Kirsty. He knew that as much as he hated the boat, she would have been more miserable on the bus. Another sacrifice made for the older sibling. He wasn't going to let himself be a martyr to it.

Kirsty looked out at the open water, towards the city of Venice. She was feeling good and was confident their trip would be a success. What was deemed a success? She wasn't sure. She was certain; however, it would be a trip to remember.

12

This was more like it. This was the Venice that Julia had looked forward to seeing. While she was sure she'd appreciated the city at night she noted how everything looked better with a good night's sleep. They stood on the Rialto bridge as Julia soaked in the view. The area was busy: popular with tourists and many amateur photographers had their camera phones ready while the more serious ones had their DSLRs primed to take the perfect shot that would get them a few likes on social media. Not Julia, no, she didn't want to see this through a lens. She wanted to see it unfiltered and raw.

The water sparkled from the blistering sunlight. Buildings met the water at either side as gondolas made their way up and down the canal, the unmistakable identity of such a unique city. Tourists jostled beside her as she leaned against the large stone balcony. A dozen languages spoken in disharmony swirled around her. She was able to block it out and bathe in the moment.

Lawrence had more trouble channelling his zen. The hustle and bustle of the bridge irritated as people bumped into him. Were they apologising, were they being aggressive? Were they ignoring him completely? He had no idea and he felt frustrated. Unlike Julia, he was still tired. He stayed up later than he had planned to. When they got back from dinner they both crashed onto the bed, but he stayed awake while she slept. Glued to his phone, he searched for information on Poveglia. How to get there, the costs, what there was to experience.

There had been tours that operated trips around the island but none appeared to be running anymore. It irked him more than it should have, he knew it was silly. Still, for whatever reason, it bothered him greatly. He had convinced himself he'd get to see it, learn a little of its history not found on a webpage and scratch the itch that had bothered him since he first found out about it.

Yes, a lifelong obsession he could trace back to the day before. He had barely been in the city a day and he was already bored. Everything looked the same and once he had seen one canal he'd seen them all. The gondolas looked like death traps and no doubt he'd be paying through the nose to experience one.

It was unfair on Julia to be this childish but it's who he was. He wasn't trying to mope around but he knew sooner or later she would ask what was wrong with him and then a fight would start. That's all he needed to be reminded of for the rest of his life, the time he ruined Venice for her on their honeymoon. He pondered getting a little drunk and seeing if that would take the edge off. It was early but was it *too* early for Italy? What drinking culture did the Italians have? What are the odds of him ending up in the water after a few too many? High if he ended up in one of those gondolas.

"It's some view," Julia said. Lawrence couldn't tell if it was a question or a statement, but either way, it required a response.

"It's beautiful," he said. "But without you, it's just some water and old buildings." A little charm initiated to hide his surly mood.

"Do you want to try and get on one of those gondolas later or wait until tomorrow?"

He'd rather avoid them altogether if that was an option.

"You choose, babe. When it comes to Venice, I'm easy."

"Careful mister, this doesn't mean you get free rein of Rome." She laughed and playfully hit his arm.

"I'm just happy to do what you're happy doing."

"Trying to butter me up so I'm more open to your little haunted island tour?"

She *had* told him she'd think about it. Julia wasn't enamoured at the prospect yet she knew he wasn't that interested in Venice. He never had been. In the arena of compromise, he had yielded it to her.

"Is that a yes then?"

"It's a yes dependent on what else we get to do here. We only have two full days. How big is this island, how long can it possibly take to get around it?"

These were all questions Lawrence knew the answer to, except that it didn't matter. No tours were operating. That he knew of. He couldn't tell her that. Once he did, he knew the idea would be dead. Even though he had no idea how they were going to get there, until he admitted that, there was still a chance. Julia was open to it. It gave him a lifeline.

"Doesn't take long. Should last about an hour to an hour and a half."

The tick-tock-ticking of Julia's deliberations played out in her head. A couple of hours at most didn't seem too bad. She would never understand why her husband loved stuff like this so much. She didn't have to, she just had to understand that he did.

"Okay. You sort it all and we'll go on your little boat trip.

Take some pics, hear some stories. Just be careful it doesn't keep you awake all night."

"I can think of better things that will keep me awake all night."

He grabbed her tightly and bit her neck gently. Lawrence's mood had been instantly lifted. He was such a child with his moody sulks that were easily washed away with the promise of getting what he wanted. Julia had agreed, they could go visit Poveglia. His attitude slightly soured as he realised he had no idea how to get them there. It was time to be creative. He was a salesman by trade. Surely, he could put his skills to good use. He smiled at the ludicrous idea of working out a deal with a gondolier and having him paddle them around the island. It was a terrible idea and not one he took seriously. His inner smile faded, yes, it was a terrible idea. But not an entirely terrible notion.

13

L'ultimo squalo cut through the water as it sailed towards Poveglia. Rino stood in the cockpit and steered the boat towards the island. He had never had so many passengers on his vessel. A couple from Florence that Elena knew from university were the first to board. Rino estimated them to be the same age as her, although he felt the man looked much older. They were soon joined by another couple, a friend from Florence who didn't go to the university and his friend who Rino suspected was from Rome but never asked.

An unexpected third man entered the fray, a German who had been passing by the pier and had overheard Elena talk about the tour. Rino didn't know what part caught his ear, although judging by the way he looked at Elena it was his eye that enticed him to enquire further.

"Hello, how are we today?" he asked in English. Rino had a decent grasp of the language while Elena was close to fluent. Lucky for the stranger, he made an interesting assumption considering she had been speaking Italian.

Elena's guests boarded as she turned her attention towards the man.

"I am very good, my friend," she said, in English.

"Did I hear your mention, *geero?*"

"Il giro dell'isola."

He looked at her blankly as he struggled to translate the sentence into German then into English.

"Island tour?"

"Very good. Yes, we are about to embark on an island tour."

"Is this a," he searched for the right word, "private tour? I have money."

"Now now, you don't even know where we're going?"

"I travel alone, I look for adventure." He smiled smugly.

"In that case you have come to the right tour. But before I say too much more, I need to know. Do you scare easily, signore?"

The man deliberated the sentence. Was she flirting with him or looking for a sale? Either way, he liked it.

"Nein," he said, and beat his chest in an imitation of manliness.

"You are welcome to join our journey for we are about to depart to Poveglia island, the most haunted island in all of Italy. And some say the world." She fluttered her eyelashes and bit her bottom lip. He was sold.

"How much?"

"Twenty euro." She considered charging more, she would have gotten away with it. Instead, she opted for fairness and charged what everyone else was paying.

He feigned insult at the price.

"Do I get a reduced cost?"

Elena tutted as she shook her head.

"You *are* getting a good price. This is the first of what will be a very popular tour. It will not be this price forever. Do you even know what Poveglia is?"

He did not. He straightened his glasses, Elena noted how

angular his nose was.

"Okay," he said. "I like surprises." He opened his backpack and produced the money. Elena could tell that despite his modest presentation that he wasn't poor. It was his tone. She regretted not charging more.

"Mi chiamo Elena."

"Til."

She ushered Til onto the boat. Rino Looked at her with slight distaste. She waved the euro note at him and shrugged. Five people all paying twenty each. Not a bad start.

Rino found it all strange. He was used to being alone on the sea. His passengers were on deck, all seated except for Elena. She gave some history of the island as they made their way there. How it was used as a quarantine station for plague victims. She had done her research and spoke well.

As they approached, Rino steered the boat so they could get a better look at the asylum. The large structure looked ominous, even in the daytime. It oozed of despair and felt as lifeless as the stone it was built from. Yet, it didn't feel absent.

"In 1922, the asylum on Poveglia was opened," Elena said. She spoke in Italian while translating in English for Til. "It was used to house those that Venice was ashamed of. To lock up and forget the poor souls who the city wished to erase from its memory. It was hidden in plain sight and shrouded in mystery. The locals turned a blind eye to the rumours that spread from the island. Those that worked there claimed to have seen things they could not explain and hear whispers in the night. No one that was ever committed to the asylum… returned."

The man from Florence shivered, he told himself it was from the sea breeze. Til was utterly enthralled with the story. So far it was the best twenty euro he had spent and that didn't include the view.

"Men that were condemned to live on Poveglia, died there. Only those that worked there were allowed to come and go. Doctors, nurses, orderlies. Each one sworn to secrecy by corrupt officials. Forced to keep to themselves the horrors that they witnessed."

Rino could hear snippets from the cockpit. He was impressed with her imagination. She had asked him earlier if the stuff she had read was true. He told her about the rumours, the mad doctor, the ghosts. She did well to fill in the blanks.

"There was one man, a doctor, who was worst of all. He would prowl the halls of the asylum in the early hours. When most of the staff had left for the night, it is said that he remained and looked for his next victim. Preying on the most helpless, this doctor, this fiend, would operate on them while they were still alive. He would take his surgical tools and pierce the skulls of his victims. Expose their brains to the cold air just to see what it would do."

The man from Rome looked unimpressed but everyone else was captivated by her storytelling. The man from Florence felt sick, again, he blamed it on the environment.

"What happened to the doctor?" Til asked.

Elena raised an eyebrow and leaned in closer. "The doctor is said to have been the last victim of the island. It is said that he was merely a pawn for the malevolent spirits that dwell there. A tool no different than the ones he used on his victims. When they were done with him they discarded him. They drove him as mad as his patients and he threw himself from the bell tower."

She pointed towards the tower. Everyone turned their necks.

That was Rino's cue. He cut the engine and allowed the boat to slow to a natural stop.

"We're going to take a quick break," Elena said. "Please take your pictures. Be warned though. It is said that those that snap the island get a surprise when they later look upon the photographs."

She excused herself and entered the cockpit.

"Having fun?"

Rino smiled and wiped his brow. "Sound like you're having all the fun."

"One hundred euro for an hour's work. I like the maths."

"How many times do you expect us to do this?"

"Who knows, we can let the word spread for now and see what interest we get. I think we should advertise though. If this goes well, you may need a bigger boat."

"Enough," he held up his hand. "One step at a time."

"Don't pretend you're not enjoying this."

"I'm not hating it. Let's put it that way."

"Easy money, no?"

Rino couldn't deny that. There was no hard labour involved. Elena did most of the work, and she seemed to be enjoying herself.

"One step at a time."

She kissed him on the cheek and returned to the deck.

"Ladies and gentlemen, we are about to embark on the second half of our tour. Please keep hands inside the boat at all times." She looked straight at Til who was dangling an arm over the side. "I feel we are quite a safe distance from the ghosts but I can't say the same for the sharks."

Til gave her a *yeah, right* stare as he left his arm over the side. Rino arrived on deck and bore a hole straight into him.

Without a word spoken, the captain of his ship delivered the message loud and clear. Til placed his hands on his lap and bowed his head.

Rino returned to the cockpit and fired up the boat. The old girl spluttered into life, a sound that made Rino smile each time. He steered the boat starboard and allowed the tour to resume without interruption.

"I hope you all got some good photographs," Elena said. "I hope you don't find any uninvited visitors in them later. Any questions?"

"Can we visit the island?" asked the woman from Florence. Her voice was crackly and lacked confidence.

"Oh no, you can't visit the island. It is strictly forbidden by the government. Besides, who here would dare to?"

The tourists all looked at each other. Even the most sceptical amongst them would think twice before setting foot on it. With one exception.

"Now," Elena said. "We are going to show you where the plague victims arrived and later discover what Napoleon's role was in Poveglia's history."

14

Aaron stood at the start of the pier, unhappy with his view of the Palazzo Dario. The angle was all off. He looked through the lens and framed his shot, bringing the building into focus. The harsh sun reflected off the water, it was beautiful. But nothing without the building. He was in Venice, he'd have a million opportunities to snap the sun and water. He took the shot anyway.

His face contorted with annoyance, a grimace that caught Kirsty's attention.

"Why don't you walk to the edge of the pier," she said, "scared you'll fall in?"

He was, a little. "I'm not scared I'll fall in," he said.

"Good, because we're in Venice. You know, water is kind of its thing."

He wasn't in the mood for jousting with his sister. He looked across the wide canal. It amazed him how the buildings looked straight onto the water. That locals would jump in a boat the way he'd use a car. Seemed silly to fixate on it but he did all the same.

He looked up the canal and noted how there was nowhere to stand right across from the Palazzo. One of Venice's most haunted houses, rumour is that a famous Hollywood director had an interest in buying it, but the curse scared him too much.

Almost a dozen people who owned the house had died over the years, mostly suicides. No one was certain when the house was built but some believed that the critical mistake was on its location. Believed to be built on a mass grave of plague victims, it was said that those that suffered most gruesomely in life exacted their revenge in death.

Another plague story, Aaron thought. It made him uneasy. The accountable history of Venice and those that died made the notion of a curse all the more feasible. He had learned about the plague in school, a history lesson that terrified him. He remembered waking up that night screaming and drenched in sweat from a nightmare. In his dream, he had been chased by a ghastly figure.

It was cloaked all in black. He ran, and he ran, frequently turning to see the figure close the distance despite its lethargic pace. He looked down at his arms to see his own flesh drip from the bone, exposing the whites beneath.

His pursuer finally caught up to him. It grabbed Aaron by his shoulders and pinned him to the ground. Aaron froze, unable to move or even scream. Paralysed and at the mercy of his pursuer.

His adversary was face to face with him. Its blank expression filled with nothing but a clinical malevolence. It was the sound of his own screaming that woke him. He never had the dream again. He'd never forget it.

The memory sent a chill up Aaron's spine. A gruesome embrace.

"What the hell is wrong with you?" Kirsty asked, noticing her brother twitch.

"Nothing. Can we do something else while we're here?

Something, I don't know, more normal?"

"*Normal* isn't why we're here youngling."

"I know exactly why we're here, I'd just like to see something that doesn't have some macabre history attached to it for five minutes."

"What's macabre about this? The sun is out, the water is pretty."

"It would just be nice to unwind for a bit before heading off to *Plague Island* or whatever it's called."

"Plague Island is one of its names to be fair. As is the Island of Madness, the Island of Death, Island of the Dead etc etc etc."

"Thank you for proving my point."

"We're in Venice. Everything has something *macabre* attached to it. Poveglia, though, that's the golden goose. We get that in the bag, everything else we do will be easy peasy. We've went at this all wrong. Starting off at the bottom and trying to find our feet? Nope. Dive in headfirst and sink or swim. Take a shot at the King."

"Stop speaking in baseless clichés."

"My point still stands. You want to be a ghost hunter? I can think of no better place than there."

The legend of Poveglia spoke for itself. Aaron understood how it had spawned so many stories. What really worried him aside from being butchered by some spirit was that the island was off-limits to the public. They couldn't just take a water taxi over and ask the driver to keep the meter running while they went for a look. If caught, they'd go to jail. That was a possibility with most places they wanted to investigate. You couldn't spell haunted without condemned, not if you wanted something genuinely spooky at least.

He never saw what scared Kirsty in The House of Reston

Mather. If he had, that would be him. Done. Finished, game over. Even though he didn't see the dead ba- the dead body with his own eyes it was still enough to force his urban exploration career into early retirement. Until Kirsty talked him round like she usually did. Aaron never understood why Kirsty wasn't more traumatised than she was by what she saw. Except she was. She just hid it well.

"Fine," he said. "You're taking me off-topic, all I'm saying is it'd be nice to do something else, something that doesn't involve anything haunted before we go. I thought that was the whole point of doing this in Europe. A holiday to go along with your weirdness. That too much to ask?"

"Fine," she said. "We can do whatever you want until that time. Then I'm in charge. I'm the producer, remember."

"Have you figured out a way to get us over there yet?"

Kirsty had not. They both knew that the island was closed off to visitors and neither had any boating skills of their own.

"I'm working on it," she said.

Aaron was sceptical. He realised this didn't bother him. He was enjoying Venice. He liked the city, despite his fear of water. He was in no rush to visit Poveglia. He was more than happy to unwind and do some sightseeing.

He also knew how relentless Kirsty was. She might not know how they were going to get there but she'd find a way. He was very concerned it would involve the two of them rowing over themselves. The thought did cross her mind, not that she would voice it. Not until it was the last resort.

15

Kirsty wasn't the only one wondering how to get to Poveglia. Across the water and beyond the Palazzo Dario, Lawrence stood within the Basilica di Santa Maria della Salute. He was studying a particular piece of art that hung on the wall. It appeared to depict a man wrestling with an angel as it tried to ascend to Heaven. Except the man was keeping him on earth, much to the dismay of what he figured to be God and Jesus. *Aren't they supposed to be the same guy?* he thought. He wasn't religious in any way. He was a proud atheist and made sure everyone knew it should the opportunity arise. He carried around his belief, or lack thereof, in deities with a smugness that often bored those in his vicinity. He had to be right in a conversation and didn't care who was hurt in the process.

Still, he did enjoy the imagery and architecture. The church was considered a minor basilica, although he noted to himself that it hardly reeked of unimportance. It was a pose, a gratuitous flex of the Catholic church to show how important they were. Some would describe the way he projected his views on others in a similar fashion.

He didn't mention any of his current thoughts to Julia. She wasn't religious either, but reserved space in her soul for a spiritual understanding of the world. Plus, he didn't want anyone to overhear. It was only polite to remain quietly disrespectful. Unless God could hear him. How would he reply? What would God say to his scoffing? That an almighty being would give his arrogant and self-serving thoughts any notice amused him. That God, *The* God, would take time out of his busy day to pull an irrelevant atheist to the side for a quick chat.

Julia wandered around the church. She studied each feature with an ardent curiosity. It was beautiful. Millions of churches existed all over the world, however she believed none were as striking as those built in Europe. Venice had its fair share. They only had a couple of days left, and they couldn't do everything she wanted. This one was near to where they were. It made sense to tick it off the list. What she really wanted was a gondola ride, although she knew that Lawrence was interested in a different boat trip altogether.

She left it to him to research the tour of Poveglia. It was his idea, not that it had mattered in the past. She had lost count of the times she had to organise something that he was meant to. She wasn't doing it for him this time. Not when they had so little time to spend in Venice. She was surprised he hadn't mentioned it much since they left the apartment. For something he had become so obsessed with he was strangely quiet. Julia wouldn't pry. Not yet. She just wanted to experience the more traditional side of Venice. The parts not haunted by insane spirits.

Lawrence took out his phone. No reception. Great. He looked over at Kirsty who was lost in her own little world. He went over and gently embraced her.

"Hey, babe," he said. "Enjoying yourself?"

"Yeah," she said, "it's nice in here. Peaceful."

"What's next on the agenda? I'm thinking we grab a seat somewhere, maybe order a drink or two?"

Julia was getting quite thirsty though she figured Lawrence was after something stronger. It was their honeymoon after all, they both deserved a little afternoon treat.

"Sure. Do you have anywhere in mind, or you happy to just see what we come across?"

"Let's just wander."

Lawrence realised he was hungry as they left the basilica and decided to grab something to eat. Lawrence had planned on something cheap and cheerful but Julia had her eye on something more upmarket. They found themselves in a very expensive looking restaurant that sat them by the Grand Canal.

They sat outside in the shade and looked at the menu. Before Lawrence had a chance to open his, their waiter appeared. A handsome man with an expensive haircut, he lit a fuse of insecurity in Lawrence. He quickly dismissed it with a snobbish swat. He was only a waiter. His waiter. *He* was the one in charge.

"Buonasera," he said with a thick Italian accent. "My name is Alessandro, and I'll be your waiter this afternoon. How may I help you lovely people today?" His English was perfect, which annoyed Lawrence even more. Jealousy made him ugly. He had intended to speak first in some sort of pathetic display of masculinity, but Julia beat him to it.

"Buonasera, Alessandro. I... I don't know what to have, can I see a wine list, per favore?"

"Most certainly," he took the wine list from under his arm. He opened it with a graceful fluidity before handing it over.

"If you need any assistance with the translations, please do not hesitate. There are some written but I don't know who was responsible. The beauty of their meaning has been lost." His smile was warm and seductive. Julia couldn't help but find it alluring.

"And for yourself, signore?" he turned to Lawrence, who was a little surprised his wife's new friend had even noticed him.

"What do you have on draught?" he said. Draught beer. Looks manlier, don't you think? Lawrence was aware of his pathetic attitude. He'll deal with it later.

"Ah, unfortunately, there is an issue with our machinery. It's only bottles that are available just now. If you let me know what you like, I can recommend something?"

Sure, you'd like that, wouldn't you? The ball back in your court. "Something local. Lager."

"Okay, signore. And for you signora?"

"Small red," she said. "Merlot is fine. Grazie." She handed back the unread list. Alessandro gave them a courteous bow and left.

Lawrence was tense. His face was tight and his eyes narrowed. His shoulders seemed unnaturally high. Alessandro had done nothing to elicit the response. It was irrational. It was something else. Julia was right. After today, they only had tomorrow in Venice and then they were off to Rome. Gone from the Floating City and goodbye to Poveglia.

He thought back to the articles he read. It was a real-life horror story. Victims of the plague abandoned on an island. Mental patients tortured by the vengeful ghosts of those victims. An evil doctor that performed lobotomies on those under his care. That same doctor's strange suicide. It was wild. He had to see it.

He loved a good scare, but he didn't believe in ghosts. The concept was ludicrous. There was no real danger to be fearful of. It would offer a safe thrill. Not that he felt he would get to step foot on the island but to get a closer look and bask in its essence? It gave him a welcome chill.

Julia sensed something was wrong. Aside from Lawrence's posture, she knew his mind was elsewhere.

"Go anywhere nice?" she asked.

Broken from his daydream, he focused his attention on her. "What? No, sorry. Just off on a little world of my own there."

"What's up?"

"Nothing. Nothing, honest. Just a little tired. This heat is pretty draining."

She leaned in and took a deep breath. Her eyes never left his. "What is it?"

"It's nothing, I told you." He followed it up with a fake smile and half-laugh.

"Okay. I'll accept that. Excuse me two minutes."

Julia got up to leave and made her way to the restrooms. As she disappeared out of sight, Alessandro appeared with the drinks. He looked way too happy for Lawrence's liking. What did he have to be so cheerful about?

He brought the drinks over and gently placed them down. "Are we ready to order or-"

"Best give us another five minutes, thanks." His voice was hollow and cold. Lawrence never once raised his eyes to look at the man. He took out his phone and noticed he had a reasonable connection. He thought about asking for the Wi-Fi code but didn't want to speak to the waiter again. He checked his Facebook. Nothing exciting. A couple of notifications wishing him well on his honeymoon. Some update from his sister about a missing dog seven hundred miles from where she lived. His aunt shared one of those ridiculous chain memes he hated that featured a cartoon character with an irrelevant quote.

He checked his Twitter and looked at the news. The President had drafted a new border bill or something, he wasn't interested and opted to scroll right past it. Another actor had been outed as a sex pest. Boring. Some woman had been cleared of any suspicion of the murder of her friends at a cottage. The story was a hot thing for two minutes. He still thinks she was involved. He was so agitated. It depressed him. Venice was dull and bland, he hoped Rome would be an improvement, at least.

He scrolled up to his search bar and typed in Poveglia. He was curious to see what others had been saying about it, if at all. It was a big world, he couldn't be the only one that had it playing on his mind.

He casually scrolled through the results, ignoring the blog posts and links. He wanted to see what people's thoughts were. Some posts were in Italian, the auto-translate showed they weren't worth his time. Except one. A recent post, a picture of the island alongside the hashtags #poveglia #Fantasmi #isoladed.

He clicked on it. It had been taken and posted that day, earlier that very afternoon. He clicked on the user, a @StAnger99. He felt his pulse race. The person didn't have a profile pic or their real name displayed but, if the posts were to be believed, they had been on a tour of Poveglia. There wasn't much more information to go on but it was promising.

He typed out a message asking for more information, "hello,

love the pics. Was that today, did you go a tour of the island? Looks fun, I'd love to do that." He hit send as Julia reappeared. He placed his phone on the table, a little guilt in his actions like he had just been caught watching porn.

Julia gave him a quizzical look as she sat down. For a second, she did think she caught him watching porn, but gave him the benefit of the doubt that it was not only their honeymoon, but it was also a little public, even if the restaurant was quiet.

"You okay?" she said.

"Yeah, fine," he said. "Much better now the beer has arrived. Cheers." He lifted his glass and took a large gulp. The lager was refreshing and cool, the gassy liquid hit his stomach with force. His mood had certainly perked up. He was excited. While it appeared Poveglia was a bust, he had been thrown a lifeline. It was a long shot, he knew that, but it was still a chance. His eyes kept flickering to his phone. He wished he hadn't left it on silent.

"Expecting an important call?"

"What? No, yes, no sorry. I'm being rude. Just enquiring about something for the trip and waiting to see how it plays out."

"Is it a surprise?"

"Well, I wouldn't want to get your hopes up if it comes to nothing, that's all."

Alessandro made his way back over to the table, his smile showcasing his perfect teeth.

"Are we ready to order?" he said.

"Oh no, I'm sorry I haven't even looked yet," said Julia.

"No worries at all, please take your time."

"Thank you," Lawrence said, and he meant it. He had no time for his insecurities, not now that his attention was elsewhere.

His eyes flicked to the phone. He made a conscious decision to stop it. It was too suspicious and he didn't want to mention anything until he had more information. He couldn't hide his excitement though, and Julia noticed the change in his demeanour. It wasn't uncommon for Lawrence to go in sulks and come out of them at a whim. She was used to him doing it to her detriment. He had to be more open with her. He had to discuss these things, they were married now.

Whatever news he received in the short time she was away clearly had a positive impact. Julia didn't suspect him of anything untoward, but still, she felt uneasy. She let it slide. She was hungry.

16

Rino sat on the docked boat and counted the money. He felt dirty, but he couldn't argue with the results. Since the inaugural trip, Elena had spent the afternoon drumming up some business. She wandered the nearby cafes and managed to get enough people for two more trips.

Rino noticed how Elena's confidence grew. She was a natural. He still couldn't understand what it was she was studying at university but it was unlikely it tapped into the natural showmanship she exuded. Confident, charismatic and cheeky, Rino could see her outgrowing him quickly if she wanted to do it properly.

He tried to split the money in her favour but she resisted.

"Nope," she said. "It's for you. I don't need it."

"You're taking something," he insisted. "You did a lot more work than I did."

"Well, obviously I'll expect something," she laughed. "It's fun though, right?"

Rino pondered the question. It wasn't unpleasant. But he wouldn't call it fun. He was a fisherman, not an entertainer. This, however, was much easier. Perhaps it was merely a honeymoon period and should they go again the next day he would see his interest dwindle. Would he be upset to see the venture so short-lived? Perhaps. He did like to see Elena smile and her enthusiasm was infectious.

It was late afternoon and the area was still busy. Elena had asked if he wanted to do more but he was happy with how the day had gone and wasn't expecting to get roped into three boat rides.

"Same time tomorrow?" she said.

"If you insist."

"Fantastic. I'll also post some stuff on social media, spread the love. I took some good pictures that I can use to drum up some business. Maybe I should set up a separate account?"

"Patience, child. Patience. The way you're going we'll have a crowd of people lining up."

"Is that a bad thing?"

"I'm old, Elena. Driving the boat is easy but it's tiring. I don't want to do fifty trips a day."

"If we do fifty a day for a week you can retire, hell I might quit university."

Rino didn't appreciate the joke and shot her a stern look. Elena was the first of the family to go to university. The only thing that would make him prouder would be her graduating. She wasn't interested in the money, not for herself. The idea of the tours was so her nonna could stop with the manual labour. He was old and despite being in reasonably good health, she worried about him. With the extra money, he could put it away and maybe even move in with or closer to her parents. That wasn't going to happen, but she was happy to help him any way she could.

"Tomorrow?" she said.

"Tomorrow", he said. "I take it you're going back to Mestre tonight?"

"Yes, I told Mamma I would be back for dinner. You're more than welcome to come too."

Rino loved his family. Yet he didn't want to go. He would rather they come visit him, prideful that he was. They rarely did, apart from Elena. It bothered him more than he'd ever say and that was to his downfall. He didn't want Elena to be indifferent to her family.

"I've business to take care of with the boat. I'm glad you're going back, it's important you spend as much time with them as you can when on a break."

"It's also important for you to spend time with them as well."

"Maybe you can bring them tomorrow and we'll all sail around the island." Rino knew it to be unlikely. His son-in-law hated the water and was petrified of going on boats. A silly thing to hold against him. The stubborn and silly old man that he was. He did consider the dinner invitation, albeit briefly. Then he envisioned the meal itself. His daughter asking why he doesn't move closer to them. His son-in-law voicing his displeasure at Elena spending her time with Rino on the boat. Rino struggling to bite his tongue, unable to resist throwing some barbs out. An inevitable argument boiling. Leaving, having ruined dinner. Stewing on the bus ride home. Going to bed bitter and convinced he was in the right, his regret buried deep inside him. It was better he declined.

"What time are you due back?" Rino asked.

"No rush. Got some time to go get ice-cream if you want? My treat."

Rino smiled. Their quaint little tradition for whenever she came to visit, a tradition that has endured through her life. Of course, he would pay. They both knew that. He wouldn't have it any other way.

17

St. Mark's Square was full of tourists who were more than happy to keep their distance from each other. This suited both Julia and Lawrence. It was a nice surprise from the bridge earlier. The pigeons cared little for the trespassers and barely flinched at the giants that walked towards them, daring them to move around them. A coolness had entered the air and promised a more pleasant evening.

Julia had excused herself to the nearest restroom, this left Lawrence to bask in the glory of St. Mark's Basilica. *Another church.* At least this time Julia wasn't wanting to go in. Venice was dull and everything looked the same. While he couldn't deny the initial beauty of the Floating City, it quickly faded as its lack of substance was exposed.

Julia could not have disagreed more. Even sat in the toilet of a local restaurant - for which she had the pleasure of paying for a ridiculously overpriced bottle of water just to prove she was a customer - she noted how incredible the décor was. The cubicle was lined with a marble-like quality with curving spirals. It was the nicest toilet she could remember visiting, the cost of the water was worth it.

Lawrence refreshed his Twitter. Nothing. No new notifications. He checked the feed of @StAnger99. Nothing. No new

Tweets. He jammed the phone back in his pocket. He looked at the tourists that swarmed around the square. He wondered what went through their heads. What their goals were, what brought them here and if any of them were as bored as he was. He didn't blame his obsession with Poveglia for impacting his thoughts on Venice. He'd have felt the same way towards it, only he wouldn't be filled with the same level of fretfulness. What was there even left to do here? A gondola ride? Rome would be better, he figured. Bigger city vibe. It was more his scene. This little tourist trap was a catfish and he hadn't fallen for it.

A twinge of guilt pulled at him. Julia was enjoying it and sooner or later she would comment on his mood. He'd just tell her. He really wants to do a tour around Poveglia and it's the only thing about Venice he's found interesting. She could understand that, right? It wasn't a slight on her or their marriage that he wasn't enamoured by the city. He realised he'd enjoyed the car ride more.

He looked over to the restaurant to see if Julia was on her way back. His remorse hurt him and he wanted to see her. That's when he felt the vibration on his upper thigh. His phone. His eyes widened as he hurriedly checked it. There it was, the notification he had been waiting for. The name @StAnger99 flashed up on the screen. He quickly unlocked the phone and opened up the message.

"Hello," it read. "We did a tour earlier that my friend organised. It was by invite only," Lawrence's heart sank, "but I think she's looking to do more." Another lifeline.

He hit reply and hastily composed his message, wanting to catch the stranger, whose name he didn't even know, while they were still online.

"Thanks so much for getting back to me," he typed. "I don't suppose you can put me in contact with your friend? I don't have much time in Venice and would love to organise a trip if possible."

He hit send. He watched the spiralling ball turn and turn, battling against a weak reception. It stopped. Message sent. There was a chance. He felt his mood lift. The banality of the city began to dissipate. The stunning beauty of the Basilica shone a little brighter than it did moments before. Even the pigeons looked happier.

He waited impatiently for a reply. He was excited but anxious. He bounced about from foot to foot as an old woman eyed him with suspicion. He smiled at her, a gesture she ignored and swatted away with scorn.

A delicate buzz in his hand. A reply. "Sure," it read. "I'll get in contact with my friend and she can message you directly." And that was that. He was back to the waiting game. He clumsily replied "Gracies," and didn't notice the typo until it was too late. But it was. It was done. A dozen different questions raced through his mind. It was indeed too late now; the conversation was over. It was out of his hands, bearing in mind he was messaging a stranger, he didn't want to harass them online.

It was over. All he could do was wait and he had faith. A good feeling. A spring was firmly back in his step and Venice glowed with a majesty he hadn't seen before. He didn't want to get too ahead of himself as a crushing rejection would end his love affair with Poveglia once and for all and he'd be done with this floating cesspit, for good. In that scenario, he pondered asking Julia if she wanted to leave early. Spend an extra night in Rome. Maybe even ditch the flights and take a car again, stop over somewhere on the way and fill their time with adventure.

He looked over and saw Julia return. She beamed with a cartoonish smile which he reciprocated.

"You seem more chipper," she said.

"I might have reason to," he said, not realising he was exposing his previous feelings. "I've put the feelers out on a trip to Poveglia. You did say you were up for it should I find something."

She did. She hadn't forgotten. Her interest in it was still at a low, but she had agreed.

"Okay, what're the details?"

"That I don't have much of yet, but I saw a guy online that was on a tour this afternoon. Apparently, it's a new venture. Might be able to get us on it."

"Might?"

"It was by invitation only. But they're going to check it out for me."

"Are you basing all this on some random from the internet?"

"Don't be like that."

'I'm not *being* like that. I just don't want you to get too excited."

"Well, ye of little faith, missy." He wasn't ready to feel dejected. Even if she did have a point there was something about the message, the amateur nature of the operation that bizarrely filled him with hope. "How about we grab a drink, I'm a little parched."

"Want some of this water? It cost me three euros so you can have two sips before I charge you."

"What magical properties does it have?"

"The magic to keep you hydrated."

"I was thinking of something a little stronger. I also read

there's a cool little bar just off the square."

Julia would have liked to have seen more of the square, but she couldn't ignore her husband's improved mood. She wanted to maintain that for now.

"Ok. But you're buying and I'm in the mood for something expensive."

Her playful jibe bounced off him. If the feelers he put out led somewhere, she could have anything she wanted.

18

Contrary to the photos she had seen, Kirsty found Venice to be dirty. There was no denying the structural beauty of the city, however like most of the world's wonders it was tainted by the unmistakable mark of humans. The litter in the canals saddened her: she felt we didn't deserve this planet. She was far from a conservationist. Kirsty was aware of the carbon footprint she left on the world. Jet setting around Europe chasing ghosts isn't necessarily essential travel.

Maybe a rowboat to Poveglia wasn't the worst idea. It was eco-friendly and it would be a good workout. Except she had never rowed a boat in her life and assumed the same of her brother. She had no experience of boats in general. Or currents for that matter. Knowing her luck, she'd end up adrift in the middle of the Mediterranean. It would be a good story at least. She thought about the Bermuda Triangle. Would that be worth visiting?

The crowds had started to dissipate and she needed to clear her head. She allowed Aaron to go do his own thing. She had dragged him all across Italy, the least she could do was give him some peace while she sorted out transport. She wandered aimlessly along the seafront, stopping at the Giardini della Biennale. She liked it there. It wasn't busy and it was peaceful.

She enjoyed the lack of buildings and basked in the greenery to her back as she looked out onto the water. Poveglia was out there.

She wondered if any of the locals would be up for a bribe and take them across. Kirsty had money. That wouldn't be an issue. Life had been good to her. Yet she struggled to enjoy it. She felt her life lacked an edge. She found little excitement working in an office, even if she was the manager. There was satisfaction to be had in starting at the bottom and working her way up over ten years but now that she was there, promoted as high as she possibly could be, what next? Take the money and sit on the beach? She needed something to stoke the fire in her.

Ghost hunting across Europe was certainly a novel way to spend your holiday. Truth is ghosts always fascinated her. It didn't matter that she didn't believe, she wanted to experience something that made her doubt her own scepticism. To see something that would make her question what's beyond this life, if anything.

A haunted island that could trap her, where there'd be no place to run should it get too much for her. It was such a thrilling prospect. Who knew the most frustrating part would be trying to get there? The few tours that got you anywhere near Poveglia had been stopped without explanation. It was said that the fishermen refused to get too close but would any do so for a price?

Or anyone, for that matter. The city was built on water, everyone had a boat. Someone would be tempted. She looked up and saw a man standing against the stone barrier. He looked younger than her, maybe late teens.

"Buonasera," she called out. He ignored her. "Buonasera," she said, louder this time.

18

He turned, startled and confused. He looked at her, his face was kind and calm. Naïve looking. He pointed at himself.

"Sì. Lei parla inglese?" she asked him.

He contemplated the question. This strange lady's Italian was okay, even if her accent was a little off.

"A little," he said.

"Poveglia. Do you know it?"

His eyes widened at the name. He translated the question in his head. He was more than aware of it. What did she want to know about it?

"A little," he said.

Wonderful. Is this the only English he knows?

"Do you know how I could get there?"

Silence. Did he have a clue what she was asking? Kirsty wasn't overly familiar with the customs of Venice, it may be frowned upon for unknown foreign women to randomly shout out questions at strangers.

"Boat? Paddle? Row? Row row row your boat?" Kirsty mimed a rowing action, albeit badly. Her new friend's blank expression remained. *Forget it.* "Never mind. Sorry."

The man continued to look baffled, but unbeknownst to Kirsty, he understood more than she knew. He walked away questioning what he had heard. Was this lunatic wanting to go to Poveglia? Had she any idea what it was? She couldn't have, he must have misheard her, something was lost in translation. She wasn't a native Italian speaker, it was clear in her accent. She must have meant to say something else. It was best he not dwell on it. He had heard much about the Island of Madness. Its dark history and what happened to those foolish enough to visit. The island was off-limits to visitors for a reason. *Donna sciocca.* He hoped she was wrong in her words. He prayed she would not find passage.

Kirsty watched the man walk away. His pace quickened as he got further from her. She looked back out towards the water and her phone rang. She looked at the screen, it was Aaron. He never texted. He always phoned. She found it an unsettling trait.

"Sup?" she said, answering the call.

"Where are you?" he asked.

"Croatia. I got bored of Venice."

"Hilarious, as always. I was hoping you'd be nearby to me. I've got some good news."

"What is it?" She wasn't sure where he was but it sounded much busier than her own slice of paradise.

"I'd rather tell you in person."

"You won't want to see me before telling me, otherwise I'll be gutting you in person."

"Jesus, always a tough sell with you."

"You know I hate surprises, so just tell me."

"I may have it."

"Have what?" She was getting impatient. Knowing her brother, the good news would be something spectacular to him yet mundane to her. He probably saw a dolphin or found a bar with a two for one deal. He was easily pleased, although the latter appealed to her.

"I think I found a way to get us to the island."

Her eyes widened. Of course he would. While she wracked her brain to develop a master plan he'd just stumble upon the jackpot. She was excited but dubious.

"How?"

"Can I not just tell you in person, it'd be easier and this call is really expensive."

She came close to throwing her own phone into the water. "Fine, just send me your location." She hung up before he could say anything else. So many questions raced through her mind. Who, what, when, where, why? Excitement flowed through her.

Her phone pinged. She opened it and her map opened with the directions. He was in a bar near San Marco Square. She didn't realise how far she had walked. She was about half an hour away according to the map. Kirsty was sure she could make it in less time. She had motivation on her side.

19

Ghosts? Ha. Til scoffed at the notion. Yet, he couldn't deny his curiosity. What was so special about Poveglia that it was prohibited? He refused to believe that the Italian government would be so superstitious as to ban visits to an island because they believed it was haunted.

Still, he could find no one to take him. He asked around the docks and shops he passed. Everyone seemed friendly until he brought up the island. Some didn't want to talk about it at all, while others were happy to regale him with fantastical tales. None were as convincing or as detailed as he heard on the tour. Ah, Elena. He wouldn't forget her in a hurry. Shame her grandfather was there. If not, he could see her saying yes to a date. And then, well, he'd get to sample the local culture some more.

He'd find someone else. He had no intention of going to bed alone tonight, and preferably not the bed back at the hostel. In the meantime, he wanted to get on the island. Take some selfies and make a mockery of those simple Venetians and their silly legends. Except, no one was willing to take him. He asked a few taxi drivers and all but one said no. Some laughed him off. Others, well, they were less than cordial to the arrogant tourist. The one that did say yes wanted a ridiculous fee. Til declined.

Fine, he thought. *I'll do it myself.* He found a place where he could rent a boat in the middle of the city. The owner was a middle-aged man with dark eyes and white hair. His smile cracked his face as he beamed towards a potential customer.

"Buonasera," he said. "Mi chiamo, Adamo."

"Ciao," Til replied. "I'm looking to hire a boat."

"Ah. Then you have come to the right place. What may I interest you in?"

Til wasn't sure. He had been on many boats, but he had no experience of driving one. How hard can it be?

"A small boat. Something easy."

"I think I have just the boat for you," Adamo said.

Til was careful not to mention his true intentions. He told Adamo he wanted to get a real taste for the city, take the boat for a spin down the canals. Not that the owner cared much, he appeared more interested in closing a sale. Til didn't get the impression that the shop was busy nor did he think there was much on offer other than what he hired. An electric Topetta, six metres in length with a six-horsepower motor. The best part was he didn't even need a license or any experience. Whether it was entirely legal or not, he wasn't sure. Considering his intentions for the boat, he felt it best to keep quiet.

As he set off, he cursed how busy the canal was. The boat was going to take some getting used to and the locals weren't forgiving to new blood in the water. By the time he got to the open sea, he felt comfortable. The engine whirred as he skimmed across the water. The map function on his phone would help him find Poveglia. He just hoped he had enough battery to find his way back.

As Til approached the island, the asylum came into view. There were a few boats nearby, and he grew concerned that he might be spotted. He steered towards Poveglia, quietly aware of how exposed he was. As he approached the dock, he noticed a gap to his right. He slowed the boat down for a better look. The island which housed the asylum was separated from a smaller island. The proximity of the land created a strait. It looked like a perfect place to hide, so he steered the boat down the narrow channel.

Trees towered over him as he slowed the boat and looked for a place to disembark. It was eerily silent, all Til heard was the small motor. The sun was high enough in the sky that he wasn't coated in the shadows of the forest. Til struggled to find somewhere to stop the boat. The banks on either side were steep and although he felt he could climb one of them, he had nowhere to tether the boat.

He had seen Poveglia hours earlier, however the tour had paled compared to his solitary journey. He recalled the story Elena told about plague victims being sent to the island in the 18th century. How the officials would overcrowd small boats, not much different in size to his own. A sombre tone fell over him as he thought about the thousands of people that died on Poveglia. The safety net of the tour was removed as the island surrounded him. His idea to visit the island didn't seem as funny anymore.

He approached an old bridge that connected the islands. A chill ran over him as he went under it, momentarily cloaked in its shadow. The brash confidence Til displayed on the tour had left him. Replaced with sobering anxiety. But he'd come this far, he couldn't back out now. His original plan to explore the buildings appealed less. The least he could do was set foot on the island. He'd regret not doing so.

He could see the end of the strait and the open ocean. It was then he noticed a dock to his left. *That would do,* he thought. Yet, he wondered if he would have rather not found somewhere to moor the boat. Despite travelling for the past few weeks by himself, it was the first time he felt truly alone. He laughed as he realised that was a good thing. It was for the best that he was alone lest he spends the night in jail. *Or worse.*

He shook his head to clear his concerns. He moored the boat to the dock and stepped onto the island. His foot hit the ground, and he noticed how soft and dry it was. The soil was fine and sandy. Where he stood, the grass was sparse as it struggled to penetrate the unnatural looking land. He felt less a conqueror, and more an intruder.

The island was cooler than the city. There was a lack of humidity, and he felt a strange bite to the air. He walked past a small wooden hut and studied the path before him. Beyond the line of trees was a large clearing. The grass was overgrown but not much more than the average garden that was left unattended. It looked to have fought valiantly against the powder-like soil, but even then, he expected the grass to be longer than it was.

On either side of him were small buildings. He wondered what they could have once been and tried to remember if Elena mentioned them on the tour. There was the asylum, *obviously*. What else...a prison, and a hospital. Was that what they were? He considered a closer look at the smaller one. It seemed less imposing. Til took his phone out to check his battery. It had drained considerably since he last checked it. *Stupid maps,* he thought. He risked using more battery and took some pictures. He hesitated to look at them in case they revealed something he'd rather not see. He looked. There was nothing.

It restored his confidence slightly, and he made his way over to the smaller building. The wind whispered through the trees and towards him. The hairs on his neck stood up as the breeze brushed his ears. If he didn't know better he could swear he heard a voice.

Til checked his phone again. No signal. Even less battery. It didn't make him feel any better to see that. At the building, he noticed it had no windows, only a broken door. He slowly approached it. He had to have a look. To silence the frightened little boy within him that told him to turn back. Yes, he would look inside and prove he was being silly. But he didn't feel silly, and no longer was he in the mood to make a mockery of Poveglia.

The wind intensified and so did the voice. They were unintelligible but much more distinct. He wasn't alone on the island. He turned to the clearing but there was nothing there. Nothing but the trees, and their shade. The shadows shimmered with the movement of the trees. At first. With only one source of light on the island, the shadows moved in unnatural ways. They defied the laws of nature as they snaked their way towards Til.

The voice got louder. Vibrant and dynamic with a cruel agony that underlined its words. He walked across the clearing back towards the dock. The lone voice became many as hushed tones swarmed him. Strident and targeted, the anguish penetrated his conscience as empathy flooded him. Til fell to his knees and wanted nothing more than to cry. To apologise for all the pain and misery that took place on Poveglia. As the shadows got closer, Til was ready to embrace them. To allow them to claim him. Then, his phone vibrated. It shook him from his trance and the voices dissolved. He instinctively checked his phone. It was the battery's death rattle, a final farewell before shutting down. Broken from his daze, he expected reality to return and the shadows to return to their rightful place. Instead, they continued stalking him. It was then he ran.

He made his way across the clearing and back to the dock. He jumped onto the boat and struggled with the engine. He could hear footsteps on wood. On the dock. He looked up but couldn't see anything. But something was there. Something was coming for him.

For a second, he thought the motor wouldn't start, then it sputtered into life. He felt far from safe or relieved as the boat made its way down the strait. He looked back, expecting to see someone on the dock, staring at him. There was no one. No one he could see. But he could feel them. He could feel eyes upon him. As he passed back under the bridge, the gaze bore into his back. He didn't look up, for fear of what he might've seen. He looked down at the water and the shadow cast by the bridge. It might've been a trick of the light, but he swore there was another silhouette. The feeling of being watched stayed with him until he was clear of the island.

The small motor strained with each rev as he aimed to get back to Venice as quick as he could. He returned the boat and avoided any chit chat with Adamo. He knew his actions were suspicious, but he didn't care. He wanted to forget what had happened.

Til wandered the streets and found himself in a bar. He ordered a large beer and found it didn't last long. He ordered another. Then another. His nerves wouldn't settle. Despite the heat, he found himself slightly cold. Feverish. *Great,* he thought. He ordered another beer but barely managed a few sips. He didn't feel well. Whether it was the sun, stress or alcohol; he couldn't say. His head hurt and he wanted to lie down. He looked at his phone and forgot the battery had died. He hoped he could at least find his way back to the hostel before he passed out.

20

Rino and Elena sat in the cooling sun. The ice-cream parlour was situated away from the canals, a bonus for Rino. The streets were still busy but had begun to quieten as the late afternoon saw attractions start to close and tourists head back to their hotels to get ready for the nightlife.

Rino demolished his ice-cream: two scoops mint with chocolate chip, while Elena baited the high temperature by taking her time with her three scoops: vanilla, chocolate and strawberry. A strange combination for a strange child thought Rino. Nevertheless, he was proud of his granddaughter. Her brains and enthusiasm had not only gotten her into university, her entrepreneurial spirit had seen them start a new venture. He figured it would be short-lived, she did have her studies to concentrate on, but he enjoyed the time they spent together.

He was too proud to mention how much he appreciated the extra income. It would cover some bills and lighten some stress. A few more trips throughout the week and they'd make a tidy profit. Elena would get more than her fair share, he would see to it. What she didn't realise is she would see most of the money sooner or later. He was a simple man with inexpensive tastes. If this new business picked up, he could invest more in his savings, all the money going to his family when he passed.

"So," Elena said. "I think we could get more business tomorrow easy. I've posted some stuff online. I'll print off some flyers for tomorrow and hand them out."

Rino smiled. The warmness in his chest grew cold as he remembered plans he had made. He got so caught up in the excitement he forgot that there was going to be a problem.

"Ah," he said. "About tomorrow."

Elena looked across the table at him. Her eyes narrowed.

"What about tomorrow?"

"I forgot, I have plans."

"Nonno," she said, her head lowered, never breaking eye contact.

"I have an appointment in Grado. An old friend is selling me all his old boating equipment."

"How long will that take?"

"I haven't seen this man in years. I can't say." He also had no intention of staying any later than the afternoon. He was an old friend, but like most of Rino's old friends, they were best enjoyed in small quantities.

Elena watched her melting ice-cream and toyed at it with her spoon. Rino couldn't help but note how much she looked like her mother at that age.

"Fine," she said. "If you must."

"I must."

"The day after?"

"Sure." Rino saw no issue with that. Truth be told he was looking forward to some rest, but he felt bad for letting Elena down. "The day after."

"That's not too bad actually. It'll give me a whole day to find business."

"Or maybe study?" *Or spend the time with your parents?*

"I can do both. I'm fantastically skilled at multitasking."

Her phone pinged. Rino didn't understand the obsession with those things. Sure, he had one, but it wasn't a computer. It was old, cheap. It did the job. Could it connect to the internet and play games? No. It could phone people. That was the point of a phone. He didn't mind texting if need be, although he hated the tiny keyboard. He noticed Elena seemed more enthused. He wondered if it was a boy messaging her. He felt the muscles in his neck tighten. It's a grandfather's right to be defensive, *I can't imagine that wimp of a son-in-law striking fear into the souls of anyone, let alone potential suitors.*

"Ooh, this is interesting, "Elena said. "It's my friend Dario, from earlier."

Rino couldn't remember any names, he wasn't even sure if he was introduced formally. His short-term memory wasn't great.

"Someone, American, he thinks, saw his posts about the trip. They want to book with us."

Rino struggled with the concept. How a random stranger, an American no less, can indirectly get in touch with an old Venetian fisherman about booking a tour on his boat, one he had only trialled mere hours ago. It hurt his brain.

"What do you think?" she asked.

"It all seems strange to me."

"It's the way of the world, Nonno. Let me be your digital spirit guide into the 21st Century."

"I feel uneasy."

"I feel it's easy money. I haven't even had to spend on an advert."

She hadn't been wrong yet. The old man had stepped out of

his comfort zone and now that horizon was being expanded at a quicker rate than he expected. Maybe it was time to embrace the modern world…to an extent, at least. There was a strange sensation in his stomach. First, he had to deal with the familiar one in his bladder.

"Excuse me, personal business."

Elena almost pressed for more details as he stood before realising where he was going. As he disappeared out of sight she noticed she had another notification, one from earlier she didn't hear. It was a reply to her own amateur advertisement, promoting the new tour to Poveglia.

See the world's most haunted island. Hear the terrifying truth about what happened there and why visitors are strictly prohibited from stepping foot on the land. Come join the only tour brave enough to dare sail its waters. Message me for details.

She felt it needed some work but it had an effect. The message was in English which posed no issue for her. It was a fairly general enquiry. She responded, explaining that there would be no tour tomorrow but that they should be back in action the day after.

Rino returned to the table. "Shall we?" he said. "We best be getting you back home."

Elena smiled, it was weak. She didn't want to go home, she was more than happy to stay with Rino, but she did promise her mother she'd be back for dinner. If only he would come. She knew better than to ask him again.

"Sure, just gave me two minutes." She responded to the American that contacted Dario, a general message similar to the other she sent. It's a shame they were losing a day. The tour had potential to make some serious money, but it was the time that was priceless.

21

Aaron read the message out to Kirsty. “Thank you for your interest. The cost is twenty euro per person, the tour will last around two hours. Unfortunately, there will be no tour tomorrow, please let me know if you would like to book one for the day after? Elena x.”

Kirsty sipped at her Bellini and thought deep and hard. *This is a good Bellini, expensive but good.* The thought derailed her as she tried to clear her mind and focus on the next step.

“I don’t really want to spend another day just wandering Venice,” she said.

Aaron leaned back in his chair and heard it creak over the music. An older barman stood serving drinks in a quaint white jacket and shirt combo. Aaron loved the bowtie, it made him smile. The bar was expensive but it was also one of the most famous in Venice. He was quite happy to spend another day sightseeing, but he could tell his sister was not interested.

“How late do they run the tours?” she asked.

“It doesn’t say. Just that there will be none tomorrow.”

“What kind of amateur outfit have you found here?”

“The only game in town, I take it you’ve found better?”

“You mistake my tone, youngling. They don’t sound too professional to me. That’s a good thing.”

"Why?"

"A professional tour has rules. Guidelines to adhere to. Did they land on the island itself or just go near it?"

"It's the best I could find, okay?"

"I'm happy you found it. It's a good find, stop being so sensitive. My point is, they may be more open to a private tour. Cross their palms with enough silver and they drop us off for a couple of hours."

"What if they don't do private tours."

"Then they drop us off and finish the tour. Come

back and get us later. It's worth a shot. You said yourself, we don't have a great deal of options here. What harm will it do? I still think we should hire a boat and head out ourselves."

"Let's file that under, no chance in this life or the next." Aaron took a drink of his own Bellini - he had to admit it was probably one of the best things he had drunk - and replied to Elena with some follow-up questions.

They sat in near silence waiting for a reply. They didn't wait long.

He read it out, "Aaron, thanks for your interest. We currently have no set times for the tour, as we are just starting out we are open to working with our guests. If you would like a later tour, that could be a possibility depending on interest. We are however unable to visit the island itself. Any attempts to do so is punishable by law and is for your own safety and ours."

"What's so dangerous about it?" Kirsty said, making spooky gestures and laughing.

"I don't know if I want to end up in an Italian jail. No, wait, I do know the answer to that. I don't."

"Cheer up, it's just added flavour to scare tourists. Ask her if they're available for a sunset tour at least. I'm telling you though, with enough incentive they'll drop us off. Hell, with enough persuasion they'll carry our bags for us."

"That's a very disrespectful view."

"All this place is, is a giant tourist trap. I've been here half a day and been fleeced every time I've sat down. Do you know I saw an old Venetian saying on a website yesterday, know what it said? *A pagar e a morir ghe xe sempre tempo.*" She sat back and shot him a matter of fact, how do you like that look.

He stared at her blankly. Kirsty had picked up the Italian she had learned quickly. It made him jealous. "And are you going to tell me what that means little Miss Versace?"

"There's always time for paying and dying," said a voice. It wasn't Kirsty. Both turned to see the older barman stand over them, a friendly yet eerie smile crept over his face.

Both siblings looked at each other with side glances. Something was unnerving about the man. His hair was thick and grey, the wrinkles on his face told a story. This was a man forged from history and experience.

"Excuse me, but I could not help overhear," he said. "You are looking for a... journey to Poveglia?"

Kirsty wasn't sure how common it was for tourists to discuss it. She was less sure how many were successful. "Maybe," she said.

"I doubt very much you will have much success, signora. The locals around here, for which I am one, have a lot of respect for the island. It deserves it."

"We're just talking," Aaron said, "you know, nothing serious." He smiled up at the man but was chilled by the man's own stony smile.

"A lot has happened on Poveglia. Some, I'm sure you have read. But much more you would never know."

"Are you in a position to tell us?" Kirsty said. She felt the same chill as Aaron except it exhilarated her.

"I have work, signora. As you can see, I'm blessed to see the bar so busy. What I will say is that the legend you will be told to scare you, pales compared to the horrors which occurred there. And would continue to do so, should anyone be foolish to disturb the island."

Kirsty knew many before her had visited the island and left unscathed but didn't mention it. She didn't have to.

"I'm sure you've read stories of those that visited the island," the barman continued. "Maybe even seen some pictures? It doesn't show the whole truth. No one that visits, that is lucky enough to leave, is ever the same again. That is just how it is."

Kirsty was enamoured by this man. As was Aaron but in a different way. She could see he was fearful of this spiel to scare the tourists. For all they knew this barman worked for the tour company and was delivering a sales pitch. Not that he needed to, she was long sold on the island. All this did was make her more determined to set foot on it.

"Grazie," she said. "I will definitely bear that in mind."

"I sincerely hope you do," he said. "Another round of drinks?" His demeanour softened. Kirsty ordered another two Bellinis, hoping that the first one wasn't a fluke. The barman left, and she looked at her brother, unable to contain her elation.

"He was intense," she said.

"That's one way to put it," Aaron said.

"How much of that do you think was true?"

Enough to put me off. "No idea. So, what now?"

"Now, I'm going to get suitably drunk. Enjoy my hangover tomorrow and hopefully visit the island."

"I told you, there's no tour tomorrow."

21

"But what about tomorrow night? Give me your phone, I've some questions of my own."

22

Lawrence listened to Julia sing over the sound of the shower. She could carry a tune, albeit, not for long. He sat on a leather-bound chair and flicked through the TV channels. He hadn't a clue what half the shows were, however he found some amusement when he'd find something familiar dubbed in Italian. He wasn't even convinced some of the languages were Italian. Was all of Europe multilingual?

His phone pinged, it was Elena. His initial optimism faded as he read the message. There'd be no tours tomorrow. His gut was tangled in knots. There it was, the circus had just left town. In a bizarre contradiction to his true feelings, he was a little glad. It was the hope that was killing him. The hope was diverting his focus and leading him along. That light at the end of the tunnel was a freight train of disappointment.

Now that it was done, maybe he could enjoy the remaining time in Venice. Julia would be happy. She was getting ready to be treated to a night on the town. Lawrence had no reason to be checking his phone every two minutes, he didn't have to concern himself with Poveglia any longer. It was over. He could dedicate his full attention to his wife.

He replied to Elena with a thank you. He expressed his disappointment nonetheless, highlighting how he only had one more full day in Venice. Maybe if they had time they could come back before heading home, perhaps he'd come back alone in the future? He didn't think either scenario was likely. *Forget about it. It's done. Move on and just enjoy yourself, stop ruining this for Julia.*

He hit, send and with a feeling of lethargy, returned to the TV.

Julia got ready in the bedroom while Lawrence showered. He left the shower and took a towel to dry himself off. As the steam dissipated from the room, he noticed he had a message. It was from Elena. He didn't feel the pang of excitement upon noticing it, not anymore. He picked up the phone and opened the message. He couldn't believe it. "We have some good news. Due to unforeseen interest, we are able to offer a tour around Poveglia tomorrow at 08:00 p.m. Please note there will be a ten euro surcharge per person due to the later booking. If this is of interest, please let me know as soon as you can – Elena x"

The extra cost didn't even register. He didn't care. He was elated. He fumbled with his reply, making sure he confirmed his interest. He wasn't fazed by the typos in his message, as long as the intent was clear. A definitive yes.

He found himself doing a little dance in the bathroom. He didn't think Julia would mind, she had already told him she was fine with it as long as he took care of the details. He'd tell her over dinner. She could choose where to go. It didn't matter to Lawrence how expensive or lavish it was, he had cause to celebrate. Extra cause, on top of his honeymoon, obviously. His last day in Venice was looking up already.

23

While they finished up their ice-cream, Elena was inundated by some crazy British tourists who were desperate to see Poveglia. They had no intention of waiting and thought he could be bought so easily. They didn't know him, not at all. He rejected their increased offers.

Rino was content to have a day off and continue with the tours the day after. He had to admit to himself that the money was welcome, but he wasn't greedy, even if he was saving it for his family.

Then his daughter called. He hadn't long waved goodbye to Elena and had started making his way back to his boat when she rang. Rino hated answering his phone in public. He specifically hated walking while on it. He dodged some crowds and ducked down a quiet alley and stood in the doorway of a closed shop before answering.

"Hey, Papa," Verona said.

"Hello," he said. "Lovely to hear from you. I've just put Elena on the tram, she shouldn't be too long."

"Grazie." A silence. "It's Elena I phoned about. Did she seem okay?"

The question puzzled him. She had spent the day with him, it had been unusual, to say the least, however why wouldn't she be okay?

"Same as ever. Why the concern?"

There was a silence followed by a sigh.

"She mentioned she was going to try and talk you into some boat tour again. Did she succeed?"

"I gave in. I couldn't stop saying no to her."

"Did you earn much from it?"

Something was wrong. Rino never knew his daughter to be straight to the point. She was never blunt, and she rarely if ever spoke about money.

"Verona, what's wrong?"

"We've had some money troubles recently. I don't know if she mentioned it."

Rino wasn't surprised that she hadn't. It sounded like a problem for the adults and Rino still saw Elena as a child despite her age.

"There may be an issue with her university fees for next year," she continued.

Rino closed his eyes and took a deep breath.

"Does Elena know this?"

"I don't think so. She knows that...she knows things haven't been right. It's bad enough that Vincent didn't get the promotion he went for, but they've also lowered his salary as part of some cost-cutting exercise."

Anger boiled within Rino. Elena's father was at fault and now the child was to suffer for it? He couldn't stand that fool. It may have been harsh to hold him at fault for what had happened, but he did all the same. He never had the highest opinion of his son-in-law. Rino never felt there was any conviction in him. Knowing him as he did, Rino wouldn't have been surprised if he was spending money he was yet to earn and that's why they were in the position they were.

"How much?" Rino asked.

"Papa, you know I hate to even bring this up."

Rino appreciated how difficult it was for her. She was proud, like him. Like Elena. That poor child. She deserved her education. Rino would see she got it.

"How much?"

"Ten thousand euro."

It was more than he had. "When for?"

"Next month, the start, so about three weeks. Four if they show leniency."

And you're just mentioning this to me now? He couldn't normally earn the money, not in that short period of time. Except, he did have another revenue stream. It would mean hard graft but Rino was never scared of work.

"I think I can help. Just one thing, don't tell Elena. She doesn't need the stress. I'll get the money."

He couldn't cancel his trip to Grado, he needed the equipment, it was an investment that would earn more than he'd spend. Yet he could no longer afford a day off. He phoned Elena and told her he changed his mind. Get back in touch with the foreigners. Tell them he'll do it. For an increased fee, although not too much. He didn't feel comfortable ripping them off. He was desperate but he still had his principles.

The journey home was a blur. The door of his apartment slammed shut and the day should have gone with it. It's how things usually were for Rino, except it was no ordinary day. It had been the most surreal day. Tour operator extraordinaire. It would have made him laugh had it not been for Verona's phone call.

He took a bottle of beer from his fridge, promising himself

he'd only have the one, which he did. He sat on his battered old chair, the grey fabric welcomed him like the old friend he was. It was a lot of money. He already had some. It was up to Elena what she did with her cut, however Verona was going to have to come clean and make sure the money was going towards her education.

That was a conversation for another time. He just wanted to sleep. He closed his eyes, worried he'd drift off on the chair. He didn't. He barely got any sleep when he finally climbed into bed. His bones creaked and the aches of his age cried out to him. It had been a surreal day. Tomorrow was about to get stranger.

24

The darkness spun around him. It grabbed and clawed. It seeped into every orifice and violated his sanity. He couldn't see anything, nothing to distinguish where he was. He couldn't remember arriving at wherever *there* was, he just seemed to appear. He knew he wasn't meant to be there, hadn't always been *there*. But there he was.

A foreboding sense of doom gripped his heart. Something was coming, something more malignant than the thick shadows that held him. The shadows separated slightly, making a pathway for this unknown entity. Whatever it was, for it to part the blackness before him, it was to be feared.

As the shadows lessened their grip, he thought about running. But where? The only path was leading him straight towards whatever evil was coming for him. Regardless, he took his chance. It was like moving through clay, the nothingness resisted his every move. He couldn't feel his limbs. They didn't want to react.

Footsteps. The damp echo of footsteps. He was in a corridor, a stone corridor with light either side of its long narrow length. His arms had returned to him. He extended them and was able to touch the walls on either side, revealing how narrow the corridor was. He looked at the light before him. The footsteps, behind him.

He ran with the pace of a man who had his lungs removed and his ankles bolted with iron. The footsteps got louder yet he could not go faster. Fear saturated him. His head boiled, a fiery landscape of torment.

The light got closer, he had no idea where it led, but he knew it must have been preferable to what chased him. The footsteps gained on him, the light was so far away. The fire in his head had now ravaged his chest. An intake of breath was like breathing smoke. The exhalation was like vomiting broken glass. He collapsed to his knees.

The light was close enough that he could see his own hands. Pulsating bulbous sores covered them. They were filled with a putrid liquid that made him vomit yellow bile. It was agony. Everything was sheer agony.

The footsteps closed in, he was too petrified to turn around. He began to crawl towards the light and stopped. He shrieked in pain as the pus-filled boils burst, and he rolled over to his side. He began to violently cough as the source of the footsteps stood over him. A figure made of terror. Faceless yet oddly distinguished.

His eyes blurred as an unknown liquid washed over them. The figure lowered a hand and the coughing intensified, as did the screams.

Til woke up with chest spasms. He struggled for breath as the nightmare lingered. As his senses returned to him so too did his breathing. He was glad to be awake. He was also glad he had paid extra for a private room. To have to explain to strangers that a nightmare had such an effect on him would have been embarrassing. At least it should have been. Instead,

Til found no reason to be shameful at the terror he felt. His sheets were drenched in sweat as perspiration rolled off of his forehead.

He looked to the corner of the room and gasped. There stood the figure from his nightmare. Tranquil in its lucidity, it aroused a primal sense of death. Paralysed by fear, he willed his arm to turn on the bedside lamp. The room filled with a dull light. The figure was gone.

Panicked, he shot upright and looked at his hands. They were uninjured. He checked the sheets for vomit, worried he had been sick. They were unmarked, or at least he thought so. Specks of red had soaked into the sheet. Still wet to the touch, Til put his fingers to his mouth and found he had coughed up blood.

A chill ran through him. He was feverish. He pulled the cover up to his neck as he slowly lay back down on the bed, never taking his eyes off of the corner of the room. If anyone had heard him, they didn't come to his aid. Maybe, just maybe, he hadn't made an audible sound, that it was all in his head.

He knew better. He also knew that he wasn't getting back to sleep. He kept the light on, and his eyes wide open. He checked his phone; the screen displayed 01:09 a.m. It was then he noticed a faint peculiar smell he couldn't explain. A menthol scent hung in the air. He dared not fall back asleep.

25

Lawrence awoke the next morning, full of energy and excitement. His head was a little cloudy due to the champagne he drank but it wasn't a hangover he had any concern for. He promised Julia extravagance and she took advantage of it. Julia was happy to exploit her husband's good mood as they enjoyed five-star dining by the sea. She also felt she had earned it in advance. To tour the islands of Venice should evoke thoughts of romanticism. Instead, she was going to do so viewed through a different prism – ghost hunting.

She didn't believe in ghosts, but she didn't want to see one either. She never understood how or why Lawrence had such a fascination with the supernatural. It was childish yet that was Lawrence. Mature and married with a mortgage, he still needed his little dopamine hits of frivolity. She may not have wanted to tour a haunted island but it meant so much to Lawrence she wasn't going to say no and crush his new dream.

She stirred, feeling the weight shifting off the bed as Lawrence got up. He stretched with an unflattering pose, unaware of how comical he looked and made his way to the bathroom. Julia was also feeling a little hazy from the alcohol. She looked at the time, 07:30 a.m. They only got in about six hours ago and even then, they stayed up until after two.

With it being their last day in Venice, and the night taken care off, Julia wanted to get as much done as she could. In terms of sightseeing, she was more than happy to explore the neighbouring islands if possible. Get a real taste of how the locals lived and soak up as much culture as she could. And ride a gondola. She wasn't leaving Venice until that happened.

The tour was booked for 08:00 p.m., which meant an earlier dinner and keeping Lawrence relatively sober lest he be refused boarding. She needn't worry about that. Nothing was stopping Lawrence from getting on that boat.

Across the city, but not too far, Aaron stared out the window of his room. The B&B he and Kirsty had rented was small and expensive but at least had two rooms. The host originally mistook them for a couple and found it hilarious when he discovered they were actually brother and sister. It was funny for a minute and got old quickly.

The room had a flowery décor, the host claimed his gran previously owned the apartment, and he never bothered redecorating. Kirsty had found it strange that he felt the need to mention it and said to Aaron later how kitsch she found it. It wouldn't be the word Aaron used, but it was much politer.

They had managed to book a tour around Poveglia island. Kirsty had the rest planned. She wouldn't tell Aaron the details and would smile maliciously when he asked. He didn't like it. There was something off about the whole thing. He had images of being held ransom at sea by a crazed local lunatic who posed as a tour operator to rob gullible tourists. It was entirely plausible, more so than what he assumed was Kirsty's plan to bribe her way onto the island.

With the day to spend in Venice, he was happy to tick off

some sights. He loved being a tourist. Kirsty hated it. Tourists stood out, she liked to blend in. He found the irony in her doing so by embarking on a ghost hunting tour of Europe amusing.

Aaron's view looked onto another building with a narrow canal below him. It felt like Venice, it made him smile. He didn't know if his sister would find what she was looking for on the trip. Aaron intended to enjoy the journey even if the destination was a let-down. He wasn't sure if he'd return home with any exciting stories, but he expected to experience something unforgettable.

The coffee had cooled enough for Rino to take a sip. He grimaced at its bitterness, having run out of sugar he had nothing sweet to take the edge off it. He had planned the day out before going to bed: visit Grado, see friend, haggle over gear, leave happy, quick bite, meet Elena, complete tour and then rest. The last part was the part he looked forward to. He had slept horribly. Finding out about his daughter's financial issues played on him. How he wished he was a rich man, rich enough to make all his baby girl's woes disappear with the wave of a cheque book.

It was Elena he worried about most. If they couldn't get the money together then she couldn't return to university. She was the first of the family to do so and Rino was adamant she would be the first to graduate. He had yet to do the math regarding how many tours he would need to complete to raise the money, but he wasn't afraid of hard work. He'd take tourists around that cursed island all day and night if he had to. It sickened him that he was missing a day, but he had to go to Grado. Besides, they were making a little extra doing a tour at night.

He was concerned about taking Elena with him at the later hour but that was part of the deal. They were a team, and he couldn't imagine trying to entertain the tourists. Her English was better while he was the old man who looked menacing and maintained a mysterious aura as he silently steered the boat around the island. At least that's how Elena put it.

Yes, he was uneasy about that night's tour, yet he knew the money was good. He had so much to earn and so little time to do so. He hadn't prayed for years, not since his wife died. But he had prayed that God would help him on his path to provide for his family. It was difficult for him to reconcile his faith. He felt it had abandoned him, not the other way around. Still, he prayed. He had to at least try. For Elena's sake, he had to try.

TIl's bedsheet was drenched in sweat yet he was cold. He hadn't slept since waking up. His eyes were raw, his brain was in a heightened state of alarm coupled with a pounding headache. He had gotten ready and checked out of the hostel as soon as the desk opened. The clerk was suspicious Til had been up all night taking drugs, confusing his jittery and sickly persona for what it was.

He was meant to catch a train to Croatia, the next leg of his backpacking holiday. Instead, he booked a flight home to Berlin. Done with the holiday. Done with Venice. He was scared they wouldn't let him on the plane due to his illness. Thankfully, he managed to conceal his ailment as a hangover and they let him on.

The nightmare had faded but the immense feeling of dread had not gone away. He couldn't shake it. It clung to him like a rotten smell. An unknown presence that was sinister; he couldn't wait to leave Italy. He just wanted to go home. He reckoned he'd feel safe once he landed in Berlin. Hopefully the virus he appeared to have caught would have eased by then.

26

The boat had seen better days. It had cracks and the deck had rot in it. Rino paced around it, shaking his head and tutting his disapproval. Enzo sucked hard on his cigarette and waved away his friend's judgement. "If the boat was in good condition," he said, "then you wouldn't be here to rob me."

"A fair price," countered Rino, "I'll offer nothing but a fair price."

The boat, a Kingfisher 33, had no business on the water. And neither did its captain. Enzo had retired from fishing due to an accident three years earlier. A motorist ran a red light, almost killing the old man. He survived, but the loss of the full use of his left leg and a mangled right hand which had calcified into a claw left him unable to work. The payoff was good. Good enough to keep him comfortable until his dying days. Rino felt with the indulgent lifestyle of Enzo, his dying days wouldn't be long away.

"Why now?" he asked Enzo.

"I'm sick of looking at her. Sick of seeing her. Sick of her being a reminder. I won't get much for her, she needs too much work. But the hauler, the creels and the rest. They're in great condition. You're getting a steal, I can't stress that enough." He began to cough, his violent outburst not deterring his nicotine need.

They were in great condition and the price was too good to pass up. Rino thought long and hard on his way over about cancelling. Reneging on the deal. It was not in his nature, he was a man of his word, and he knew he was doing Enzo a favour. And his old friend was right, it was too good a deal to pass over. The electronics alone would cost him thousands brand new, and here he was in a position to get much of it for half that. He needed to save as much as he could, but he was a fisherman by trade. Soon Elena would be back at university, and he'd need to return to the day job. It was likely the university fees would wipe him out. This equipment would help him get back on his feet quickly.

"I can take some of it," Rino said. "I can make good use of it."

"That's what I like to hear."

The men relocated to Enzo's apartment to discuss final costs. The flat was modest, more so than Rino's, and less tidy. They haggled back and forth with both men agreeing a price that made their bartering pointless. Enzo offered his guest a beer, but he politely declined. One beer wasn't going to kill him, but he wouldn't drink any alcohol knowing he would have Elena on his boat. Especially at night.

"Not like you," Enzo said. "Getting soft on me?"

"I'm going out later."

"If one beer has you unable to steer that shit hole of a boat of yours then you have bigger problems than me my friend. Why you go out at night anyway, you hate taking the boat out at night."

"I have a little bit of business to take care of."

"Ooh, do tell..." Enzo lit up another cigarette. He did so one handed with ease, having mastered a way to continue his habit in spite of his injury. Rino really didn't want to tell him but knew he wouldn't let it go. He thought about lying, but Enzo would see through it and it would only fuel his curiosity.

"Not that it's any of your business, I have a little side-line going on. Just for now."

"What would that be, you trafficking for the Mafia?" Enzo wheezed as he laughed.

"Tours, okay? I'm taking some tourists out around Poveglia."

Enzo's eyes widened at the name. A plume of light grey smoke fell from his lips.

"Oh, now that is interesting. Are you mad, friend? You know better than to meddle in those waters."

"I know better to not be scared of stories. I did it yesterday. It was fine, it's easy money."

"Better you than me." Enzo appeared to forget about his cigarette, his focus was elsewhere. His face was sober and Rino could see that his eyes were troubled.

"What?" he asked, wishing he had lied.

"Nothing. Nothing at all. You know...you know the stories though."

"Yes, I know the stories. I'm very aware. Of the *stories.*"

"We both know what Livio saw and heard."

"*We* both know what Livio *told* us he saw and heard."

Rino knew the story well. In the 90s, Livio, a fellow fisherman, told how he got too close to Poveglia one October morning. The sun was still to rise and Livio allowed his boat to drift into Poveglia's waters. The early morning sky was black, as was the sea. He felt his net tug on something big. As he checked on his catch, there was a scream. His head jolted to the source of the commotion. The asylum. It had to be. He ran to the port side of the boat and tried in vain to adjust his sight to the darkness. It was then he heard the scream again. A woman. She was crying out for help. He had never heard such agony. Livio didn't know what to do. He froze to the spot. He had to help her. He decided he was going to drive the boat closer and call for help if need be. And that's when the shadows moved. From the silhouette of the asylum, a vile mist blacker than night drifted along the pathway. Livio had enough experience at sea to know what a natural mist was and how it moved. This was sentient. And it saw him.

The men sat in silence. A gentle breeze caught the smoke and blew it in Rino's direction.

"I hope it's worth it," Enzo said.

"It's just for some extra cash. I'm old, older than you. I'd love an easy life."

"Well, I can't say retirement hasn't been good to me. Almost cost me an arm and leg though." Both men laughed. *I hope it doesn't cost you more, my friend.*

27

There are many things that Julia was told about Venice. From the canals to the architecture; friends who had been raved about the wonderful delights the city had to offer. What they didn't tell her about was the sudden rain. Minutes earlier she sat with Lawrence, enjoying ice-cream as the world passed them by. Now she stood in the doorway to an apartment complex watching the water bounce off the pavement. She'd never seen rain like it, especially for it to come out of nowhere. Where once an immaculate blue sky reigned, a grey cloak covered the city and unfurled its fury onto those below. She could tell the tourists from the locals by their responses. As some ran for cover, others casually took shelter as if the rain was nothing but a minor inconvenience.

They had been on their way to book a gondola ride when the heavens opened. Julia hoped the weather wasn't going to prevent that from happening. To leave Venice without drifting down the canals would have been a disaster. Lawrence was also concerned about the weather, but it was his own boat ride that played on his mind. He'd feel cursed if the trip to Poveglia was called off due to bad weather. For all the scorching sun the country got, now it chose to rain. The stress rose in his stomach.

27

With the same unexpectedness as it came, the rain stopped. The grey sky turned back to blue. Tourists cautiously stepped from their shelter while the locals carried on, business as usual. The rain had cleared the air and brought with it a cool freshness. It was both welcoming and unsettling. As the clouds separated, the sun returned. Glowing as before, it shone its warmth onto the streets and removed any traces of the rain.

The gondolier was a man in his early thirties and despite his Italian accent, was not local. Julia didn't know what region he was from, but it was a harsh dialect. She felt her Italian was enough to get her by only to realise that her Italian was generic. It was phrase words that would mean nothing should she engage in a proper conversation. Thankfully the gondolier, Genny, was fluent in English.

Julia was blissfully at peace as the boat drifted down the canal. The water was busy with other vessels, mostly carrying tourists throughout the city. It wasn't the postcard she envisioned, but she loved it all the same. With her back to Lawrence, she cuddled into his chest, his arms placed gently around her. The honeymoon could have ended there and then, and she would have been happy.

Lawrence would not have been. He enjoyed the ride: it was smooth and peaceful despite the noisy traffic that the gondolier navigated through. But it wasn't the boat ride he looked forward to. He imagined slipping the driver some money and asking him to take them to Poveglia. The thought was frivolous but tempting.

"Excuse me," he said to Genny.

"Yes, signore?" the man answered, his eyes never leaving the water.

"How far out do you travel on one of these?"

"Not too far signore. I prefer to keep to the canals. It's good for business."

"So, you wouldn't, for instance, take it out to a neighbouring island?"

The question stirred Julia. She pretended not to listen while fine-tuning her hearing to the conversation.

Genny laughed. "No, signore. That's a little too far out for me. I keep to the canals. Good for business and the water is calmer."

Lawrence was happy to leave his curiosity at that until the gondolier spoke up again.

"Where did you have in mind?"

Julia rolled her eyes, she knew where this was going.

"Oh, off the top of my head," Lawrence said. "Poveglia, maybe."

Sombreness washed through Genny. He lost focus for a moment and allowed the boat to coast. He snapped out of it, thanking God that his passengers didn't notice. Genny wasn't from Venice, Julia was right in her assumption. He grew up in Tuscany and had only been working in the city for two years. He didn't grow up with the fear of Poveglia the way the locals had, but those same locals warned him not to get too close. He had no reason to doubt them. Those that felt brave enough to share their stories were convincing. Most notably, Livio, the fisherman he worked for when he first arrived in Venice. Genny was a good Catholic man, he believed in the human soul and that Poveglia had imprisoned its fair share. He had faith that evil existed and he knew without any doubt that it lived on Poveglia.

"That's a serious island you speak of, signore," he said after what felt like an eternity. "I can't think of any reason a man would go searching for it."

"Could be fun," he shrugged his shoulders, disregarding the severity of Genny feelings.

Fun? Genny spat the thought. *Foolish American. Fun? May God forgive your ignorance, brother.*

"You ever been?" Lawrence asked.

"No," Genny said. He didn't mean it to be as blunt as he did. He was, after all, on duty and had to put on a smile for the customers. "No, signore, it's not a place that is of interest to me. Too many scary stories for Genny." He laughed a hollow laugh. Again, Julia picked up on it.

"I suppose. But that's where the fun comes in, right?" Lawrence persisted.

"Signore, if you don't mind me, you are not going to Poveglia?"

Lawrence was careful with his answer. He didn't want to give too much away. He wasn't entirely sure how legitimate the tour was. There was something amateurish about the whole thing.

"Maybe," he said. "I might hire someone to take me out, haven't decided."

"Well, I implore you not to, signore. There is wickedness on that island. It's forbidden to visit for good reason. Besides, you wouldn't find anyone foolish enough to take you." *And if you did, then God help you.*

Genny knew he had overstepped a boundary. Lawrence too was uneasy at the change of tone in the gondolier. He found him unprofessional, even though Lawrence himself broached the subject. He decided he wouldn't be leaving a tip. Julia, on the other hand, decided the gondolier deserved a tip for her husband's boorishness. And why was Genny so spooked? She didn't know him, perhaps he was inanely superstitious. Perhaps he was selling fear to build up the legend. Scare the dumb tourists and get them to spread ghost stories. The island was forbidden. A phrase that could instantly make it more desirable to the gullible. Julia was curious, she couldn't deny it. Most likely the hype would be too much and the crumbling ruins of the asylum would be a major disappointment to Lawrence. It amused her to think of her enjoying the tour more than him.

They finished the gondola ride in silence. Julia thanked Genny and made sure to tip him generously. Genny liked her, she had kind eyes. He wanted to grab her arm as she turned to leave, to warn her of visiting the island. To listen to his instincts. To believe that the island was a home of evil, a malevolent entity that should not be disturbed. But he didn't. He feared how he would come across. Instead, he watched her as she disappeared into the crowd. He stood clutching the money. His next customers waited patiently on the dock. He painted a welcoming smile back onto his face and tried to forget the unease he felt. It didn't go away.

28

Kirsty left her brother to do his own thing as she sat in her hotel room. It was better that way. She was bored with Venice and her focus was elsewhere. Yes, she was content at having passage to Poveglia, but that was only half the battle. She didn't just want to see it. She wanted to set foot on it. To spend the night. She was aware that the latter was ambitious. To start with anyway. If, and it was a big if, she could convince the tour operator to take them to Poveglia and give her time to look around, maybe they'd take them back the next day for an extended stay.

It would require cunning, but she was confident in her abilities. The tour they had booked seemed amateurish. Social media posts but no official website. She didn't believe them to be charlatans or con artists, but opportunists looking to make some coin from the naive tourists. She may have been a tourist, naïve she was not.

Kirsty didn't have an endless supply of cash, if she did she'd buy her own boat with her own captain. She believed she had enough to bribe her guides. They had already reneged on their policy that they only did day tours. They were either simple or greedy. Hopefully both.

That night would be a trial run. Test the resolve of the guides.

It crossed her mind that the island itself might not live up to expectation. That after an initial inspection she might not want to return and explore it. The thought saddened her. She wasn't as invested in the island as Lawrence was, a man she was yet to meet and had no idea existed at that point. But she did have her own stake in her adventure. To chase the rush and have her own scepticism questioned. It excited her.

The House of Reston Mather provided her with excitement until that fatal discovery. A discovery that left her cold. The thought of that child's lifeless eyes, those doll eyes, didn't even sadden her anymore. It left her numb in a way that frightened her. She could still feel empathy for the child, but the numbness brought with it a cold vice-like grip.

Kirsty would never fully appreciate how much she had been traumatised by that incident. She hoped to find something on Poveglia that would terrify her in the same way a rollercoaster shoots you with adrenaline. Finding that baby scared her, but there was no rush. In a way, she looked for something more frightening so that it would replace that memory. It was unlikely she would come face to face with any evidence of the supernatural. If she could experience something to at least have her doubt her own beliefs, she felt that would be enough.

The lifeless corpse of a child taken too soon provided no such doubt. It was real. There was no other explanation for its existence. *Her* existence. It was once a girl. Never to become a woman.

She took out a notepad and jotted down some rough ideas. She rehearsed a script that would be an opener to the guide. Ticking off the ways she would charm them into negotiating passage to the island. She had to be prepared, she was getting one shot at it.

Elsewhere, Aaron was glad to not have to think about Poveglia. He had just left Doge's Palace having enjoyed the gothic architecture. He loved his sister and as much as he would have been happy to wander Venice with her, her lack of enthusiasm for anything that wasn't haunted had grated on him. He couldn't understand why she couldn't just enjoy the simpler things in life. They were travelling Europe with the opportunity to see some of the most beautiful sights on offer, and she wanted to see the most macabre.

Kirsty might not have been afraid of finding a ghost but Aaron was. He was much more superstitious than his sister and was in no rush to set foot on Poveglia. The barman they had met may very well have just been trying to scare them. It worked, in Aaron's case, anyway. For Kirsty, it jolted her with enthusiasm. He didn't get it. He was long beyond trying to figure her out.

And there he was regardless. Following her. If she did manage to convince the tour to drop them off, he knew he'd follow her onto the island. She would go without him, and he couldn't allow that. A part of him hoped the tour guide said no and stayed firm in the face of monetary persuasion. Then again, he was worried about what it would do to Kirsty. What she'd do if she got desperate. He didn't fancy getting a small boat over with her at the helm. No, as much as it concerned him, the tour was the better idea. Jump off, have a look around and then back on the boat. Satiate her desire then off to the next place.

How naive he was to think it would be so simple. He knew he was kidding himself. He could worry about it later. He wanted to enjoy the rest of Venice, the touristy parts of Venice, while he could. The sun would set eventually. And with it, his optimism.

29

The arguing quietened. Too suddenly. The way a room will quieten when someone is interrupted and it's clear they've been talking about you. Elena's hand hovered over the door handle to the living room. She wasn't trying to be discreet. She didn't approach the door with trepidation. Who does in their own house? The voices on the other side were her parents. Raised voices, borne out of frustration, not anger. Not quite. Silence filled the gap. It was uncomfortable.

To ignore it and turn around would raise suspicion. She didn't pause because she wanted to hear something. She hesitated due to the silence. It told her much more than eavesdropping would have.

Her parents seldom argued that she was aware of. When you spend so much time away from home, how could she be sure of how much they fought? She took a deep breath, composed herself and opened the door. It was evident by the atmosphere that she had interrupted something that was not for her ears. Her mum sat on the couch while her dad stood by the fireplace. It didn't paint a good picture.

"Everything okay?" she asked, her eyes darting from each parent.

"Yes, why?" her dad answered, a little too defensively. It

probably sounded better in his head.

"I'm going to head out now, I just wanted to say bye."

"At this hour?"

Elena looked at the clock on the wall. It was 07:00 p.m. Not exactly what she would call late.

"I'm meeting Nonno, remember?"

"I've no idea what he's playing at taking you out on that death trap of his. Especially at this hour. He's not a young man anymore, his senses aren't as sharp as they were and believe me -"

"Vincent, please," her mother interjected. Verona wasn't happy about her daughter on a boat at night either. She also knew it was necessary. Vincent didn't agree. It was what they were arguing about before Elena approached. Verona knew they needed the money. Vincent also, but his pride refused to put the burden onto his daughter. Or his father-in-law, although he was more concerned about being indebted to the old man.

Vincent averted his gaze from his wife. He stared at the floor, his fist clenched, albeit not aggressively. It was frustration at himself, no one else. He lifted his head and stared his daughter in the eyes.

"I just worry, that's all." He tried to soften his tone, with less success than he'd hoped. "It's a father's duty to worry so much."

"I get that," Elena said. "I'll be fine. Nonno would never do anything to put me in danger and I do everything he says when on the boat. He's the captain, I'm merely the first mate." She saluted and Vincent laughed. Verona felt tears well in her eyes, she suppressed them and smiled.

"Just be careful," Vincent said.

"Aye Aye," Elena said. All three laughed. It was like nothing was wrong. She approached her dad and kissed him on the cheek. She did the same to her mother, who pulled her in close and hugged her.

"You will be careful," Verona said.

"Always," Elena said.

And she left.

The tram from Mestre to Venice was roughly a twenty-minute journey. Then, Elena had about a ten-minute walk to the dock. She checked her watch, it flashed 07:10 p.m. A tram was due soon. Plenty of time.

The shelter was new and modern. Wide and open, it would keep her dry from any sudden downpour but not protected should the wind choose to blow. She texted Rino to let him know her status. He replied with expected typos and his usual curtness, which she viewed with affection.

As the time passed, Elena realised her tram was running late. She wasn't concerned. She had plenty of time. Even if she was cutting it fine, a brisk walk would do her good. She wasn't worried. A few minutes later the tram came and she boarded. Plenty of time. She might even stop off for a coffee.

30

There was no harm in being prepared. Rino ran over the same safety checks. Over and over, never doubting himself. He wasn't taking any chances, not with Elena on board. He didn't want to be sued off of the tourists either should something go wrong. It was just then that it occurred to him he wasn't insured for the passengers. *Foolish old man.* It was too late now. He'd worry about it another time; besides, he was certain he wasn't the only one in Venice to operate out with the law. The city had a reputation for fleecing tourists. A reputation Rino never denied, and now he found himself participating in it.

No, his was a fair price. He could have gotten more out of them, especially the British duo who seemed so eager to come aboard. They had asked him if they could visit the island. Only an outsider would ask something so silly. Rino needed the money and was happy to break some minor laws, but he wasn't putting his granddaughter in jeopardy. He wondered where she was. He thought she'd be there by now. He pulled out his phone and called her number. It didn't ring. She must be on the tram, the bridge into Venice was known as a bit of a black spot for signal, or so Elena had told him before lest he worried.

He looked up and saw a young couple walk down towards

him. The man looked happy, excited. There was a spring in his step. His companion looked content but much less enthused. He wasn't sure why but Rino took a liking to her more. There was something about the way she carried herself. It was earnest.

They approached Rino, who quickly deduced that these were his customers, but who, the Americans or the British?

"Hi, sir," Lawrence said.

It was the Americans.

"Is this the tour for Poveglia?"

"Si," Rino replied. "You're early."

Lawrence was slightly taken aback by the tone. It was true, they were early but better early than late.

"Spiacente, signore," Julia interjected. "We didn't want to be late."

Rino was right in his initial thoughts. He did like the woman better.

"Come aboard, we don't leave until eight."

Julia thanked him and both boarded the boat. It was a quaint vessel, the rustic nature tapped into Lawrence's sense of adventure while Julia was concerned whether the boat was serviceable. The seats on deck weren't the comfiest. This was a boat built for a sole function and it wasn't to accommodate tourists.

While Julia and Lawrence got comfy, Rino tried to hide his agitation. Elena should have arrived by now. He didn't think she'd be late, but he had no desire to make small talk with the customers. That was her task. He drove the boat and looked moody. That was the agreement.

He was certainly adhering to the latter part of the deal. Julia could tell something was making the man uncomfortable. He hadn't even introduced himself. It had suddenly occurred. That they had taken this stranger's word for it that this was the right boat.

"Hey," she whispered to Lawrence. "Are we sure this is the right boat? Doesn't something seem off?"

It didn't. Maybe it was his natural naivety or overwhelming desire to see Poveglia that clouded his judgement.

"No," he said. "Pretty cool though, right?"

Julia sat back, defeated. She was being paranoid. It was obvious from what Lawrence said that the tour would be far from luxurious. The way he described his correspondence with the girl Elena, it had a DIY feel to it. The captain of the ship certainly filled the surly grandfather role that was mentioned in the tweets he saw.

The captain's surliness increased along with his concern. He tried phoning Elena again. No answer. He continued the safety checks, repeating the same process over and over mechanically. He barely even registered the two strangers on his boat and the woman's uneasiness.

It was then that his final two passengers arrived. Kirsty and Aaron walked up to the dock, both carrying backpacks. They reminded Rino of the German tourist and the instant dislike he took to him. It wasn't a good start. Where the hell was Elena?

"Buonasera," said Kirsty. "Rino?" she looked onto the boat and locked eyes with the older man.

He nodded. It was the Brits. He appreciated their Italian greeting and wondered how much they knew, hoping he wouldn't have to engage much in conversation. Where the hell was Elena?

"Benissimo," she said, although the context confused Rino.

"Permission to board?"

He nodded again.

"Parla inglese?" she said with a tone.

"Si," Rino Replied. "Take a seat. My granddaughter will be along soon to... brief you before we go."

As she went to board, Kirsty noticed the other two for the first time. With raised eyebrows, she assessed the situation. She was under the impression it would be a private tour. It was what she asked for and it seemed to be what was agreed.

"Excuse me," she said to Rino. "Have we got our times mixed up? Is there another tour later tonight?"

"No. One tour," he said, his eyes never leaving his task.

"Oh, it's just, I'm certain we booked a private tour with your granddaughter."

"No other tour. This is the tour."

Julia and Lawrence couldn't help overhear. Kirsty was neither subtle nor quiet in voicing her displeasure. This wasn't part of the deal. This wasn't what was agreed. Was it? She was faced with a choice. Rock the boat, so to speak, and be proved wrong. Or, stick to her guns and have the interlopers ejected so she could fulfil her goal. It wasn't going to be as easy to get to Poveglia with these two. Unless they were into it. That could work to her advantage.

"Are you sure?" she said. "Aaron, check the messages."

"There is no private tour," Rino said, his tone final. "This is the only tour. One late tour. You don't like it -" he cut himself off. He didn't have to put up with this on his own boat. Neither could he afford to lose the business. He swallowed his pride, as heavy as it was.

The unease Julia felt had now found collusion. It was comforting to know she could at least justify her worries now.

Her eyes locked with Kirsty - just for a moment - who smiled a smile that said *I'm sorry, this is so embarrassing but can I ask you to leave? I'm sure you understand.* Julia might have been underwhelmed at the situation. She wasn't ready to back down either.

"Ah, here we go," Arron said as he scrolled through the messages. The look of conviction on his face softened and was replaced with uncertainty. "Oh."

Kirsty's smile faded and she pursed her lips. Her gaze slowly swung to her brother.

"It might be that something was lost in translation."

"There is one tour," Rino said. He had little to no business acumen. If he had, he'd have realised the potential of charging extra for a separate tour. Still, no Elena.

"Well...," Kirsty said. "Looks like it's going to be cosy."

They both boarded the boat and took seats opposite Julia and Lawrence. Despite her comment, there was plenty of room for the four of them. Lawrence looked over and tried to make eye contact. Julia had her head down and eyes glued to her phone. Aaron returned his gaze.

"All right?" Aaron said. "Looking forward to the tour."

"Yeah," Lawrence said. "Should be fun. What brings you here?"

"Something a bit different. Although it's my sister here that's more interested." He hoped his comment would include her in the conversation, but she wasn't ready to speak yet. She had embarrassed herself and presented a terrible first impression which caused her to retreat into her shell.

"Yeah, my wife isn't that into it either. It's a favour to me. You believe the place is haunted?"

"Ha, let's just say I'm open-minded to it. You?"

“I’m sceptical, but maybe there’s no smoke without fire.”

Rino’s phone rang. It was Elena. He retreated to the cabin and answered it.

“Where are you?” he said.

“Nonno, I’m so so sorry,” she said. The regret in her voice was real. He could hear sirens in the background. Rino felt a spike of adrenaline as worry flowed through him.

“What’s happened, are you okay?”

“I’m fine, I’m fine. There’s been an accident. I’m fine, don’t worry, I wasn’t involved. But the road is all closed off. Nothing is getting in or out of the city.”

Rino sat back. He was deflated. All the air had left him. The tour was over. He couldn’t do it by himself. Over one hundred euro, money that was going towards Elena’s education, gone. It wasn’t a great amount, not compared to the sum he had to earn. But what if something else went wrong? He needed every penny he could gather to be on the safe side. He’d have to work even harder the next day, he dreaded more things going wrong, how he’d be continually chasing the money all summer.

“As long as you’re okay,” he said.

“I’m sorry I can’t be there. What are you going to do, has everyone arrived?”

“Yes. I’ll tell them the bad news. Maybe I can reschedule with them.” *Perhaps this is an omen.*

“You could do it without me?” she laughed. But Rino didn’t. “It’s not the worst idea. If they’re already there. It’s easy, and you know the stories.”

No, it was out of the question. Rino wasn’t a tour guide. “I don’t think so. You get home now, message me when you do.”

“Okay. I’m so sorry. I was looking forward to it.”

Rino was sorry also. But not for the same reason.

31

He returned to the deck, his passengers eyed him with curiosity. There was an air of concern that cut between them. All eyes turned to him looking for answers.

"The tour is cancelled," he said. He was sorry, despite not sounding it. Rino's tone could be blunt in his native tongue, in English it was cold and matter of fact.

Lawrence was devastated. What did he mean the tour was cancelled? This was a joke, surely.

"Um, sorry," he began. "What do you mean?"

"No tour," Rino replied. "We meet again tomorrow."

Julia thought she'd be glad at the news. Instead, she felt a pang of guilt.

"But we can't make tomorrow," Lawrence said. His voice was weak. Desperate. "We leave tomorrow, this is our only opportunity."

"Sorry," Rino said. "No tour."

Lawrence was so devastated he didn't even think to question why. Kirsty was more alert.

"What's going on, why?" she asked.

Rino's eyes darted to her. He didn't like the tone of her question, but she did deserve an explanation.

"My granddaughter speaks on the tour. She cannot make it."

"So? You drive the boat, right? Why don't you just take us out?"

"I drive the boat, si. I am not a tour guide, I don't tell stories."

The devastating news meant Lawrence switched off. He wasn't paying much attention to the conversation. Julia, however, was. There was a bullishness about the other woman she disliked, although she was curious as to where she was going with her interrogation.

"What needs told? I don't need to be told anything. I just want to see the place, I know a lot about the history of the island as it is."

She was really starting to irritate Rino. Who was she to be so forward? He tried to remain professional and calm, knowing he was close to snapping.

"Sorry for…how you say, your trouble. You may know many things, do the others? Don't they deserve a proper tour?" He waved a hand over to Julia and Lawrence. Julia didn't feel the question merited a response from her so stayed quiet.

"I know a little," Lawrence said. "I'd rather see it than not. We don't have the option of coming back tomorrow. It would be cool to hear some stories, but anything is better than nothing at this stage."

Kirsty nodded approval at Lawrence. His response vindicated the plan she was concocting. A part of her did consider scheming to get them off the boat but felt Rino would be more inclined to take all of them than two of them. Besides, she got the impression she hadn't exactly warmed herself to him. That was fine. She wasn't there to make friends and if they remembered her years from now, she doubted she would return the favour.

"See," she said to Rino. "You'd be letting those two down."

31

"Get to your point Rino said to her.

"My point is, there's hardly a queue of people willing to take us anywhere near Poveglia. Believe us, we've tried."

They were all silent in agreement.

"We could come back tomorrow," she continued, "but who knows what can happen between now and then. Those two? They can't. We're already on the boat, all ready to go. I know my stuff. I've done my research. I'm quite happy to answer any questions anyone has."

It was an interesting proposition and not one Rino wanted to accept. Yet, there was no harm in it. There was no valid reason for him to deny it. He felt uneasy about taking Elena out at a later hour. Her absence could be a blessing in disguise.

"And you?" he directed his question at Lawrence and Julia.

It didn't make much difference to Julia. She had little interest to begin with. Lawrence realised he was handed yet another lifeline. It didn't make much difference to him either. He had no less affinity to this stranger he just met than to the missing granddaughter. Granted, he felt there would be some authenticity to Elena and it disappointed him how uninterested Rino appeared to be. The whole situation got more amateurish by the second, yet that only excited him further. It added an element of the unknown. Whatever would happen, he was certain not to hear regurgitated stories told to every other tourist who boarded the boat. He was in for a unique experience. How could he refuse?

"Sounds good," he said. I'm happy with that. Julia?"

"Fine, whatever," she said, unenthused and weary. Weary of what sort of situation she had found herself in. It was certainly not the tour she had in mind, somehow exceeding her already low expectations.

"Okay," Rino said. "Let's get this done." He collected the money from everyone – pleasantly surprised he didn't have to give out change - and untethered the boat. He made his way to the cabin and fired on the engine. The boat spluttered into life, none of the passengers were familiar with boats, but they all felt that it didn't sound too healthy. Nevertheless, they left the dock and were on their way and ahead of schedule. The sun was still in the sky but was already on the descent. Venice looked even more beautiful from the water as it began its preparations for the approaching darkness.

They had barely left the city and Julia was already looking forward to returning. Aaron and Rino shared similar thoughts. Lawrence couldn't believe that after all the hassle and false promises that they were now on their way. Kirsty, well, she had to put the next part of her plan in motion. Convincing Rino to take them to the island. It wouldn't be an easy task, but if she could get Lawrence on her side, it might make things easier. She had time before they got there. And she was a fast thinker.

32

The sun had lowered as the boat cut through the lagoon. The blue skies were a darker shade and the water mirrored it. For all the other boats left in the water, only theirs travelled in the direction of Poveglia. For all the drama she endured, Julia adored the view. The trip was surprisingly smooth, she was expecting the boat to cause her more discomfort. She was enjoying herself, company aside. A tense atmosphere lingered on deck. The young guy, Arron, he seemed nice. His sister, on the other hand, was not Julia's cup of tea.

She had managed to convince Rino to depart as planned and even offered to act as an impromptu guide. Julia wasn't sure what it would entail exactly or if she was even capable. There was a confidence about her. Julia couldn't ascertain if it was justified or if she was bluffing. Perhaps, it was a little of both. Julia herself could live without hearing ghost stories, but now she was on the tour it'd be nice to get her money's worth. She remembered Lawrence reading about it online, maybe he could fill her in.

"How you finding Venice?" Aaron asked. He had hoped to dissolve the tension and introduce some civility.

"It's okay," Lawrence answered. "Not a lot to see, though. Quite a small city. You?"

"I love it," Aaron said.

"Me too," Julia said. The conversation in its infancy caught Kirsty's attention, but she did not speak.

"Beautiful place," Aaron said. "You been here long?"

"Couple of days," Julia said. "Then off to Rome for the second leg of our honeymoon."

"Congrats. We were in Naples before coming here. Not sure what's next to be honest."

"Sounds quite the life," Lawrence said.

"Can't complain. First world problem, I know, but it's nice to just kick about and be a tourist."

The comment struck Julia as strange. What did he mean by *be a tourist*? If they weren't tourists, then what were they? She didn't pay much attention when he spoke to Lawrence earlier. What was their motive for going to Poveglia? She was reading too much into the situation. Yet her intuition was setting off alarm bells.

"You doing a whistle-stop tour of each place?" she asked.

"Something like that. Kirsty gets bored easy." He had hoped his comment would bring his sister into the conversation. She declined. Her mind still raced with ideas. Her stomach was doing flips at the prospect.

"Well, this is certainly different," Julia said. "Here's hoping after the effort you've made to get out here that it lives up to your expectations."

Aaron smiled as he bowed his head. He was nervous. He wished he and Kirsty were on the boat without them. They seemed like nice people, he could only visualise Kirsty ruining their experience by hijacking their trip.

Julia had no idea what to look for, what the discernible feature of the island was. Everyone else did, though, they all waited for the spire of the bell tower to come into view. They didn't wait long. Kirsty was the first to notice it. Her eyes locked on the pointed spire as it shot towards the heavens. It wasn't a huge tower by any means, but as the highest feature on the island, it carved its place against the dawning sky. It was fitting that the tower would direct people to the island being that it was previously used as a lighthouse. The light within had long been extinguished by darkness, and soon the night was ready to fall over the island itself...and those that approached it.

33

The sun looked bigger as it disappeared into the ocean. Poveglia revealed itself, the silhouette of the asylum carved out its claim against the orange sky. The island was noticeably small yet long. It was incredible to think it had once been inhabited by settlers.

The boat started to slow as Rino allowed his passengers to get a good look at the island. Aaron and Kirsty had to crank their necks slightly to see. Lawrence felt his heart race a little. Even Julia admitted to herself that there was something ominous about the place, and she knew little of its history. Speaking of which, Kirsty was still to fulfil her proposal and act as a tour guide.

"There it is folks," she said, apparently reading Julia's mind. "Poveglia."

"Was that really an asylum?" Lawrence asked.

"It was. Fully operational with patients and everything. It was built in the twenties and closed down around forty years later."

"Because of the scandal?"

Julia rolled her eyes at the incoming urban legend, yet she was still intrigued.

"That's one way to put it. It was rumoured that a doctor was experimenting on his patients. But the grim history goes back longer than that. They used the island as a quarantine station."

"For plague victims, right?"

"Correct."

A sense of self-satisfaction swept over Lawrence. It pleased him to have some knowledge of what was being discussed.

"So," Kirsty continued," as you can imagine, the island has seen its fair share of death. Great place to build a loony bin. The patients would complain about vengeful spirits haunting them. But who was going to believe them? Apparently, the good doctor did, not only because he believed in ghosts, but because he himself was being haunted by them. It's said they whispered in his ear. Guiding and corrupting him. Manipulating him into fulfilling their own dastardly deeds. It's possible they were attracted to him because of the darkness already within his soul. Either way, one day he found out the authorities were onto him. The net was closing in, and he was going to be in serious trouble." She pointed to the bell tower. "He was seen entering that tower over there. He climbed his way to the top the hard way and came down the easy way. Some say he jumped. Others, that he was pushed. What's confirmed is his body was never recovered. For a black mist smothered his dead corpse and when the mist cleared... it was gone."

A thrilling chill ran up Lawrence's spine. He had read about the doctor but learned much more from Kirsty's story. Julia was less impressed. It was a nice story, sure, and considering it happened in modern history it wouldn't have been too difficult to verify. There'd be newspaper clippings, police reports, eye witness testimonies. Julia doubted any of these things existed. She thought about questioning it. She was aware it'd likely rub Kirsty up the wrong way if she picked holes in the story. Considering how quick Lawrence had been to pick apart religion in the past, she noted his hypocrisy when it was something of interest to him.

Her thoughts were interrupted as the boat came to a halt around a mile from the island. Rino had positioned the boat at an angle so his passengers could get the best view. He arrived on deck.

"Good spot here for pictures," he said, his English a little rustier than he remembered. "Take your time, you have five, maybe ten minutes." He disappeared from deck.

Aaron removed his DSLR from the backpack and started setting it up. Lawrence got lens envy as he removed his phone from his pocket and used the camera on that. With all eyes on Poveglia, Kirsty's gaze was elsewhere. She saw this as her opportunity and went to speak to Rino.

"What do you think?" Aaron asked Lawrence.

"It's pretty cool. Pretty cool. That was some story your sister told."

"She has the gift of the gab as our grandmother always said."

"How much truth is there to it?" Julia asked. She didn't mean to be rude, not to Aaron anyway. She was curious.

"In what way?" Arron said.

"The doctor. I can't say I'm buying the ghost angle but did he exist? Is the legend based on a real person?"

"I'm not actually sure. Kirsty might know. Actually, our good captain might. He grew up when the asylum was still open."

"He doesn't seem the most approachable of people."

"Ha, true. We were promised a surly old native and I suppose he plays the role well."

33

It just registered to Aaron that Kirsty was missing. He looked into the cockpit to see Kirsty saying something to Rino. She was whispering so he couldn't hear her. Suddenly, they all heard the old man laughing, and he stormed onto the deck.

"Time's up," he said. "We move."

It had barely been five minutes, let alone ten and Julia was feeling nervous. He didn't know what was said, but whatever it was, Rino had not taken it well. Aaron had more of an idea, and he could feel his stomach flip. Kirsty slunk behind Rino with all the grace of a child who had asked for a pony and was not ready to accept that no was the final answer.

"I don't think you've thought this through," she said to Rino.

"No," he replied. "I told you no."

"What's going on?" Julia asked.

Rino bit his tongue, literally, and grimaced at the pain. "Nothing. Take your seats, please." The courtesy was without emotion, his voice was cold yet it trembled. Whether with anger or fear, it was difficult to tell.

"Whoa, what's going on?" Lawrence asked.

"I offered a suggestion to make the tour more interesting," Kirsty said.

"And what was that?" Julia said.

"I asked him to drop us off on the island."

While Julia was angry at her brashness, Lawrence was intrigued by the proposal. He wanted to express his interest but Julia spoke first.

"I don't know as much about the island as everyone else on this boat but I do know that it's illegal to visit."

"Yes," Rino said. "It's what you would say... prohibited?"

"We're not asking you to do anything too outrageous," Kirsty said. "Just take us to the dock. Let us look around for ten minutes then boom, we're off."

"It could be sort of-" Lawrence began and was quickly silenced by a look from Julia.

"Sounds stupid," Julia said.

"What's the matter?" Kirsty said. "Scared of the boogeyman?" She pouted her face and gave Julia the puppy dog eyes. Maybe Rino should drop her off. And leave her there while he's at it.

"Guys," Aaron stepped in. "Come on, this is supposed to be fun."

"We are having fun." Kirsty flashed a manic grin at her brother. "Rino, I told you I'll make it worth your while."

She had offered him extra to drop them off. An extra twenty euro. He scoffed at the suggestion, the money didn't even register. Was he tempted? Not by that amount. Maybe if he didn't have the other passengers. No, it was foolish and irresponsible. He wished Elena was with him. He hated dealing with situations like this.

"You," Kirsty pointed at Lawrence. "You look like someone with a sense of adventure. Don't you want to step foot on the island? Feel the ash of ten thousand bodies beneath your feet. To bask in the gruesome history of a genuine legend."

He did. He couldn't deny that he did. But he didn't say anything. He didn't have to, his silence betrayed him. Besides, Julia would never go for it.

"I dunno," he said. "Could be fun to get a closer look, I guess."

Julia rolled her eyes back into her head and closed them tight. It was a long blink. When she opened them, nothing had changed. Her husband was still a child and the captain wasn't for budging. The trip had become uncomfortable and she just wanted to get back to the city.

"See?" Kirsty said to Rino. "You're outvoted."

He scoffed and muttered something in Italian before replying in English. "I'm the captain. I have the only vote."

"I'll give you an extra fifty."

He shook his head, a derisive smile on his face.

"A hundred."

She had his attention. The smile had faded, but he was still fuming at her insolence.

"An extra hundred. Each. From me and Aaron."

Everyone looked at Aaron, who had just found himself potentially a hundred euro lighter despite not opening his mouth. He kept it closed. His beaten expression told all how little say he had.

Two hundred euro. On top of the money he was already making for the trip. He had his principles and they told him to refuse. His principles also advised him against doing tours in the first place. Yet there he was. Things had changed and Elena needed the money. His family needed him. He wasn't happy about the situation, and he was being forced into making a choice.

He looked at his American passengers. "And you? You're okay with this?"

Julia wasn't sure she understood the question. Was Rino asking them for money to visit the island also or was he looking for them to object? Was he wanting them to object?

Julia spoke. "There's no way in hell I'm setting foot on that thing."

Lawrence was more open-minded about it. He also knew Julia wasn't going to be happy with him leaving her on the boat while he went exploring. He did want to see it up closer though. That was an opportunity he couldn't pass up.

"We're quite happy to sit in the boat," he said.

Julia turned to him. How dare he speak for her. She felt Rino was giving them the chance to derail this entire thing and instead Lawrence had gifted Kirsty validation. Julia looked over at her. Her smile had an innocent smugness to it, the sort of smile she'd be more than happy to remove from her face with a left hook.

"Well," Kirsty said to Rino. "Those two can stay on the boat with you. We'll have a little wander, we won't go too far. Or you can leave us, do a round trip and grab us on the way back."

"No," Rino barked. He inhaled his deepest breath of the day and exhaled through his nose. "No. I stay. You don't go far. If at any point I change my mind - I shout, you return."

Kirsty nodded politely. She'd won. She expected Rino to cave quicker. She had underestimated that a man of his stature would be opposed to some extra cash. Or, he had played her. But she didn't think so. No, he really didn't want to do it. Yet he couldn't say no to the money despite how reluctantly he agreed. There was something about the old man she couldn't figure out. It wasn't until the boat had fired back up and they were on their way that she realised he hadn't even asked for the money upfront.

34

An orange hue cast the asylum in darkness. It certainly looked more impressive the nearer it got. Julia couldn't tell if it was the building or the island itself, but she felt something emanate from its direction. Its aura covered her. Embraced her. It guided the boat to its shores as it welcomed its visitors. A fortuitous event spawned by a chance meeting. If their plane hadn't landed in Rome would Lawrence have even known of this place? She reckoned he'd have discovered something. Yet, she did wonder.

Rino steered the boat towards the wooden pier. It had seen better days but he figured it was safe enough. Kirsty and Aaron had swung their backpacks on, ready to explore. Aaron had his camera ready to shoot. The boat gently came to a stop and Rino tethered it to the pier. It bobbed gently in the calm water.

"Thirty minutes," he said. "Both of you. Back here in thirty minutes."

"Come on now, you wouldn't really leave us, would you?" Kirsty said. She smiled. Aaron did not.

"Thirty minutes. From now."

"How about an hour?"

"How about you keep your money, and we go back. Before I

forget. Money?" He had almost forgotten. He even considered leaving it until they came back. It's not that he didn't trust them, besides they'd be stuck there without him. He didn't want to give Kirsty any advantage. Not that he'd leave them, paid or not. He didn't need Kirsty to know that.

Kirsty intended to honour the payment. She did want to make him squirm - just a little. Thirty minutes wasn't long but it was enough for a taste. Now she had Rino in her pocket they could return tomorrow. Just the three of them. He could give them more time then, she had enough cash on her to make it work. If she liked what she saw, that is. The island could be a total let down. It didn't look like it would be though. It didn't feel that way at all.

She removed the money and handed it to Rino. "See you in thirty minutes." She turned to Lawrence and Julia. "Don't wait up."

Aaron waved sincerely before following Kirsty onto the pier. It creaked under his weight, a slight panic froze him to the spot before he realised he was safe. His next steps were much more careful. They made their way along the path by the water. It was badly overgrown, they had to duck for most of it. Within minutes, they had disappeared from view. Swallowed by the branches.

A creeping uneasiness washed over Rino. He looked at his watch as if thirty minutes would pass in an instant. He regretted his decision. He felt he had made a mistake. Whether Poveglia island was haunted or not, the buildings were condemned. It wasn't built as a tourist attraction and had fallen into disrepair over the years. He'd be responsible for anything that happened to them. He took them there, and he allowed them to set foot on the place. On top of that, he had ruined the other couple's trip. Well, the woman's at least. The man didn't seem too troubled by the detour. Still, he felt bad. He contemplated making small talk, maybe even apologise. He decided against it. He wanted to go home.

Julia sensed something was troubling Rino. He had taken the money and yielded to Kirsty's demands, but something didn't sit right. He appeared stressed and overtly concerned. About what, she couldn't tell. She looked over at the open water. The ocean was blackened by the approaching dusk. Enough light still shone on the island, although she feared it would be dark the time her fellow passengers made their return. It'd be a shame if *one* of them fell into the lagoon on their way back. Just the *one*.

The asylum looked so accessible to Lawrence, yet it remained forbidden fruit. A part of him would love to have gone with Kirsty and Aaron. He didn't even think they'd have minded. Thirty minutes? He'd have slipped Rino some extra money to partake in the bonus tour. He seemed a good guy, he could trust him enough to leave him alone with Julia.

Ah, yes. Julia. Who would have been perfectly fine with Lawrence's fantasy scenario. She would have been more than happy to see him off while she waited on the boat like the good little wife that she was. Hey, she may even go with him. To share in his experience of a thirty-minute ghost hunt and answer the question once and for all regarding the existence of the supernatural.

It was as if Julia could see his ludicrous daydream by the look she shot him. She was far from amused at the situation.

"What?" he asked her.

"Really? You really need me to explain this?"

"I didn't know we were going to end up here."

"But you're loving it, aren't you?"

"Don't be like that. I didn't know."

"You hardly objected to it."

"Neither did you if we're playing that game."

"For your sake, let's not play that game."

Rino wasn't sure what they were saying. He only made out certain words. Julia's tone translated in any language and Rino's guilt tugged at him again.

The minutes dragged as all three sat in silence. Julia and Lawrence hadn't spoken for ten minutes and Rino's agitation increased by the second. He reminded himself of Elena. He could make peace with himself later, but as he waited for the others to return he couldn't help feel he had made a huge mistake.

He walked to the port side of his boat and stared down at the water. Looking at Poveglia made him feel uneasy. The dark water that stared back at him allowed him some comfort. He noted how black the sea was. It reflected back his own doubts at him as the bond he had formed with it began to dissipate. As if the sea itself was turning on him, his anxiety rose as a lifetime of regrets plagued him. The water had an oily sheen, he wondered if his own greed had somehow poisoned it.

No, it wasn't his imagination. There was another layer to the water. Something lay on top of it, blacker than the sky. Panic took hold and he marched over to the cockpit and frantically checked his instruments. The sudden manic burst in his movements startled Julia.

He returned to the deck and swore loudly in Italian while wiping his face with his weathered hands.

His actions frightened Julia.

"Is everything okay?" Lawrence asked.

He grumbled something in Italian. Neither Julia nor Lawrence knew the words, but they'd bet their mortgage on guessing it wasn't pleasant.

He turned to the two of them, his hands fixed to his hips. His jaw was clenched tight, a vein throbbed in his temple.

"We have…" he said, struggling for the words. "We have problem."

"Problem?" Julia said. "What do you mean by that, what's happened?"

Rino looked at the sky for strength. He found none.

"There's a leak. A…the fuel…" His English had abandoned him.

"Wait, what? You have a fuel leak? Are you serious?"

Julia found the sentence Rino looked for. He nodded his head.

"Is it bad?" Lawrence said.

Rino nodded. "We go. Soon." He couldn't tell how bad the leak was, but they weren't haemorrhaging fuel. Not yet anyway. How long they had he didn't know. What he couldn't do was take any more chances. None of them spoke but all thought the same thing. They had no means of contacting the others. None at all.

Rino clenched his fists tight, then flexed them out. He stretched his fingers hoping to exert all the tension that coursed through him. He knew what he had to do. He went back into the cockpit and returned with a large torch and a handheld radio.

"Whoa, where are you going?" Julia asked, pre-empting Rino's move.

"I go get them. We leave."

"You can't leave us here?"

"I won't be long. I get them, we go. Capisci?"

"Capeeshi my ass, you can't leave us alone on this boat. What if something happens?"

"You'll be safe, just stay in boat. Sooner I go. Sooner I'm back. Sooner we leave."

"We should all stick together," Lawrence said. "Maybe we should all go."

"No," Rino barked at him. "I go. You stay. When I find them I'll contact you on this." He held up his radio. "If anyone comes to the boat...just..." He didn't know what to say.

Julia's glare was abrasive. Lawrence turned to her, slowly. He was scared to catch her eye, yet it was inevitable. It was like pulling a plaster off the hard way.

"It was only a suggestion," he said.

"We're going to have some serious words when we get back to Venice," Julia said. She looked over at Rino, who had ignored them and was making his way towards the pier. At his age, he struggled more than the others as he climbed onto the platform. The wood creaked under his weight and for a second, he thought he was going to fall through.

"Wait here," he said. Where they were going to go was anyone's guess. Rino felt terrible for leaving them. The fuel leak had spooked him. Did he hit something at the dock? He couldn't say. There was no way to investigate it and certainly no time. He didn't want to take any chances, he had to get them all back to Venice as quickly as possible lest they find themselves stranded. He didn't want that, especially with four tourists he'd just taken to a forbidden island on an unauthorised and uninsured tour. He felt so foolish. And a little frightened. He tested the torch, hoping he wouldn't need it. There was still enough light in the sky for him to see what was in front of him, but it was fading. And fast.

He didn't look back at his boat as he made his way up the path by the water. The trees had overgrown through years of neglect. He had to be careful to resist their attempts to force him into the water. He ducked under branches and pushed others back. The thicker ones required more force on his part, and he began to tire. Youth wasn't on his side. He took one look back at his boat. Lawrence and Julia watched him as fought his way up the path.

He turned from them. And he was gone.

35

Rino pushed back the branches. There was resistance as the thicker ones swung back at him. He had to be quick to protect his face from the provoked assault. He looked down at the water, perilously close and uninviting. The stone path was uneven and hazardous. He had to be very careful or he'd fall. At his age he was concerned he wouldn't get back up.

He felt alone. More alone than he had ever felt in his life. His boat, less than five minutes away, appeared lost to him. He knew, or assumed, the siblings he sought couldn't have been too far ahead of him. Except they were young and he was old. He worried how much distance they had on him.

He looked up at the endless sky. He had an eye for a storm but he couldn't see any on the horizon. He also had enough experience at sea to know how quickly one could form. That's all he'd need. He powered on through.

He arrived at a clearing, the trees fell back from the path and in front of him stood the remains of the old asylum itself. The building was adorned with scaffolding. A restoration project that was quickly abandoned. It chilled him to think why. He shouted, "Hello," realising that he had forgotten the names of those he sought. "Hello. Time to go."

There was no response. Nothing. He waited impatiently and

cried out again. Rino expected a snarky reply. An argument by the woman that this wasn't part of the deal, and they had paid for more time. Instead, he was greeted by silence. The asylum was large, he had no intention of going in there looking for them. There was more chance of them turning around and passing him while he ventured off in the opposite direction. The old superstitions rose in him also. He felt exposed out in the open yet safer. He cursed himself for even being there.

The hairs on his back stood up. There was an unbearable sense of eyes upon him. Staring at him from a direction he couldn't pinpoint. What he knew for certain was it wasn't from behind him, not from the open sea. He could feel a malicious gaze, eying him with morbid curiosity. It was coming from the asylum. Not in the building, but the essence of whatever inhabited it looked upon Rino with interest.

Old superstitions indeed. Decades of urban legends and silly ghost stories began to plague his rational mind. He looked up at the bell tower, the place where the fated doctor was reported to have fallen from. His eyes fixated on it. On its spire sat a cross. Whether Christ hung from it he couldn't see. It's possible he once did, long ago removed by something he'd rather not think of. Rino sensed the Lord wasn't welcome on Poveglia and neither was he. He called out again. No response.

If he opened the door, they might hear him better. The idea of touching any part of the asylum alarmed him. He reached out to touch the door when a glimmer of light caught his eye. Further up the path was a smaller building. A light flickered from inside. Clearly, the English found the asylum too daunting and found the other place more inviting. Rino walked towards the building, hating the idea he would have to walk past the asylum to get back to the boat. With apprehension, he walked closer to a window. The light was gone. The glass was missing but the frame remained. Its crisscrossed design made it impossible for anyone to climb through. He called out into the building, his voice trembled as it echoed throughout the empty space.

He was frustrated and angry at being ignored. They must have heard him, even the others at the boat would have heard him. He became concerned that a passing boat might have heard him, the Carabinieri, even. He turned on the light and shone it through the window. The inside of the building was derelict. The abandoned and rusted bed frames reminded him of a hospital. There was rubbish littering the place, remnants of disrespect. But no sign of life. No indication his passengers were inside.

He went to call out again when he heard a whisper. His heart momentarily stopped before relief washed over him. Voices. That was good, right?

"Signora? Signore? Ehi!" His voice echoed through the room but the murmurs remained. He strained his hearing but couldn't make out what was being said. It had to be them. The alternative wasn't worth thinking about. He made his way around to the side of the building. A strong breeze was carried in from the ocean, the cold fresh air stung his cheeks. There was a door. Slightly open. He approached it and prised it open further. It was heavy and a struggle for him to move by himself. Those two idiots more than likely saw an opening and squeezed through it.

Little natural light made its way inside. A fading twilight lay over the room, soaking up any natural light that made its way in. Rino turned on his torch. It offered little illumination, yet he felt safer with it on. The whispering remained, but it was no less intelligible. It crept across the walls and lingered in the air, which was thick and musty.

Rino's senses pleaded with him to leave and head back to the boat. As if he could without the others. He couldn't leave them. It was out of the question. His legs shivered as he walked further into the room. A low voice crawled towards him from a corridor on his left. He turned on instinct, gazing into the blackness. He swung his torch towards the source. Nothing. The light wasn't powerful enough to brighten up the corridor. Beyond its reach was more darkness.

"Time to go. Time's up. We leave now. I'll leave you here. I swear." It was an empty threat, albeit one he was starting to consider as fear strengthened its grip on him.

The voice was garbled. It was unmistakably a woman, saying words Rino didn't know. It gave him hope. It could've been English, that's why he didn't know what was being said. But why was there no response? He made his way towards the corridor. Ice ran down his spine as sweat formed on his brow. His light shone deeper down the hallway, never reaching the end. The whispering got no louder, yet neither did it quieten. It remained at a constant level, teasing Rino with a promise that never came.

Robbed of his reason, he continued down the hallway. The sounds of outside had disappeared. He estimated that he'd reach the end of the corridor soon, the building didn't seem that big. In a panic, he shone the torch behind him. Darkness on both sides. With only two directions to travel, he was still worried about getting lost. The whispering got louder. It wasn't English, it was Italian. Not a dialect he was familiar with but definitely his mother tongue. It startled him. He tripped, stumbled and found himself lying on the ground. The torch was thrown from his hands. It smashed, taking the only source of light from him.

He felt a cut on his lip and grazes on his hands. He stood up and composed himself as best he could. He was disorientated but sure of his sense of direction. He was going no further. It was time to leave. He didn't know the source of the whispering, but he did know it was not who he was looking for. He held onto the wall for guidance as he made his way back, hoping he was moving in the right direction. The stone was cold and damp. There was a slick wetness as his fingers traced over the wall. He could see nothing but black.

As he progressed he was able to distinguish between shades of darkness. Shadows moved towards him as the whispers got louder. He was still unsure of what they were saying. It wasn't friendly and it wasn't courteous. It was a warning.

The shadows glided over the wall and made themselves towards Rino. He failed to convince himself that his senses were playing tricks on him. He thought of Elena. The reason he was there, the reason he now found himself more scared than he'd ever been. *La Madonna,* he thought as the shadows closed in. The whispering stopped, replaced by a clear and succinct voice that only said one word to him. Run.

But he couldn't. His legs had betrayed him. And the shadows claimed the rest.

36

Panicked seagulls squawked their displeasure. Whether they were annoyed at being disturbed by the invader's shouting or they sensed something malignant stirring was known only to them. Julia looked up as a flock flew towards the horizon. How she envied them. To get up and go whenever they felt like it. To be unrestricted by petty obstacles like the ocean.

Her head started to hurt. Likely brought on by stress. She hoped that's all it was. Julia was prone to migraines. It's something she could do without as she sat in a fishing boat tethered to a haunted island. The things she did for love.

The sun was setting, taking with it the heat. A devious chill threatened the boat's passengers as it made its way across the water and towards the island. While the seagulls fled, the wind was drawn to Poveglia as if the island drew in breath. Except there was no exhale and Julia didn't want to be around when it did.

What was taking him so long? It had been a few minutes since they last heard any shouting. Only one voice emanated from the island. Neither Lawrence nor Julia heard any response. Rino's own voice got further away, they assumed the old man had ventured deeper into the island to find the others. How long did they have before the fuel was gone? It had spooked Rino. That was enough for Julia. Not that Lawrence seemed as phased by the whole thing. Ignorance and optimism had partnered with him as he found himself enjoying the thrill of the situation. He couldn't fathom anything going wrong. Rino would return in time and they'd have enough fuel to get back. He wasn't concerned.

What he was, though, was envious. Envious of Rino, Kirsty and Aaron. They were walking the island as he sat on a rusty old boat. He should've been grateful for getting as close as he did. It was fortuitous that he not only found out about the tour, but he happened to share it with people more ambitious than he was. He thought of Kirsty, his excitement at her appearance in his mind confirmed his attraction to her. That, he would have to conceal better than his giddy boyishness at being on an adventure.

"He's been gone too long," Julia said.

"It's only been about five minutes."

"More like ten minutes."

"Kirsty and Aaron were supposed to get thirty, to be fair."

"You saw the look on his face? That's someone who has a clue about boats and he was freaking out."

"We'll be fine. I'm sure the others will be back before him and we'll all laugh about it." Even Lawrence wasn't kidding himself with that one. Rino and Julia certainly wouldn't be laughing. And neither would he when Julia was through with him. She was unhappy, and rightfully so. Her mood bordered on furious territory and he'd be the one feeling the brunt of it. An argument was on the cards. It was booked for back at the hotel when they were alone. Julia hated to make a scene, and she was capable of boxing up her rage, ready to unleash it at a time of her choosing.

36

After the argument, they'd go to bed. Wake up still angry, not speak for an hour or two, then everything would be sorted before they left Venice. This little mishap wouldn't spoil the honeymoon as a whole. It wouldn't even tarnish the better memories she had of Venice. She knew he had to suck it up and take any blows aimed at him. He had to admit, it was partly his fault. He wasn't taking full responsibility, though. That was out of the question.

The boat gently rocked on the calm water. Julia looked at the clear skies, spreading out endlessly across the ocean. She thought of the sudden thunderstorm earlier that day. How quickly the weather could change. She didn't have faith in the boat keeping them safe in that scenario. Where the hell were they?

A burst of static shattered the silence as the boat's VHF radio shouted out for attention. Neither of the couple had any idea what was being said. Rino would know what to do. Except he wasn't there, and he'd left behind two Americans with little Italian between them. They looked at each other.

"Should we answer it?" Lawrence asked.

"I guess. It might be important."

"I hope your Italian is better than mine."

"She might speak better English. Other cultures are less ignorant than ours."

Lawrence approached the radio as if it was a bomb. He carefully lifted the receiver as if afraid it would detonate. He clicked the button, "Hello?"

Julia watched him from the edge of the cockpit. He could have at least greeted the speaker in Italian.

The reception was terrible. Even if the woman on the other side was speaking in English, they'd still struggle to hear what she was saying. Julia's faith in the sanctity of the boat continued to fade.

"Hello," Lawrence said again. "Buongiorno. Sorry, I don't speak Italian. American. I speak English." The woman at the other end continued to speak Italian. Lawrence didn't know if she didn't know English or just couldn't understand him. Either way, it was frustrating for all. The radio cut out abruptly. Lawrence's eyes widened as he turned to Julia for help.

"What did you do?" she asked.

"Nothing," he said. "I didn't press anything." He started fiddling with dials in an attempt to get the signal back. The radio made noise, that was a good sign. It squealed as he struggled to regain any sort of signal.

"Stop it, you've no idea what you're doing. You might make it worse."

The radio hissed briefly before the static started to clear. The crackle returned but it wasn't the same voice. It was music. The sound of a record playing. Neither were familiar with the piece of music, but it sounded old and that it was being played on something even older. Thoughts of a gramophone appeared in Julia's mind even though she wasn't sure what a gramophone sounded like.

As different as the music was, it wasn't what they were looking for. But before Lawrence could change the channel, it was gone. Replaced with white noise.

"I've no idea what I'm doing with this thing."

"I don't like this."

"We need to get a hold of Rino."

Julia could almost see the lightbulb appear above her husband's head. He couldn't possibly be stupid enough to be suggesting-

"I don't think we can wait any longer," he interrupted her thoughts. "I think we're going to need to go onto the island and get him."

Her heart sank so heavily that Julia was worried it would rock the boat. He could not be serious, had he lost his damn fool mind? It would have been so easy to just push him into the lagoon. Perhaps the shock of hitting the water would straighten his head out and cleanse him of his terrible idea.

If Julia had a paranoid mind, she'd be able to convince herself that this was Lawrence's plan all along. That he was in some sort of strange scheme with the others so that this would all play out to its natural conclusion: Lawrence walking the island.

No, that was absurd. It was far-fetched and unfeasible. Lawrence didn't have the conniving wit to plot such a plan. He was more an agent of chance who would drift on the wind and allow it to take him where it chose. And it chose here, dragging Julia along with it.

She wanted to slap him. To scream. Instead, she couldn't argue with the logic. They did need to find Rino and fast. Best case scenario, they bumped into him as the three stooges returned from their jaunt. Worst case scenario...

"No," Julia said. "No, I'm not going."

"I understand what you're saying. I'm not suggesting we go exploring. I just think that Rino has somehow missed the others. They're probably ships in the night out there. I don't want to delve too deep into the island, just scout the perimeter and make sure we don't miss them on the way back."

Scout the perimeter. He was loving this. He was in full-on adventure mode.

"And what if they come back to the boat when we're looking for them? And they decide to leave *us*?"

"They won't. I'm just wanting to walk up past those trees. Take a look. Make sure Rino hasn't missed them." He was repeating himself, he had no further argument. Regardless of his intentions, Lawrence wanted to keep his wife happy. If that meant going onto the island and finding Rino so they could get as far away as possible, so be it. If it so happened he had an even cooler story to tell people when they got home then all the better.

"If you're really against it," he said. "You can wait here." Although his tone was kind and thoughtful, the words were not. Julia felt her anger boil. She agreed to go on the stupid tour to begin with. She didn't object loudly to going to the island. For him to leave her had proved to be the last straw.

"Lawrence," she said, composed yet stern. "If you leave me on this boast, I assure you that you had better not return."

The radio spewed forth a garbled transmission. It fizzed and screeched a chaotic dissonance that had Julia gritting her teeth. The voice was clearer this time but it wasn't a woman's. It was a man's. A familiar voice. It was Rino. Julia could swear it was Rino. "Aiuto," the voice said. "Aiuto."

They both looked at each other. The anguish in the voice usurped any need for a translation. Lawrence tried the receiver again.

"Rino? Rino, is that you? What's wrong? No comprende, captain…over."

As the voice faded, Julia opened her phone and quickly typed in the word. The spelling was wrong and autocorrected to a word she still didn't know. The translation app found a match. *Help*. Rino - if it was even Rino - was in trouble.

36

A grim silence filled the air as Julia and Lawrence locked eyes. Any sense of adventure Lawrence had was gone. He was scared. Selfishly he was scared at the prospect of Rino being too injured to get them home. Scared at whatever caused his injury. No, that part was just ridiculous. He was an old man; the island had its pitfalls. He'd likely tripped and sprained his ankle. Nothing more.

An unspoken understanding passed between husband and wife. Neither wanted to depart the boat, not anymore. Yet both knew they couldn't ignore the call. Chances are it was a cross-transmission, just like the music. But it was unlikely. The quality of the communication was poor but it sounded so much like Rino.

Despite Rino telling them to stay on the boat, it seemed like their captain was now in need of aid. Julia felt sick at the prospect while the excitement that lay in Lawrence had betrayed him as it clawed at his stomach. Without saying a word, it was settled. They were going onto the island.

37

Venturing into the unknown, they left the boat and braved the wooden pier. Lawrence went first, making sure it was still sturdy enough to hold any weight. The now familiar creaking of the wood made the hairs on the back of his neck stand up. He offered to help Julia up but she preferred to wait until he had left the plank. She didn't want to jinx it. As she climbed into the dock, her eyes remained down. She looked at the water towards the boat but couldn't see any boat leak. What did she know anyway, Rino saw it. He knew more than she did.

The path before them was filled with the same obstacles that their predecessors faced. Branches had been disturbed and damaged. Leaves lay on the ground. A stronger wind had formed, it battered the waves against the shore wall. It felt like a warning that dared them to go further at their peril. A blue twilight shone over the island as the sun surrendered the night to the moon. The clear skies allowed for better illumination. They had a spare torch they found on the boat. Julia prayed they wouldn't have much use for it but it was better to have it than not. They had no other source of light aside from the moon. All it would have taken was for a cloud to manifest and they'd be plunged into darkness.

37

They arrived at the other end of the overgrown path. The asylum stood to their right. What once looked like a derelict building from the water loomed over them with menace. It's history permeated through the brickwork, confined by an unknown force that struggled to contain what it held.

It was just stone, bricks and stones. The rational side of Julia's brain was screaming for her to get back to the boat. It also wanted her to get far away from the island but that wasn't much of an option. What she wouldn't allow it to do was infest her with foolish thoughts. Yes, it was intimidating, but she was more worried about finding Rino and the condition of the boat than she was about the dead.

Thousands of dead, left to rot on the island over centuries. True, most of the casualties had perished long ago. But what about those in more recent times, those that inhabited the very walls of the building that stood before them?

Julia thought about the doctor that Kirsty mentioned. The experiments he would perform. It was plausible. There were many cases of evil doctors that abused their position of trust. The one on Poveglia could have been a serial killer.

What Julia refused to buy into was that an otherworldly force influenced him. Stories grew arms and legs over time, as much fun as Lawrence may have found Kirsty's stories, they did little to entertain or frighten Julia.

Or had they? There was a lurking uneasiness in her stomach that rejected her reasoning. Yes, she was trespassing on a restricted island. Yes, they might not have enough fuel to get back, and they had no idea where Rino was, or the others for that matter. All understandable reasons to feel the way she did. Except there was something else, something more. Something unknown that she was unable to reconcile.

Lawrence had a similar feeling in his own stomach. There was no denying that the excitement had returned. His nerves were close to shredding his insides yet he got a thrill from doing something so illicit. Events had quickly escalated. He wasn't even sure he'd get to see the place and now he walked on its surface. The aura of the place had a nauseating allure that drew him in the moment he clapped eyes on it. The forbidden fruit he knew he shouldn't touch, but when presented with the temptation, he couldn't resist.

Besides, what harm was he doing, and he had a valid reason for being there. They had to find the others and get back to the city. Did he feel guilty about enjoying the potential jeopardy he put Julia in? A little, but he was so naïve he didn't feel there was any real danger. He walked his own private funhouse of horrors. The fear was an illusion. Safety was never far away. In theory.

They walked further up the path and stopped at the door of the asylum. Rust had set in the metal, but it remained in sturdy-looking condition. Despite the age and obvious disrepair, the building had undergone, it still looked like a fortress.

Lawrence looked at the path before him. Back the way he came, out towards the ocean. Finally, his eyes lay to rest at the entrance to the asylum.

"What do you think?" he said.

Julia was beyond arguing with him. Every issue she challenged resulted in the situation worsening. *No, there's no way I'm going in there,* would end up with them both going in. It was more than likely it's where Kirsty and Aaron went. It was entirely feasible it's where Rino would look first. Why neither had come back out, she wasn't ready to answer. There'd be a rational explanation and if it wasn't to her liking, she may add to the island's body count.

"Sure," she said. "Why not? We've come this far."

She didn't hide her tone. She didn't want to. If anything, she exaggerated it to drive the message home. It almost baited Lawrence into a response, but he caught his words before they left his mouth. It wasn't the right time to ask her what was wrong.

"The door is open," he said. "I'll just shine the light in, shout on them."

Julia nodded, eyebrows raised. They both suspected they'd end up inside.

Lawrence shone the light through the open doorway. Slivers of moonlight accompanied the torch. The room was dilapidated, devoid of any recognisable furniture that allowed him to identify the room.

"Hello?" he shouted. His voice echoed throughout. "Guys? Fun's over, we need to leave. Rino? You in there, amigo?"

The ocean breeze stung Julia's cheek. The city at night was a lot warmer than Poveglia was. Her optimism at quickly resolving the predicament they'd found themselves in had faded.

Lawrence turned to look at her, validating her thoughts. He shook his head, then eased himself a little further through the doorway. He called out again, his own voice the only reply.

"I'm going in," he said. "See if I have more luck."

"Of course." Julia raised her eyebrows, her lips flattened out her mouth.

"What's that supposed to mean?"

"Nothing. Go on, I'll wait here."

"I'm not going in for any other reason than to try and find them so we can get out of here."

"Didn't suggest anything to the contrary."

Taking a deep breath, he entered the asylum. Julia instantly regretted letting him out of her sight. His absence made her colder. She felt exposed with her back to the ocean but she wasn't taking her eyes from the doorway. He had barely been gone seconds. The stench of being alone clung to her. She felt naked and vulnerable. She had no idea what was behind the door. No idea as to how she would feel when she walked beyond the frame. What she did know was that she had no desire to remain outside alone, even for a further second.

Without a second glance at her surroundings, Julia bit her lip hard enough that it hurt and entered the asylum.

38

The air inside was thick. Thick with dust that carried with it a stale smell of the past. Coldness washed over her as her eyes adjusted to the dark room. Lawrence scanned the room with a methodical artistry, painting a picture with the light for Julia to see. What surprised her most was the amount of graffiti on the walls. *So much for a secluded island.*

"Place must be more popular than I thought," Lawrence said, apparently reading her thoughts. "Or it was, anyway."

"It's not hard to get to if you have a boat," Julia said. "Who in Venice doesn't have a boat? Can imagine a lot of kids coming here."

"Well, let's hope they're still not here."

"Scared of Italian youths more than the ghosts?" There was a playfulness to her tone that Lawrence appreciated. The situation wasn't easy for her, and he wasn't as jovial as he once was. Ghosts couldn't hurt him, but a bunch of delinquents that are disturbed could.

"I just had a thought," he said. "Do you think the Mafia might use a place like this to hide drugs and guns?"

"I think we should stay focused." She smiled a smile he didn't see.

Lawrence walked around the room. Slowly. Carefully. His

imagination had branched out to other dangers, earthly ones. The place was very secluded. No one would bother you. He imagined drug addicts using it as a shooting gallery, leaving used needles in their wake. He kept that theory to himself. It was impossible to tell what the room once was, although he guessed it must have been some sort of reception area. The walls had vegetation crawling along them. Nature had laid claim to the asylum.

To his left at the end of the room was a staircase. He approached it with trepidation. It was badly damaged with missing steps. It was possible to climb, but it would have been difficult. He didn't know Kirsty well, but from the brief time he did, he didn't envision a hazardous staircase being a barrier to her curiosity.

"I don't really want to go too far into this place," Julia said. "We don't want them to double back on us."

"Yeah yeah yeah," he said with a soft voice, allowing the last word to trail.

Julia could feel eyes on her. As if the walls themselves were alive and able to see. She felt more exposed in shelter than she did by the ocean with nothing behind her. Despite this, there was also a gradual claustrophobia serenading her. The darkness didn't feel like emptiness. It felt tangible. Like she could hold it in her hands. Like it could hold her.

She rubbed her arms. Shadows moved around the room. Her eyes played tricks, she hoped. Lawrence made his way towards the staircase, and she followed, staying as close to him as possible. From the corner of her eye was a green glow. She turned, it was emanating from a room at the end to her left, just up ahead.

"Lawrence, look?" she said.

He shone the light but it didn't answer her question. What the hell was causing it? They both approached the room. Upon entering, they realised the light was coming from another room connected to the one they stood in. A green glow flickered in the darkness. An invitation. Like moths to a flame, they followed. The source of the light was surprising but unspectacular. It was a glow stick. Likely left by Kirsty and Aaron. It illuminated the room much better than their torch did. Lawrence turned it off, leaving them doused in the fluorescent light.

"Looks like they came this way," he said. But what now? Julia had no time for games or any intention of following a neon bread trail.

The plaster on the walls was cracked. The roof was falling in, she wondered if she would be able to see into the upstairs room with more light. Julia was glad of the light they did have. She could see broken glass on the floor: broken beer bottles. It looked like the asylum was party central, she just hoped it was closed for business.

The next room had nothing but blackness. It wasn't as inviting and Julia had enough. It was time to go back to the boat. The asylum was a death trap due to its mistreatment by people. Living, selfish people. She made a mental note to try to get a tetanus shot before leaving for Rome. Just to be safe.

Lawrence turned his torch back on and shone it into the darkness. It failed to penetrate the gloom.

"What now?" he asked Julia.

"I'm done. Let's go back. For all we know they're all waiting for us." She didn't believe that but she could hope.

Julia could feel something enter the room. Its eyes bore into her back so hard she could feel the pressure between her shoulder blades. She turned hesitantly, but quickly. Nothing. Nothing she could see, anyway. Lawrence turned to match her gaze, swinging the torch around. It cut through the green glow but was of no help. She felt foolish. She wanted out of there.

While her focus remained on the nothingness before her, something she couldn't sense approached her from behind. It made its way towards her, silent and cautious not to disturb. Moving with a malicious glee, it didn't want to play its hand too quickly. It savoured the build-up as the payoff promised to be exquisite.

A crunch of broken glass betrayed its plan but it was too late. The figure was behind her, its cold hands were on her shoulders before she had the chance to turn and face her stalker.

The voice said one word as it gently jolted her. "Boo."

39

Julia felt her heart miss a beat as she turned to face Kirsty. The prankster laughed with a devilish wickedness that was almost childlike in its glee. The recipient did not find it as amusing. Julia felt her fist tighten, it took incredible restraint not to punch Kirsty right in the mouth. It would have made for an awkward boat trip back to the city, but her conscience told her it'd be worth it. In the end, she resisted.

"Sorry about my sister," Aaron said. "What she finds funny and what polite society laughs at are always at odds." He was holding his camera, looking through the viewfinder.

"Do you find it funny?" Julia said with an accusing tone.

He looked baffled and a little hurt by the accusation. She pointed at the camera which was pointed right at her.

"What? Oh, no. I'm not recording you. I'm using the night vision function."

Julia noted there was a large flash on top of the camera as well. And a mic. He had a lot of equipment. Kirsty had her backpack and little else.

"I'm sorry," Kirsty said, struggling to repress a smile.

"Just, don't talk to me and we'll be better that way."

"It was a joke. Seriously, I'm sorry. What are you two doing here anyway? How much did Rino fleece you for him to let you off the boat?"

"Actually," Lawrence said. "That's why we're here. Rino left the boat to come and get you guys."

"What, why?" Kirsty said. "We've not been gone thirty minutes, that was the deal."

"There's something wrong with the boat. He said it's leaking fuel."

"It must have really rattled him to leave you two on the boat. Or, he's found a convenient excuse to cut our time." Kirsty stroked her chin comically. "So, where is he?"

"If we knew that," Julia said. "We wouldn't be standing here talking to you now, would we?"

"We haven't seen him," Aaron said. "Or heard him for that matter. It's quiet in here, we heard you two."

"You must have heard us calling out for you then," Julia said.

Aaron felt sheepish that he did not. "We didn't. I wasn't ignoring you, honest. I didn't hear a thing."

"So," Kirsty said, her voice snapping. "The gang's all here but we've lost the captain, the one guy that can get us home."

"Exactly," Julia said. "That's why we need to get back to the boat. Rino is probably waiting for us as it is."

"Wait a minute," Kirsty said. "Why did you come looking for Rino, why not stay on the boat?"

"There was a radio transmission," Lawrence said. It was difficult to make out at first. We thought it was the coast guard or something, we couldn't tell. But there was something else. It sounded like Rino. He sounded hurt, we think he's had a fall or something."

"Considering the condition of this place, it's likely," Aaron said. "I don't imagine there was anything else to go on?"

"Nothing," Lawrence said. "I think there's something wrong

with the radio also. It kept cutting out."

The four of them all stood in silence. Each one had their own thoughts on how to proceed. The one man with any experience to get them off the island was missing, presumed hurt. If he had come into the asylum, Kirsty and Aaron didn't notice him. They also didn't hear Lawrence's calls. That was strange. The sound of the ocean could be heard the room was so quiet. Lawrence's voice echoed throughout but didn't reach anyone. Aaron said he didn't hear them. Julia didn't trust Kirsty, but she had no reason to suspect Aaron was lying.

A malignant essence permeated the air. The darkness swirled around them, held at bay by a glow stick. They had to act, no one wanted to be the first to speak. Seconds passed, they felt like minutes.

"So," Kirsty said. "Since Rino is somewhere on the island, I take it there's no immediate rush to get back to the boat." Her words hung in the air. Julia couldn't believe what she was hearing. The opportunistic nature of this woman, her ego. It made her sick.

Aaron also felt sick, although in his case it was nausea. He blamed it on something he ate, or maybe it was the boat, or both. Most likely it was a combination of everything with Rino's disappearance and potential misfortune being the cherry on top. He wanted to sit down. There was nowhere to sit other than the floor. He wanted some fresh air.

"Is that the best idea?" he said. "For all we know Rino is back at the boat. Maybe we should call it a night."

"You can go back to the boat and wait on Rino if you wish but if he is lost somewhere I'm going to feel a lot warmer in here."

Julia accepted that scenario. She had no qualms about

leaving Kirsty in the asylum. But it wasn't realistic. If they went back to the boat and Rino was waiting, they still wouldn't leave without her, unfortunately. *If* Rino was even at the boat. They had to look for him. There was no easy solution. She cursed the moment she'd ever heard of the damned island.

"We all go back together," Lawrence said. "And that includes Rino otherwise none of us are going to get very far."

"You think he'd leave us here?" Aaron said.

"I don't know," Lawrence said. "He seemed a decent enough guy but for all I know this is a scam by him."

For all I know, you two are part of it, Julia directed her thought at Kirsty and Aaron.

"He won't," Kirsty said. "Call it intuition. There's something off with him but I can't see him leaving us here. We'd find a way off anyway and when we did he wouldn't want the review I'd leave for him."

Instinctively, she pulled her phone out and checked the signal. Dead. She said nothing as she put the phone away.

"So, what do we do then?" Aaron asked.

Suddenly, there was a faint knocking from above. The weight on the ceiling shifted as if someone was moving on the floor above them. Bits of old plaster fell from the ceiling followed by dust.

"I say we go see who that is," Kirsty said.

40

They returned to the darkness of the main entrance. Kirsty produced a fresh glow stick and lit up the room. As the room illuminated, all eyes fell upon the stairwell. They were badly damaged with steps missing. The gap was large but there were enough broken steps in-between that made the journey possible. Dangerous, but possible.

The question was who goes? They all thought about it, but no one wanted to be the first to bring it up. Neither Julia nor Aaron wanted to go. Lawrence was hesitant also while Kirsty was more than happy to. Albeit not alone. She was brave but she wasn't stupid. Someone had to speak first. She decided to take that burden.

"Who's coming with me?" she said.

They all looked at each other, Julia looked to Aaron. It made sense for Aaron to go with her, they came here for this sort of adventure. Let them go up and check it out. Still, Julia was wary about letting Kirsty out of her sight. She couldn't trust her to come back down. It pained her to admit it, but they had to all stick together.

"We all go," Julia said, much to everyone's surprise. "We check it out, if it's not Rino, we come back down." She didn't think it was Rino, she found it difficult to consider that he'd climb those stairs. Then again, maybe he did and that's how he got injured. "Rino," she shouted. "Rino, are you there?"

Calling on him first was the sensible thing to do. A catalogue of bad decisions got them to the point they were at. Hopefully, Rino would call back down. Say he was okay, he'd just got a fright and now he was ready to take them all home. A hope that was crushed by a silent reply.

"It still might be him," Lawrence said. "He could be hurt worse than we think."

"Either way, I agree, we all go," Aaron said. "It'll be safer." He was reminded of the drug den of Reston Mather's house. He didn't see anyone, that was Kirsty's burden to bear. But it still stuck with him. How lucky they were. At least there were four of them now. And if anyone was upstairs then their silence hinted they were afraid and wanted to be left alone. He'd have been happier if they didn't have to investigate it any further, but the decision was made. They agreed they would all go.

The remaining steps were badly damaged. Large cracks and chunks were missing. It was uninviting and hazardous. Kirsty agreed to go first. The stairwell was narrow enough that she could stretch across to hold onto both bannisters. She clipped her glow stick to her belt. She was bathed in a radiant green as she tested the first broken step. It held her weight and she sighed relief. The next step was more of a stretch, she used the bannister for momentum and was thankful it also held. Her next move was easier as she jumped a step onto the rest of the stairs. The upper staircase spiralled in a square. It was in much better condition, but she took no chances as she held her grip on the supports. Julia followed, with Lawrence not far behind. Aaron wasn't happy at going last but someone had to. The nausea in his stomach remained, slightly more intense than before. He struggled a little as he climbed the stairs. He thought about making himself sick to see if it would help.

At the top of the stairs, Kirsty aimed the glow stick down the hallway. The upper level was cleaner. There was no graffiti on the walls and little debris or rubbish littering the floor. She worked out the dimensions of the area and noted that the room that was directly above them was to their right. She slowly walked up the hall, every creak of the wooden floor was amplified by the quiet. It made everyone carefully contemplate each step they took.

A gentle chill drifted down the hall, it hit everyone as it passed them. It was unsettling, another reminder of why they shouldn't be there. They entered the room to find nothing but a lone wooden chair placed right in the middle. Aaron was tempted to sit down, although he was worried it would break, and he'd find himself on the floor, humiliated.

"That was a little anticlimactic," Kirsty said.

"Other than Rino, what were you expecting to find?" Julia asked.

It was a good question. Kirsty wasn't sure. She was glad it wasn't drug addicts. *Those lifeless doll-like eyes.* The memory was unwelcome. From a side glance, she could see the child lying in the corner of the room. In the darkness. That glassy stare fixed on her, damning her for her inability to help. She knew it was her mind playing tricks, all she had to do was remove doubt by bathing the corner with light. The memory would dissipate and reality would return.

But she couldn't. Fear had gripped her. If she was wrong, if she aimed the light into the corner and the memory was real, then what? She wanted adventure, she wanted her scepticism tested. If the past was to haunt her, it had to remain a memory. All she had to do was shine the light and expose her paranoia for what it was. Except she wouldn't take the chance.

The paint on the walls had peeled over time. The floors were bare, exposing the raw floorboards that had aged badly over decades of neglect. Julia felt safer on the stairs. Each creak served as a reminder that it was not a place she wanted to be. Especially if it wasn't Rino that made the noise. If not Rino, then who? Or what?

"Can we all agree that we can tick this room off our list?" Julia said.

"Maybe it was a rat," Lawrence said.

"Must have been a big rat," Aaron said.

"How big do the rats get in Italy?"

"I'd rather not know if I'm honest."

"The rats are the least of your worries here," Kirsty said. They all looked at her, waiting on some ghoulish diatribe. "It's the scorpions I'm more concerned with."

Julia let out a sardonic laugh. She couldn't help it. As if things weren't bad enough, she now had scorpions to contend with. At least it was a rational fear. Maybe that's what happened to Rino. A scorpion stung him. She hoped not, it went beyond her first aid expertise.

Aaron shone his light into the adjoining room. He activated another glow stick and threw it in. The room was as unremarkable, yet no less creepy, as the one they were in. There looked to be no reason to enter.

"I say we go back," Aaron said.

No one disagreed. Julia found herself gravitating towards the room. She was curious and wanted to be sure. She had to see for herself that it wasn't worth going any further. As much as she wanted to leave, she didn't want to do so without Rino. She stood next to Arron and looked into the room. Nothing.

She was about to agree with Aaron when she heard the sound of wood strain. It wasn't clear where it was coming from but it got everyone's attention. Lawrence and Kirsty found themselves on one side of the room, looking at Julia and Aaron on the other. Everyone froze as they honed their hearing on the sound. The sound of wood struggling to support its burden. A final warning to everyone that something devastating was about to happen. And with no further caution, the floor gave way.

41

The floor that had once been there was gone. It disappeared in an almighty crash as the rubble fell to the room below. A dust cloud rose from the opening, its filth sprinkled in the neon light. Kirsty and Lawrence had found shelter in the doorway they entered from. Kirsty's eyes stung from the dust. They all got off lightly, considering what could have happened. Julia and Aaron were at the far side of the room. Aaron and Lawrence shone their lights over at each other.

"Jesus," Lawrence said. "Julia, you okay?"

"I'm fine," she said. "Just a little shaken."

"What the hell just happened?" Aaron said.

His eyes fell to the chasm in the room. At his side of the room, there was barely enough floor left for him and Julia to stand on. The other side was gone completely. It forced Kirsty and Lawrence from the room, both stood in the doorway. As sudden as the collapse was, the four of them were lucky they weren't injured. Even if it did mean they were separated. They were safe, that was the important factor. But what now? As they stood across from the gap it was clear that no one was capable of clearing it. The drop below was too deep and with all the debris that had formed, the dangers were magnified. They were separated, it was time for a new plan.

"We need to calm down," Lawrence said. "And think about what to do next."

"This is fucked up," Aaron said. "How the hell do we get back out of here now?"

"Bro," Kirsty said. "Chill, please."

"Easy for you to say. You can get back the way you came."

'I'm sorry, but I'm not taking the blame for the floor falling in like that."

"No," Julia said. "How about everything else though?"

"Excuse me," Kirsty said. "No one forced you to get off that boat and no one asked you to come in here."

"We wouldn't be here if it wasn't for you." As her voice cut through the gloom it wasn't clear who she aimed her vitriol at. If it wasn't for Lawrence she wouldn't have been aware the island even existed. He organised the boat ride and he was the one that had little objection to Kirsty getting off the boat. But Julia was aware of the part she played. She was angry at herself. No one had forced her to do anything. She may have been reluctant in her actions, but they were still her actions.

"This isn't getting us anywhere," Lawrence said. "Look, this is…I don't know. It's not ideal. Look, Kirsty and I will be able to make our way out if we just double back. If you guys keep following the corridors around, you'll see another staircase."

"Lawrence," Julia said. "For all you know that's the only staircase in this pit."

"We'll go back to the boat then. Get some rope to throw across, that might work?"

She wasn't sure how. What Julia was sure of was that she no longer felt safe. Forget the threat of ghosts or drug-addled teens, the asylum was condemned for a reason. It was a derelict ruin that threatened to swallow her. To bury her with the other relics of history.

She needed to get out and fast. She wasn't going to achieve that by staying still. As dangerous as the building was she had to move. There were trials to be overcome. It was a risk worth taking to get the hell out once and for all.

"Go back to the boat," she said. "But stay there. We'll find another way out."

"What?" Aaron said. "We should stay here, wait for help."

"It's best we keep moving. The sooner we get out of here the sooner we can get home."

Kirsty was impressed. She didn't think Julia had it in her. She already had a pre-loaded argument to counter any hysterics. Instead, she found herself in agreement with Julia. In a way, she was envious. They were getting to explore the asylum further while she was expected to go back to the boat and wait. *Well, we'll see about that. We'll see.*

"Okay," Kirsty said.

"No," Lawrence said. "I'm not leaving you."

"You have to," Julia said. "Go back to the boat and wait for me. It's not my preferred plan but it's the best we have. Aaron, do you have any of those glow sticks left?"

Aaron was dazed, he wasn't paying attention. He couldn't help but feel the lack of concern by his sister. The nausea in his stomach had gotten worse and now he was feeling hot. As if things weren't bad enough.

"Aaron?" Julia said. She spoke with a warm authority. Like a school teacher that consoled a child while reminding them they can trust the listener. "Are you all right?"

He snapped out of it. "Yeah", he said. I'm fine."

"Do you have more glow sticks?"

"What? Yeah, yeah. I've a few."

41

"Lawrence, where's the flashlight?"

It suddenly dawned on them all that the only light in the room was from Kirsty and Aaron's glow sticks. Lawrence looked at his hands, almost shocked to see he wasn't holding the flashlight any longer. He looked at the chasm before him and brought his gaze back up to see Julia.

"It's fine," Kirsty said. "I've got some glow sticks in the bag. We'll be fine, they're much better than that torch anyway."

Julia wasn't convinced. She also felt bad about losing Rino's property although she imagined it was the least of his issues.

"See you back at the boat," Julia said. She smiled over at Lawrence, his face lit by the fluorescent green.

"Just for the record," he said. I hate this idea."

"I'm not a fan of it myself but I'm done with being here."

"I love you."

She hesitated in her reply. Of course, she loved him but his words carried with it a finality. They'd be reunited soon, it wouldn't take her long to find a way out. Then there was Rino. They still hadn't found him. If they got back to the boat, and he wasn't there… No. Don't think like that. Think positively and one step at a time. Deal with the Rino situation when it comes. First, find their way out of the asylum.

She locked eyes with Lawrence. She couldn't not say it. "I love you too."

42

Lawrence and Kirsty stood as the others disappeared into the darkness. He had no idea what lay in store for Julia and Aaron. Or himself and Kirsty for that matter. He was frightened. Fearful for Julia's safety amplified by his own guilt. Julia may have her own free will, but he didn't help. He steered her towards the rocks.

Lawrence and Kirsty made their way back towards the staircase. Kirsty took the glow stick from her belt and dropped it down the opening in the stairwell. It hit the bottom with a faint click and lit up their path. They looked upon the shattered stairwell with a heightened respect as they carefully made their way to the bottom. Each strain they heard clawed at them. It was as if the asylum was taunting them.

At the bottom of the stairs, they found themselves back where they came in. Lawrence made his way towards the door, his hand reached out to touch it when Kirsty spoke.

"Are you in a rush?" she said.

Lawrence stopped. He turned to her, her face in shadow as the green light shone from behind her.

"What do you mean?"

"I mean, Aaron and your wife aren't going to be back at the boat anytime soon. I don't see why we need to be."

Lawrence was lost as to what was going on. Was she coming on to him? Did all the danger turn her on? He was flattered, but faithful. Faithful, but tempted. He felt a hot flush grow in his stomach.

"What do you have in mind?" he had no intention of doing anything, but he couldn't help push the situation. How far would he take it? He was aroused by the prospect, the cheap thrill of it. He relaxed his posture and leaned against the door.

"The others could be ages trying to find their way back. And we still have no idea where the good captain is. The way I see it, we've time to have a little nosy at the rest of the place. You wanted a tour, I did promise you I'd be your guide."

The warm feeling in his stomach turned sour. He felt sick at his stupidity. The fragile male ego had been punctured and with it, guilt oozed out from the wound.

"Let's just go back to the boat," he swung the door open. A fresh wind hit him. It was cold and welcoming. He stood outside, looking over the ocean. The moon shone brightly in the sky and with it his optimism had returned. He was out. Julia would be fine. Rino would be fine and soon they'd all be together and gone from the island, laughing at the high jinks they got themselves into.

Kirsty was less enthused about being back out of the asylum. She wanted to see more. She wasn't satisfied. If he wanted to go back to the boat and wait like a loser, then fine. He'd be going alone.

Alone. Alone was something she'd rather not be. The building was falling apart, what if something happened to her? It's probably what happened to Rino. He was likely injured and alone. A part of her also wanted to find him. She wanted to be the hero in the story. If she returned to the boat with its captain, it didn't matter how annoyed they were with her she'd be instantly redeemed. People say they don't care what others think about them, but they often do. Maybe not at that moment but later, when they're alone. That's when the despair comes to visit.

"Your call," she said. "But you'll be sitting on the boat by yourself."

"Not if Rino made it back first."

"Maybe. But even then, do you really want to sit with Captain Howdy waiting for everyone else?"

"I'm not going back in there."

"Me neither. Place is falling apart. Plus, it's huge, we'd likely get lost."

"So..."

"We want to find Rino. We also want a little more adventure. It's why we're both on this island, right? You may have left the boat to go looking for Rino but be honest with yourself It excited you. Being in there excited you." She pointed to the asylum. He looked at it. It looked at him. It did excite him. The adrenaline pounded through his body the entire time he was inside. Now he was out, it had faded. All that was left was the remorse and pain he felt at being separated from Julia. He needed a distraction. It'd be good for him.

"So, you don't want to go back to the boat," he said. "And you don't want to go back inside."

"We could loop this entire island in about an hour, it's tiny."

They both looked up the walkway. A smaller building sat on the corner of the island. They didn't know that's where Rino went. If they did, they might have rushed to it and looked for him. If they knew what he encountered they'd have swum for shore.

"What do you think that is?" he asked

"I think that was once a hospital."

"It looks pretty small to have been a hospital."

"Small island. I don't think the majority of people that came here did so to be healed. Poveglia isn't just somewhere to treat or rehabilitate. It's damnation. People sent here weren't expected to return."

Lawrence didn't really understand her explanation. Regardless, he was transfixed by her words. Kirsty knew how to tell a tale. He wasn't sure if what she said was accurate. If anything he had learned of Poveglia was indeed true, it didn't really matter as he could believe it was. The island radiated an essence that caressed him. Or maybe he was still thinking of earlier.

The thrill within him reignited. For a second, he forgot that Julia was lost somewhere within the asylum. He had faith she would be fine. She was tougher than he was and he felt no threat from Aaron. No, he had earned this. It was in his interests to take a look. He looked at Kirsty. His gaze flickered to the overgrown path, back towards the boat. It wasn't nearly as alluring as the unknown.

"I'm not too keen on going in. Even from here it looks in worse condition than the asylum."

"It could be where Rino is."

"Rino could be anywhere."

Kirsty stood, plotting her next move. He had a point, where was the fun in keeping to the outskirts of the island. The building did look pretty damaged in the moonlight. She pictured an aerial view of the island that she saw. It came to her.

"Follow me," she made her way up the path.

"Whoa," Lawrence said. "Where are we going? We look like we're heading towards the hospital."

"I just want to have a quick look. It's on the way anyway."

"On the way to where?"

She turned to him and winked.

"Spoilers."

43

A scraping noise woke Rino up. He wasn't sure how long he'd been out for. He didn't know whether he fainted or if he was knocked out. He hoped he was still in bed and was waking from an awful nightmare. Except he wasn't in his bed. The surface was cold and hard against his back. He was on the floor. The scraping noise was his back against the stone.

His eyes were wide, yet they may as well have been shut. All he could see was black. Nothing obscured his vision. Nothing covered his eyes. There was nothing to see.

A presence he couldn't see filled the emptiness. His memory slowly returned and he tried to scream. He was horrified to find no noise came out. His lips hurt. They were pressed together, he was unable to prise them apart. He could feel the blood trickle from where the wire was inserted to tighten his mouth closed. Sewn shut to prevent him from crying out for help or perhaps just crying out in general.

He struggled in vain to move his arms, his legs. To flail out at the unseen hands that dragged him down some godforsaken hallway. He felt his legs lower, then the rest of him. His heart skipped a beat and his stomach lurched into his throat. Rino could feel his body being dragged over a ledge. The relief that he was being taken down a staircase was short-lived. The back of his head hit the first step then was carefully held the rest of the way. A perverse show of concern.

A heartless screech passed over him, the response was a guttural groan. The words spoken were inhuman yet appeared to be some form of language. There was a clear subordinate relationship between the creature that held his head and the one out front. How many things were holding him? He couldn't see what they were but had already assessed they weren't human. Maybe once, but not anymore.

As they reached the final step, his head remained elevated as he was dragged along the stone. The floor was cold. Damp. He thought of Elena. Tried to comprehend never seeing her again. And if he did how he could possibly explain what had happened.

He was there for her. He had done it all for her. He didn't blame her, not one bit. He was glad. Glad that she wasn't there with him. Would he have travelled to the island let alone got on in it if she had been? No, he wouldn't have endangered her. If she had been there she most likely would have prevented all of it from happening. He was a fool, one that others will say died due to greed. Few if any will understand why he took the money, why he allowed the British to leave his boat.

The grating of his back against the floor made his skin crawl. His shirt mostly protected him from any real damage. Every metre or so a sharp stone would snag and pull at his shirt. The fabric would rip slightly, thankfully his flesh did not.

It was such small mercies he clung to. He flooded his mind with happy memories. Elena, Verona. Eleonora. His beloved Eleonora who he hoped to be reunited with. *It's been so long, my love.* He could only pray that he was worthy enough to spend eternity with her.

43

A sudden, damning realisation hit him with force. What if he was already dead? He had been killed while walking the island and now he was being dragged to Hell by Satan's spawn. No, he was still breathing. His heart still beat. Wherever he was, he was still alive. For how much longer, he didn't know, but he wasn't optimistic of seeing the ocean again. To breathe the salt air into his lungs.

His eyes were of no use but his ears still worked. He could hear music. A record player. The crackle on the vinyl was unmistakable. The sound was peculiar, it wasn't a modern setup. It sounded old as did the music itself. He didn't recognise it but it must have been from the 1920s at least. Some sort of jazz. He tried to make out the lyrics but the male singer sang in French.

He was forcefully lifted like a sack of potatoes and thrown onto a steel chair, sat upright at a 70-degree angle. He wanted to urinate badly, it hurt so much to hold it in. If possible, he would depart the world with as much dignity as possible.

A flicker of light teased him from above. Gradually a dull orange glow lit up the room. Staring at the high ceiling he was still none the wiser to what was going on or where he was. The wall before him was undistinguished in the poor light. He couldn't move his head, unseen hands held him in place. Without warning, a leather strap was placed over his forehead. It was quickly followed up on both wrists and shins. He could feel the hands leave him, their work no longer required.

A fresh burst of fear took hold. He thrashed in his restraints. A futile gesture. He tried screaming again but to no avail. The attempt hurt his mouth. The best he could conjure was a strained splutter as blood and saliva spat from his pursed lips.

Footsteps approached him from behind. He wanted nothing

more than to turn and see who it was they belonged to. To be given a chance to plead, bargain or fight for his life. He didn't want to die. He never felt he was afraid to until then. Not like this. Not at the hand of a malevolent entity.

No, don't be foolish, he thought. *It's just a man, a sick and twisted man.* He had obviously disturbed some crazies and had been attacked. That was reasonable. Plausible. But not a theory he truly believed. He knew in his soul it wasn't true. That same soul burned with the evil energy that powered the island. Centuries of death had formed Poveglia, assisting its growth into something ungodly. He thought of the others, hoping they'd at least escaped. Get the money he left on the boat to Elena, somehow. He cursed them. He cursed himself for his own foolishness. He cursed God for allowing an evil like this to exist. Finally, he prayed.

The sound of metal being sharpened made his skin crawl. An instrument that would no doubt be used to inflict pain and likely his demise. His mind reeled with the possibilities. *Eleanor, I'll see you soon.* The sharpening of metal stopped. *Verona, Elena. I'm sorry.*

He felt a sharp point at his right temple. It was gently pushed into his skin, drawing blood. The sound of the hammer was terrifying as it struck the object. The clang rattled his skull as he felt the sharp point pierce his head. Again. And again. His skull punctured as the bone splintered. He felt a strange sense of relief as the pressure in his head was released. It was short-lived as he remembered what pain was. The agony of his broken skull shot through him. The hammer hit again, and he could feel cold steel find its way into his brain. He could hear the squelch of the fleshy matter in his head move as the foreign object within was pushed deeper. His tongue convulsed and tried to leave his mouth, forced to remain in its prison by the sewn lips.

The object was carefully removed. It hovered within his peripheral vision. A glob of white dripped from the edge of it. He knew little about the human brain but wished the incision would rob him of some senses. Sight, sound, pain - anything. He had once read somewhere that the human brain didn't feel pain. He disagreed. His head was on fire, and he could feel oozing from the hole in his skull. Something thick and warm trickled down the outside of his head.

Rino tried to close his eyes as the object, a thin metal spike that reminded him of an ice pick, was gently lowered. The owner of the instrument came into view. What was left of Rino's logic struggled to make sense of what he saw. To rationalise the form before him. He wondered if his brain was damaged, affecting his sight as the figure before him didn't make sense. It was both tangible yet nothing. A black smoke pretending to be a man. Whatever it was, he was forced to watch it as it slid the spike under his right eyelid and push the point upwards. He prayed for the darkness to wash over him but it would not. He remained awake the entire time.

44

The fever had gotten worse. Aaron's body shivered with cold sweats as his temperature rose. It was too dark for Julia to notice how physically ill he was and Aaron didn't want to draw attention to it. The situation was bad enough without him coming down with the flu. Julia concentrated the glow stick in front of them as they made their way down the hallway. It was yellow which provided a warmer atmosphere that Julia was grateful for. This part of the asylum was in better condition than the rest. The walls were still cracked and vegetation covered them, but the structure was more intact.

They came to the end of the corridor and entered another room. Julia shone the light inside. Rusted steel bed frames lay in a row against the far wall with some dented lockers on the other side. The realisation that people once lived there hit home with Julia. That anyone had to be subjected to this place made her shiver. She turned to check on Aaron. Something wasn't right. His face looked ashen, and she could see beads of sweat on his forehead reflect off the yellow hue.

"You okay?" she said. "You don't look well."

"I'm fine," he lied. "I'll feel a lot better when I get out of here."

"Yeah, you and me both."

They walked across the room, careful of their step. The

recent memory of their near-miss was imprinted in their minds. Every creak of a floorboard was a reminder that each movement brought with it the threat of serious injury. It was a risk they had to take as there wasn't really a viable alternative. They had to get out and fast.

The air was thick. A tangible musty odour lingered. Decades of abandonment had conjured a revolting ether. Left to manifest, it was never intended to be breathed in by anyone. Aaron could swear there was an underlying perfumed and minty odour. *I must be going crazy,* he thought.

Except Julia could smell it too. She was able to identify it as menthol. Peppermint, even. Yes, an unmistakable hint of peppermint. It was faint yet strong enough to cut through the stale stench that occupied the room. It should have been a pleasant fragrance. Instead, it unnerved her even more. It was a foreign entity, an anomalous scent intended to mask something awful. It didn't belong in the asylum, and neither did they.

As the smell got stronger, Julia felt she was starting to lose it. Amongst the mint was a sweetness that reminded her of roses. It was fleeting as the menthol-like fragrance dominated the air. There was no hiding from it as it became the most potent odour in the room, so much so it stung Aaron's nose.

"What the hell is that?" he said.

"No idea," she said. "Let's keep moving."

As they made their way towards the exit, the door of one of the lockers slowly creaked open. The rusted joints strained as steel grated against steel. Julia and Aaron both turned to see the door gently come to a stop. Neither wanted to openly speculate as to what caused it to open. Julia privately noted that their movement on the floor must have set off a reaction. She was reminded of an old cupboard door in her grandmother's house. Whenever she stood on a certain part of the floor, the door would open. All it was and nothing more.

"Julia," Aaron said. "I think that's where that smell is coming from." His own fear prevented him from investigating any further. Julia could sense the palpable fear oozing from him. He was spooked. She understood. She struggled to maintain her own composure. But she would not be defeated by cheap parlour tricks. Everything had an explanation. The reprobates that used the place as a den of iniquity had probably left behind some Tea Tree oil to mask their dope-smoking. *Yeah, sure, like they'd need to do that here.*

Slowly and with caution, she approached the locker. She placed her hand on the cold steel which was hostile to her flesh. She opened the door slowly; each scrape of the rust was like nails on a chalkboard.

The glow stick lit up the locker. She almost dropped it as she gasped. Taking a step back, her eyes looked in horror at what was revealed. Aaron recoiled in fear yet ran to her side to share the awfulness that lay within.

Large black eyes stared at them from an aged face cloaked in shadow. A long-hooked nose protruded from its grotesque features. It wore a black cloak which was covered in dust and grime. Aaron's heart refused to slow its pace even as he realised what it was. It wasn't a person, it was a costume. Or, to be more precise, a uniform. One not worn by anyone for centuries. The attire of a plague doctor. But why was it here, in a locker? And the smell was so potent. He'd learned that the plague doctors would use pleasing odours to mask the stench of death. But that was centuries ago. Not now. *Not here.* Then it hit him. His dream. The visual rekindled his childhood nightmare. That ghoulish figure that chased him. After many years he could put a face to it. And it stared back at him from the darkness.

"Time to go," Aaron said.

"I second that," Julia said. "I'm really getting sick of this place."

They both turned and made their way from the room. The exit had no door and took them out to another corridor. Julia felt they were walking deeper into the asylum. Every room took them to another corridor that appeared to lead them further from their goal. They had to find another stairwell soon, there just had to be one.

As they made their way up the corridor, the smell of mint reappeared. It moved through the air with grace, tingling their nostrils. It stopped them both in their tracks. Julia put a hand up to motion Aaron to stop. They both stood in silence. The faint sound of the waves could be heard as the night tide hit against the island. A floor creaked, likely settling from where they just walked. Then it creaked again. And again. Footsteps. Gentle and methodical. Aaron turned but was faced with darkness. He turned his camera to the night vision mode. He could see the corridor in a bright monochrome. But nothing was there. Nothing had followed them. But the footsteps got louder. Closer.

"Aaron," Julia said, her voice soft and faint. "Can you hear that?"

Aaron couldn't answer. Fear had paralysed his vocal cords. He wanted to scream at Julia to turn the light around. To ease his concerns and prove he was being silly. He then remembered the flash he had attached. It was more powerful than the default. He pointed it towards the sound of the footsteps. With trepidation, he hit click. A bright flash lit up the corridor. Julia was alerted to the sudden burst of light. But it was the sound of the camera falling to the floor that made her turn around. Beyond the yellow glow, shrouded in the darkness, stood that familiar figure. Grotesque in its appearance and draped in black, the attire had filled out. No longer lifeless, the cavernous eyes burned with misery and judgment. The figure took a step towards them. Then another.

"Stop," Julia shouted at it. She grabbed Aaron's arm and inched backwards. Taking two steps for every one the Plague Doctor took. "I have a gun, I will shoot." Her empty threat wasn't heeded. The thing before her continued to advance. No, not a thing. A man. Just a man. Some idiot prankster in a costume looking to scare anyone dumb enough to stumble through the asylum. Or, it was Rino. Yes, she was the pawn in this entire charade. Aaron and Kirsty were probably in on it. No, Aaron's fear exceeded her own, his entire body quivered in shock. It could still be Rino, or even his granddaughter. Yes, that was it. It was a likely story that she couldn't make the tour. How devious and all part of the show. Tell your friends of the near heart attack you suffered on Venice's scariest ghost tour.

Except she didn't believe that to be true. It was a desperate attempt to invalidate the danger they were in. The menace that emanated from the Plague Doctor manifested itself in absolute terror. They quickened their pace before Julia gave up any pretence of defiance, and they both ran. The corridor seemed a mile long as they sprinted towards a door they couldn't see. It had to be there, there had to be an end to the passage. The floor below them shuddered and Julia felt the bottom of her spine tremble. The asylum threatened to collapse in on them. It was a risk she was prepared to take as she refused to slow down. Aaron panted with exhaustion close behind, his lungs heavy. They came to a metal door. She grabbed the handle and pulled. It was heavy. Too heavy for one.

"Aaron, help me with this," she said. Her composure was rocked but her determination was not. With all their might they pulled the door open. It swung lethargically as the hinges woke after decades of slumber.

They didn't look back as they walked through the doorway. Safely through they both looked back. The Plague Doctor was a black silhouette that appeared to blacken the darkness around it. With all their strength they closed the door shut. A metal clang echoed through the room. If it was merely a man, God she hoped it was, it might have difficulty with the door as well. Like a rabbit in the headlights, she stood staring at the door, waiting to see if it would open.

Aaron was slumped against the wall. He coughed violently. His pain echoed through the darkness. It brought Julia to her senses, and she grabbed him by the shoulder.

"Are you okay?" she said. "We need to keep moving, but I need to know you can make it."

He looked at her, his face grey and filled with perspiration. She hoped it was just a trick of the yellow light, and he didn't look as bad as she feared.

"I'll be fine," he said. He stood up straight to prove it. It was an unconvincing show of might.

"Good. Let's get out of here, we can discuss what just happened when we have some distance from that thing."

Julia wanted nothing more than to sprint as fast as she could. She knew it would mean leaving Aaron behind, despite his protestations he was clearly ill. The previous exertion had taken a lot from him, and he struggled to keep up with her brisk pace.

As they made their way into an adjoining room, the metal door they closed began to groan as it slowly opened with apparent ease.

45

The waves were now hitting the shore with more force. The taunts of a brewing storm. Lawrence didn't want to be on the island and out in the open when it hit. He thought he felt water hit his face but that could have been ocean spray. The night sky had begun to cloud but the moon still offered its assistance as it looked down upon Poveglia.

They made their way to the hospital. Like the asylum, it was covered in old scaffolding. He found it hard to believe that at one point it could have been operational. To imagine anyone living on the island as late as the sixties. He thought of Rino and wondered where he was. Was he in there? Maybe they should go in. Have a look. The building wasn't that big, it wouldn't take them long. He then thought of Julia, trapped in the much bigger structure. A potential labyrinth of corridors and pitfalls, designed to make escape difficult. And there he was, safe, ready to get his money's worth and make use of his time.

Kirsty approached a window and shone her fresh glow stick inside. The room burned orange as she looked at the residue of history, a forgotten past that society didn't even have the decency to board up and forget about. For the first time since arriving she felt like a tourist. An uninvited one at that. She also felt empty. That maybe the whole thing was a waste of time. Not for Aaron though. She was envious of her brother. She could only imagine the fun he was having, or the fun she would have been having in his place. He'd probably be hating it. She felt bad for him. In a twisted way, she reckoned she owed it to him to have a worthwhile experience on the island. To have a story. He would have one. To do nothing and go back to the boat would be an insult to what he was enduring.

"See anything?" Lawrence asked.

"Nothing worth writing home about," she said. "Fancy seeing something that is?"

He did. Despite his culpability in all of it, that spark of excitement still flashed within him. He nodded and followed Kirsty behind the building. He noticed the terrain change. It was odd. The dirt felt loose beneath his feet. Dry and powdery. He stopped and looked down, it was too dark to see.

"Kirsty," he said. "Can you shine some light down here please?"

She turned and shone the light at his feet. He crouched down and lifted the soil in his hand. It was black and fine. He rubbed it between his fingers. It stained his hands.

"Looks like someone had a fire here," he said.

"Oh, there's been plenty of fires on here," she said. "Remember what I said this place was used for back in the day. *Way* back in the day that is."

He looked at her, but he wasn't following. The plague victims came here. Poveglia was a quarantine island. Hold on, she mentioned something about the ash. About...

The colour drained from his face as he vigorously wiped the ash from his hands. Noticing it on his clothes, he frantically tried to rid himself of any trace of what once was people. It was everywhere. The remains of victims, long ago, incinerated and left to fuse with the island. The dead were as part of the terrain as nature. He felt sick.

"I wouldn't worry too much about it," Kirsty said. "Aaron once knocked over our great granny's urn and scattered her over the carpet. She didn't seem to mind too much."

"How many people died here?"

"Hard to tell. Enough to cover most of the island surface. And that's only the victims of the plague. Who knows how many the good doctor disposed of in his experiments. Then, there are the patients themselves. No chance those wackos didn't get into it with each other. I don't want to make assumptions and seem insensitive. But they felt the need to build a separate prison that kept the more dangerous patients from the others."

She raised her light, but it had little effect out in the open. The building looked to be an extension of the asylum, yet it sat separately, surrounded by the forest that had claimed the land. Large black trees cradled the moonlight. The forest was on Poveglia before a brick was laid and looked to be dominant on the island. It flourished without habitation, spreading throughout the buildings, a reminder of its might. Except it was not something natural that was in charge. The energy that crackled through the air was as unwelcoming as it was inviting. A quiet agitation lingered. Growing stronger.

It should have been enough to get them to turn back. Instead, they made their way into the old prison. Kirsty's pursuit of the thrill had ensnared Lawrence in a way that eluded her brother. While Aaron followed out of loyalty, Lawrence did so in the hopes of adventure. At the betrayal of his wife's wishes and his own fight-or-flight response.

46

Aaron fumbled with his glow stick. His hands were so sweaty, he almost dropped it twice until he finally worked it and the yellow light was activated. He held it to reveal the room they found themselves in. What once was an old lab had rotted into another vacant room in the asylum. A steel bench was nailed to the wall, hanging on by one solitary bolt. Some lockers leaned against the wall, others were dented and damaged on the floor. It filled Julia with a strange relief to know that the room looked like it had been vandalised. That meant people had been there. And left.

How they left she didn't know. Could they escape the same way? Yes, that's what they had to do. Escape the cursed island and get away from whatever was chasing them. *It's just some sick freak in a costume.* The more she told herself that the less she believed it.

She wanted to keep running, to put as much distance from them and that thing as possible. She looked over at Aaron, he looked awful. His skin was sallow and glistening with sweat. She had no idea what had happened to him. It was a hell of a time to pick something up. He seemed fine on the boat and didn't look ill when they met in the asylum. He was sick and there was nothing she could do.

"We need to keep moving," she said.

"In a minute," Aaron said. "I just need to rest. Please." He stumbled over to an upturned chair. Julia had to help him lift it, he was so weak. He sat down, relieved not to have to stand.

Julia placed the back of her hand onto his forehead. She'd never felt such heat from another person before. It was probably a bad flu. Which meant she would get it. No matter, she'd happily spend the rest of her honeymoon in bed than another second anywhere near Poveglia.

"We can't stay here long, Aaron," she said. "I'm sorry." She tried to be more sympathetic. She felt for him, she really did. Her concern was genuine. But she knew they couldn't afford to be complacent.

"I know," he said. "Believe me, I'll die a happy man if I never have to see that face again. Believe in ghosts now?"

"No," she said. Yet her scepticism had been rocked. What she believed or didn't believe in didn't matter anymore. What Julia would have labelled preposterous hours earlier bore no relation to the predicament she was in. There was no point in trying to rationalise why they were in danger when all that mattered was that they were. An icy breeze crept through the room and slithered its way over her flesh, making it crawl.

"What do you think it was?" Aaron asked.

"Some deranged bastard who thinks it's funny to scare people," she said, for his benefit more than her own.

"Heh. That'd be preferable to what I'm thinking of."

"You don't really believe that's the ghost of that doctor you told us about?"

"I have no idea who that was. The doctor my sister mentioned worked here in the last seventy years. I can't imagine he'd be dressed like that. Unless..."

"Unless what?"

"I don't know. Maybe he dressed up like that to scare his patients. It's certainly scared me."

"Well, rather than hypothesise what a ghost would or wouldn't wear, let's just stick to the real-life lunatic in a mask theory."

"I'll happily sign up to that." Aaron felt an itching sensation on his neck. It burned. He raised his hand to it and recoiled even quicker. He caught Julia's attention who looked down at him. "What the hell is that?" He raised the light to his neck to give her a better look.

She failed to hide her disgust as she looked at him. There was an infection. A large swelling pulsated from just under his jaw and to the side of his throat. Julia could see the pus and blood swimming beneath the layer of translucent skin.

"I'm not sure. Could be an infected boil."

"Great. Suppose that makes sense." He was oddly calm. It unnerved her. They'd already spent too long resting and it pained her to have to get him to move.

"Might be an allergic reaction to something. God knows there's enough things in here that could trigger it."

"Don't suppose you've any cream I can put on it?"

"Aaron, I know you're unwell but we really can't stay here."

"Julia." He looked up at her. His calm demeanour had been replaced with sorrow. "I don't want to die here." He dropped the glow stick. It was a burden to hold.

"You're not going to die here. You're not going to die for a very long time. But we have to get moving, I'm sorry."

The gentle wind picked back up, it caused the glow stick to roll over the floor, away from the door. Footsteps echoed from beyond the room. Julia looked around her to see if there was a weapon. She picked up a piece of brick that once belonged to the wall. It wasn't heavy enough to do any real damage, but she felt safer with it. She picked up the glow stick and looked out into the hallway. She threw it into the dark as the yellow light revealed what she feared. There it was. Walking towards her with no urgency. The Plague Doctor was coming for them. It was in no rush, it had no reason to be.

"Aaron," she shouted.

She ran back into the room and lifted him from the chair. She struggled to get him to his feet as he fought to assist her. They stumbled from the room and crashed hard into the wall. Julia took most of the impact. Her shoulder stung and she dropped her brick. All the while, the Plague Doctor continued towards them.

It walked with deliberate malice. Methodical in its cruelty, it slowly stalked them with a single intention. Julia crouched down and looked for the brick. It was difficult to find but she found it. She lifted it and threw it towards her target. It hit the Plague Doctor on the shoulder. It stopped its pursuit but made no sound. *Interesting. Maybe you can be hurt.* Her renewed optimism was a welcome surprise. As it resumed its pace, her fear was replaced with anger. She ran back into the room and started throwing bricks into the corridor. Happy with her arsenal, she returned to face it.

She threw brick after brick but it only slowed it down. The Plague Doctor continued its approach. It was only a few feet from them. Soon, they would be within its reach unless Julia acted. She refused to back up any longer. She picked up a broken brick, a larger one, one with sharp edges and threw it straight at its head. The brick crumbled as the Plague Doctor reeled. It took another step before collapsing onto its knees. When it fell, Julia felt victorious. She was vindicated in her scepticism. It was merely a man after all. A newfound confidence fuelled her. She picked up another brick and marched over to it. *To do what,* she thought. Kill it? Kill whoever was in the costume? She believed she was capable of doing so and would do if need be. When she looked down upon her would-be victim, her jaw trembled in fear. Her adrenaline spiked so hard her back tensed up to the point it hurt. There was no figure lying on the floor. All that lay were empty clothes and a mask. Lifeless.

"Did you get him?" Aaron asked. He was slumped against the wall, staring at the floor. His joints were in agony, it was a challenge to even look up.

"I got him," she said. "Now let's go before he wakes up." Terrified to take her eyes from the old clothing, Julia edged backwards down the wall towards Aaron. She didn't know what she believed in anymore. Her fingers hurt from how tightly she gripped the brick.

47

When Kirsty and Lawrence entered the prison they soon found themselves in the cell area. It was small which reminded Aaron of a sheriff's holding cells as seen in an old western. Each individual cell was only big enough for one person. The bars had rusted with greenery intertwined around the bars. The air in the room was acidic, each breath left a sour taste in the mouth. Lawrence had a slight concern that it was harmful. He kept it to himself.

Kirsty waved her light over the cells. Mercifully vacant, little remained apart from what was left of a bed. They hadn't been occupied in years. Kirsty wondered how troubled the patient had to be for the staff to lock them in the cells, away from the others. She noted the metal bars. It seemed odd, dangerous.

The temperature had dropped significantly. Lawrence regretted his summer attire. He regretted much. *Hope you're okay, babe.* He kept close to Kirsty, making sure not to lose her in the shadows. The cell area was narrow. He kept close to the wall for guidance.

"What do you think?" Kirsty asked.

"Something doesn't feel right," he said.

He was right, she felt it too. Her heart pounded as the adrenaline swirled in her blood. It was close to what she wanted to experience. To feel pure fear and laugh about it later. Was she insane herself? Would she even know if she was?

The corridor cut at sharp and abrupt angles. They followed it obediently, unsure of where it led. There was no going back now. The complex was small, they'd be out of there soon and still have time to see more of the island before the others were on the boat. They came across a stone staircase that spiralled downwards. It seemed unusually out of place: much older than the rest of the building. A large metal door hung open in the entry. Whether it was there to keep something out or something in, Kirsty wasn't sure. She was sure she wanted to see more.

"Maybe we've seen enough," Lawrence said. He was frightened. Frightened about where he was, where he'd been and where he was going. Frightened for Julia, hoping to the God he didn't believe in that she had made her way out of the asylum by now. Frightened of incurring her wrath when he saunters back to the boat late, and they've all been waiting for him and Kirsty, so they can leave. It was the more desired outcome.

"Look," Kirsty said. "You didn't need to join me. I'm glad you have, it's nice to have company. But I won't twist your arm to come down here. If you want to go back, I won't stop you."

And what, leave her? He couldn't do that. He wouldn't, he'd never forgive himself if something happened. *What could happen?* He shuddered. He thought of Julia. Then Rino. Where the hell was he?

"No, I'm not leaving you. We've already lost enough people."

"They'll be fine. My brother can take care of himself and by the looks of it it's your missus that will be taking care of both of them."

Lawrence nodded, a slim smile cut through the fluorescent light. They made their way carefully down the steps. The decline was steep and the steps had a rounded polish that made them perilous. No light penetrated the lower level, and they found themselves plunged into darkness. Kirsty's light cut through the gloom to reveal more cells, except these ones didn't have bars, they had solid doors. They were all closed, except one. One was a quarter open.

"What do you think's in these cells?" Kirsty asked.

Lawrence didn't answer. Her question asked more than she said. What she was really saying was *hey, let's see what's in these cells.* Lawrence hoped they were locked. It'd make things easier. Except one was open. He wanted to leave, he'd seen enough. Icy hands wrapped themselves around his chest and gripped his lungs as the temperature plummeted. He would have seen his own breath if it wasn't so dark.

Kirsty made her way towards the open cell. It was then that a light flickered. Not from her. From above. The room briefly illuminated in a dull orange glow, stronger than the glow stick. Power was generated into the building. It was absurd that the electricity could still be active. That there'd even be a working bulb in the place. Kirsty and Lawrence briefly locked eyes before the room was plunged back into darkness. The room was so silent Lawrence could hear his heart beating. His breathing was short and sharp, the cold air stung him with each inhale. He went to speak when they were suddenly interrupted by radio static. It was followed by the high pitch of feedback. An excruciating assault that was painful to the ears. As suddenly as it arrived, it was gone. Replaced by hissing. The low hum of white noise gave way to a piece of music. Some sort of swing band. It was old. Very old. And it was coming from the unlocked cell.

This was it. It was what Kirsty wanted. An unexplained occurrence that would shake her beliefs to the core and make her question her own senses. Then why did it feel so ghastly? It wasn't fun. Instead, Kirsty struggled to breathe as her instincts urged her to run. But she could not. She was unable to remove her eyes from the open door. Fear prevented her from taking them from it.

"Kirsty," Lawrence said. "I don't think I want to know what's in there anymore. Playtime is over."

His words woke Kirsty from her trance. The sounds, the static. A radio. Rino. Rino was behind the door. That's all it was and nothing more. They couldn't leave him. They wouldn't get very far without him. Unless…if something bad happened to him. If he was severely injured, then what?

The keys. He'd have the keys at least. If Rino was… They could leave without Rino if they had to. She didn't want to, no one wanted to. But if they had to - only if they had to.

Every fibre of her body told her to run. She fought against all of it as she found herself creeping closer to the door.

"Kirsty," Lawrence said, his voice barely audible.

I need to see. The light was in front of her. She made her way towards the cell. It resisted her gentle push at first. It required more effort and was soon willing to assist. With slight force, she pushed on the door. It scraped against the floor as it opened. The hinges groaned, a cacophony of sounds echoed throughout the hallway. The silence as they faded was an instant reminder that Kirsty and Lawrence found themselves deep within the bowels of an abandoned building. Trapped on an island. Still, the door had been opened. There was no backing away from what lay behind. Kirsty took as deep a breath as she could as she looked within the room.

The room was small. The light provided her with good visibility. Desolation hung in the air. She wasn't sure how she knew but it was clear to her that someone once lived in that room. That tiny inhospitable place that would have been difficult to lie down in. The thin padding on the walls showed signs of distress, burst from apparent clawing. Her light began to dim as the life left it. The corners of the room were plunged back into darkness. But not before she saw those eyes. So recognisable, the eyes that haunted nightmares. A child's eyes. Doll-like eyes, made of glass and lifeless. Staring at her. Damning her. Frozen to the spot, she was unable to move. The air left her lungs. She struggled to breathe.

Lawrence sensed something was wrong, he joined her side. An audible gasp filled the air as he saw it as well. It wasn't a hallucination, Kirsty wasn't imagining the horror before her eyes. It was real.

"That's a little freaky," he said, calling on his reserves for any composure.

Her breathing returned, heavy and panicked. It was only a doll. It looked old but in good condition. As her eyes focused on the cracked porcelain of its face, it became more evident that it was only a doll. It didn't matter. She had seen enough.

"The sound?" she said. Her voice had cracked. The inside of her mouth was dry, she felt like she couldn't have formed spit if a gun was to her head.

"Must've been another cell. We've come this far. If Rino is here, we owe it to him and to ourselves to keep looking." He had to find Rino and earn his redemption. It wasn't about being a hero, he wanted no thanks or recognition for it. It just felt like the right thing to do.

Kirsty couldn't have felt any different. Her adventure was over. She got what she came to Poveglia for. *Be careful what you wish for,* she thought. She no longer cared about Rino or the keys, she just wanted to get back to the boat. How she would get away from the island is something she'd concern herself with when she felt safe.

The small torch on Lawrence's phone was inferior but it's all he had. He left Kirsty and explored the rest of the area. The quicker he found Rino, the sooner they could all leave. He didn't want to pry as to why Kirsty was so disturbed, it was only a doll. There'd be time to ask her later. He didn't want to waste any more time.

As Lawrence's footsteps echoed behind her, Kirsty felt alone. The realisation she always was hit her, and she didn't want to feel that way anymore. She turned to leave the room and that's when she heard it. A crawling whisper, a voice like the midnight wind. It called to her in a language she didn't know. The language was one she didn't understand, yet she knew it was for her. It spoke to her. From the corner of the room. Where the doll lay.

She aimed the light back towards the corner. It continued to fade and struggled to brighten the small space. The doll had sunk back into the darkness. The eyes glistened against the remaining light, as lifeless as before. The face was still. Until it moved. The head tilted upwards. The doll sat up and refocused its attention on Kirsty. She tried to call out but her voice had been stolen. The doll stood up in a fluid motion. Slowly, it rose off the ground. It didn't move of its own free will. There were hands on its side, someone was manipulating the doll. It was thrust out towards her, like an offering. Behind the doll, hiding in the shadows, was a little girl. Her smile was spirited. She looked just like any other sweet little girl, she couldn't have been older than six.

Kirsty raised the fading light towards the darkness. The shadows masked the girl's face as the light exposed her true form. Pieces of rotted flesh dripped from her angelic face as pulsating sores oozed a yellow fluid. Pieces of her skull shone black where her skin had deteriorated to nothing. Her smile was gruesome yet genuine. It had a warmth to it, the contrast sickened Kirsty.

Kirsty found herself with her back to the wall. The child held the doll up to Kirsty, its voice transformed. Unmistakably a child's voice, it spoke a language Kirsty didn't know. The child said one word that Kirsty understood. *Play.*

Kirsty's legs trembled as she fled the room. Tears fought to be released from her eyes as she ran back towards the stairwell. Hearing the commotion, Lawrence turned.

"Hey," he shouted. "Hey wait up. What's wrong, what happened?"

She didn't answer; she just ran, almost aimlessly, down the hallway. Putting as much distance between herself and the cell as she could. Lawrence chased after her. He was scared. Scared of being left alone, or worse, alone with what she was running from. The pain in his lungs intensified as he chased her. His foot hit something hard and he hit the floor with force. His phone was thrown from his hand and with it his only source of light. He looked up to see Kirsty's dim light slowly fade. Winded, he couldn't even call after her. He was alone. What troubled him more was he didn't feel alone.

48

Stairs. Going down. This was good, this was a good sign. Julia couldn't hide her excitement as she realised they could leave the floor they were on at last. It didn't matter where the stairs went, they went down. That would do.

Aaron had deteriorated further. His face was sallow and glistened with a thick layer of oily sweat. The fatigue had set into his bones, he wanted nothing more than to lie down. Curl up on the floor and close his eyes. They both told themselves it was just a bad flu. Once they got back to Venice he could rest easy and within a few days, he'd be fine.

Neither of them believed it. Aaron wasn't a stranger to the flu. He once caught it before heading to Austria on holiday. He was determined to power on through and not let it ruin his trip. He would never forget how he felt. How he felt in Poveglia didn't compare. The flu was sitting by the pool at a five-star resort by comparison. He knew what the flu was. This wasn't it.

It was difficult to remain sympathetic while fleeing from an unexplained entity, but Julia tried her best. She didn't know Aaron. He was partly responsible for the mess she was in and now he was slowing her down. It was likely he had already infected her with whatever the hell was wrong with him. It crossed her mind to leave him. Make a run for it. Whatever was chasing them might even be slowed down if she left Aaron to it.

She hated herself for thinking it. No, they were both getting out. If she had to drag Aaron onto the boat and drive the thing back to Venice herself.

Rino. Oh, how she hoped the others had found him. She envisioned Lawrence, Rino and Kirsty all sat on the boat waiting for them. It would be an uncomfortable reunion yet one she yearned for. How to explain what they'd seen is something she would need to rationalise with herself. By the time they got back to Venice and had a good rest the night's events would most likely be put into context. It was dark. Spooky. The mind plays tricks. Everything had an explanation. A reasonable one.

The problem was when the explanation didn't fit with what you wanted it to. She could see Kirsty's smug face, clamouring for more details from her brother as he lay at death's door. Julia would take great satisfaction at the opportunity to unleash her fury on Kirsty. To put her in her place and maybe even knock out some teeth.

It made her smile. It was nice that something did. That a blazing argument with a stranger and falling out with her husband for having ruined the day was preferable to where she was. She missed Lawrence. She wasn't even angry anymore, she just wanted to see him. To make sure he was all right. Of course he was all right, he was back at the boat. And Rino was there too. If anything, *they* were the ones annoyed as they had to wait for *them*.

She looked over at Aaron who was using the wall to support himself. She looked back at the stairs. They seemed sturdy enough. It meant nothing. An empty guarantee. There were no promises in the asylum.

Aaron's body shivered with the fever. His bones ached as the muscles strained to keep him upright. The cool stone of the wall was like ice against his back. He needed it. It was his crutch.

"I'm not going to lie," Julia said. "This is going to be the hard part. But we can do this, me and you. After we get down those stairs, it's easy street."

There was no response. Julia wasn't even aware if he could hear her. She'd never seen someone deteriorate so quickly from illness before. *Yeah, right. I'm an expert.*

"Aaron!"

It was a burden to raise his head. His eyes had glazed over. The man behind them had faded. The last spark of optimism that he was going to leave the asylum flickered faintly in the low light. An immense feeling of dread shrouded him.

"I don't want to die here, Aaron. Neither do you."

He nodded. With all his strength he stood to attention, a statement of intent. Of defiance. Julia grabbed a hold of him and gently eased him down the stairs. Step by step.

49

The fresh air was like a punch to the gut for Kirsty. She collapsed to her knees and spewed bile onto the ashy soil. The tears came thick. Her own self-preservation shamed her. Her cowardice had likely condemned Lawrence to God knows what. No, not God. God wasn't welcome on Poveglia. God wouldn't allow the place to exist. Not any god she knew of. She clawed at the ground as she turned to sit. Face to face with the entrance to the prison. There was no explaining what happened. There was no explaining to anyone on why she left Lawrence.

It didn't matter. There'd be no one left to explain it to. There'd be no reunion at the boat. Rino wouldn't be there to get them home. Aaron… *God, Aaron. I'm so so sorry. I never wanted this, please believe me I didn't want this.*

Her worst fears all hypothesised, staring back at her in her mind's eye, reflected off of the doll's eyes. And what held the doll. *Jesus Christ.* She felt trapped. Alone. Having no idea of the fate of the others, she came to her own conclusions and it wasn't pretty. Her imagination was capable of conjuring up vile imagery. She was sick again.

Kirsty stood up, her knees trembled as adrenaline rushed through her body. She had abandoned Lawrence. Violent clouds made their way towards the island. They didn't concern her. Lawrence's safety did. She hoped and prayed that he was right behind her.

All Lawrence could hear was his own breathing. Shallow and rapid, the damp walls claimed it and returned no echo. He shouted out for Kirsty. She was gone. She left him. He was angry that she would do that. And terrified as to what had made her run. He stood in the darkness alone. Scared. Unsure what way to go. His eyes tried to adjust to the absence of light. There weren't even any shapes to distinguish between objects. The black of nothing surrounded him. He knew there were walls. A stairway. All he had to do was make it to a wall to help guide him and pray he was walking the right way.

Pray. Oh, now you want my help, he imagined the God he didn't believe in responding to him. *Now you want something from me. Pathetic. I don't see why I should.* Fuck him. He didn't need God's help, he just needed to find a wall. He wouldn't do that standing still. He took a step. Then another. His balance was precarious without anything to anchor his vision to.

Slowly, he made his way through the gloom. His fingers scraped stone and he felt relief. He placed both hands against the wall. Cold and wet. An oily residue secreted from the stone. It didn't matter. It was a start. He just had to figure out which way to go. Fifty-fifty chance he'd choose wisely. To choose poorly would be catastrophic. It would lead him deeper into the bowels of the prison.

Left. He'd go left. He wasn't sure why, he just had a good feeling about it. He was careful. Baby steps. Slow and steady wins the race. Each step hopefully brought him closer to the exit. The stone gave way to steel as he realised he'd come across an open cell. He took a large step as he passed the entrance. A sharp point in the frame cut his hand. It wasn't deep, but it stung. *That'll require a tetanus,* he thought. *Going to be fun explaining that one.*

A sudden burst of static filled the area. So loud it hurt his ears. The noise warbled and screeched as the frequency changed. A voice struggled to make its pleas through the white noise. Lost in the maelstrom, it was drowned out by chaos. And then it was gone. Replaced by the music that was now familiar to him. The same music he first heard on the boat.

"Rino?" he shouted. His voice full of pain and desperation. The music got louder. It was the only response he received. Electricity crackled in the air, an accompaniment to the melody. Lawrence looked up to the ceiling as the bulb emitted a dim glow. A small spark of life. It flickered like a blurred strobe. The cells briefly illuminated, intercut with obscurity.

He could see the stairs. He honed his hearing to the music. The music came from behind. Jackpot. He ran from it. Disoriented by the flickering light, a sickness swam in his head, and he had to stop. Metal scraped loudly as the doors of the cells all swung open. Hinges untouched for years squealed in exquisite anguish as they unlocked. Voices swirled all around him. An unholy union of agony and desire. The words were unknown to his ears but he sensed them. Pain. Fear. Delight. Hope. Despair. No two voices were the same. Shadows moved towards him. Murky hands made of smoke pawed at him. Some threatened. Others reminded him of the same desperation he now felt. He clasped his hands to his ears and tightened his eyes shut. His senses were overloaded by the disharmony, his brain felt like it would split if he had to endure it anymore.

Then, the music stopped. The light ceased flickering and remained on. All the voices stopped, the formless shapes backed off, some skulked back to their cells. Afraid, but not of Lawrence. The stairway was only a few metres away. He could make it. But he couldn't run. His legs wouldn't move. It reminded him of being in a dream.

He couldn't hear whatever approached him. But he could feel it. At the core of his being, he could feel it. An empty warmness covered him like a blanket. A strong sense of euphoria fought to violate him. Unnatural and invasive, it looked to dominate his senses and calm him. Cold hands with a tight grip clasped his shoulders. They weren't solid, it reminded him of water. He thought of Julia. Their wedding day. He clung on to it like a lifebelt. He wanted it to anchor his sanity. The image stayed for as long as he could hold it in his mind. Eventually, he knew he would have to submit to the tranquillity. As he did, the memory remained. The serenity of blind faith.

50

Kirsty looked at the entrance. Her exit. A doorway into Hell itself. A cavern of nightmares. The den of the macabre. Moonlight shone upon it. The building was basked in a twilight embrace. Almost ethereal she was unable to keep telling herself it was only a building. That the island was merely a tale of urban legend. It had touched her. She could feel its grip on her soul. Icy cold and sharp, its claws had hold of her. She had never felt so helpless. It was a feeling she thought would never go away.

He wasn't coming out. She couldn't go back in. It was horrible to write Lawrence off. To accept that whatever she had seen had now claimed him. She hated herself for her selfishness, her cowardice. There was no redemption in futility. If she could find her brother, if she could at least escape with him, then maybe she could live with herself.

Kirsty rose to her feet and dusted herself off. The ashes of a thousand victims fell from her clothes as she wiped the sin from her. Her hands were stained black. The shame wouldn't wash away so easily. All she had to do was follow her way back around and she would be on the path. It was easy to find the boat from there. Then, she would wait. Wait on Aaron. Julia. Hell, let's even hope Rino and Lawrence make a last-minute appearance.

She wasn't sure how she would get the boat running without keys. She thought of untethering it and just letting it drift. To be lost at sea would be paradise compared to the island.

The trees rustled behind her. Her heart froze as she turned. Something small and dark shot from the undergrowth. A rabbit. It darted towards her before changing its mind and returned to the confinement of the forest. Kirsty had read that the island had a large rabbit population. Why, she had never bothered to find out. It wasn't interesting enough. Wasn't exhilarating. It lacked the thrill she sought. The rabbit had more right to be on Poveglia than she did. The rabbit called the island home. As did whatever else haunted it. She was the invasive species. The unwelcome. The naïve fool, full of arrogance and lacking any respect.

She mouthed the words, *I'm sorry.* Kirsty just wanted to go home. There was a loud snap from the forest. If something stepped on a branch, it weighed more than the rabbit. The odds on it being someone she'd be happy to see weren't strong enough for her to investigate. Nevertheless, unlike the rabbit, she was unable to flee. Her eyes fixated on the trees. They rustled. Not the wind. Something, hopefully someone, was making their way towards her. Whatever it was, it was upset.

The little girl appeared. Her grotesque features masked by the night. Kirsty was terrified. Yet, not of the girl. Not quite. As otherworldly as she was, Kirsty felt no threat from her. The girl was holding the rabbit in her arms, cradling it. The rabbit's head flopped. Lifeless. It swung like a sick pendulum as the girl walked towards her.

The girl sobbed. Despite the situation, Kirsty felt sympathy for her. That big sister instinct overruled her common sense. She would have found the situation funny if she wasn't paralysed with fear.

"The bunny won't move," the girl said. At first, Kirsty thought the girl spoke English. But it wasn't that. No, it was strange. The girl didn't speak English, but Kirsty understood her anyway.

"What happened?" Kirsty said. She couldn't believe she was engaging in a conversation with a gho... No. She wasn't quite there yet.

"He doesn't let us play," the girl said. Both spoke different languages yet managed to understand each other. Her voice was soft with an underlying harshness. There was an innocence that was smothered beneath her words.

"Who, who doesn't let you play?"

"He doesn't... He doesn't want us to talk to you."

"Why is that?"

"I like you. I wish you could play with me. No one is ever allowed to play with me anymore."

"Please you have to help me understand. Maybe I can help."

"You're not allowed here."

"Why, why not? Who are you talking about?"

She raised her face and looked at Kirsty. The girl's eyes glistened. Her frown was strong, the bottom lip quivered. "He doesn't want me to tell you. He'll hurt me. He wants to hurt you."

Run, Kirsty thought. *Run you idiot.*

"I have to go back," the girl said. "He doesn't like it when I go outside." She turned and made her way back towards the prison. Hugging the rabbit's body tight.

"Wait," Kirsty said. "Do you know where the others are?"

The girl stopped and turned to look at her. Her head tilted

the way a doctor would before they're about to deliver bad news. "He's here."

The girl screamed a ghastly and frightening shriek as she was torn apart. Her body turned to ash as it scattered before Kirsty's eyes. The rabbit fell to the ground and the girl was no more. The remnants of her form snowed down upon the rabbit's corpse and returned to the ground. From within the building, the darkness took form. The shades of black were distinguishable as a figure walked towards her from the gloom.

The feeling in Kirsty's legs returned as did her senses. *Run.* And run she did. The adrenaline coursed through her veins as she ran as fast as she could. So consumed with escaping the thing that pursued her, she didn't even realise she was running in the wrong direction. Away from the path, she ran into the forest. Deep into the thicket. It didn't even register as the branches snapped and cut at her face. She was just thankful to be moving.

51

The corridors of the asylum all looked the same. The silver lining for Julia was that she was seeing graffiti again. It felt right. She clung to that little sliver of optimism. It drove her to keep moving. They hadn't had sight of the Plague Doctor for a while now. She doubted they had vanquished it so easily, but she was happy with how much distance there appeared to be between them.

She activated the last of Aaron's glow sticks and held it up. It was blue. Cold. The corridor was short and turned to the right. Aaron clung to the wall for support as they made their way down. As Julia turned, she noticed a room to her left. A glimmer caught her eye. She lowered the glow stick and looked into the darkened room. There was a light coming from it. It was faint but unmistakable.

"Wait here," she said to Aaron. "I need to check on this."

She walked to the doorway and looked in. Her heart filled with joy at what she saw before her. Moonlight. Shining through a window. The glass was gone and a rusted metal guard remained. She ran over to it. It was high, she had to tiptoe to look out. It didn't look towards the sea like she'd hoped but it was a way out. It was still a welcome view. She looked at the trees outside, how vines and branches crawled along the building. The forest was as part of the asylum as the stonework. It had invaded the room she stood in. It was welcome to it. In years to come, the building would be consumed by the forest. She hoped she'd be alive to see the day that the place was no more. She just hoped they'd both stay alive...

She ran back to Aaron with the good news.

"I found a window," she said. We'll need to climb a little and remove an old guard from it, but we can get out. Aaron, we're going to make it."

He wanted to share her enthusiasm. It pained him to even lift his head and look at her. He might just make it in getting out. With some help, he could get to the boat. He didn't feel like he would recover. Aaron could sense the end.

"Sounds good," he said. He coughed violently, the bulbous sore on his neck pulsated with each spasm. "Julia. Julia, if you...if I'm slowing you down in...any way..."

"Hey. Enough of that. We're getting to that boat. Even if I need to drag you onto it."

Tears welled up in his eyes. Julia didn't know what to say. She had no more motivational speeches to give. She couldn't blame Aaron for his defeatist attitude. It pained her just to look at him. If he was contagious, she would be next. She didn't feel ill. Tired, angry and scared but fine otherwise. If it was working away inside her then at least she had time on her side. Something that appeared to abandon Aaron.

"No one is dying here, Aaron. We've come this far. Die on me now and I'm going to be pissed."

They shared a laugh, one that caused Aaron substantial pain.

"Do you think the others are at the boat?" he asked her.

"Why wouldn't they be?"

"Heh. My sister..."

My husband. Julia decided she'd kill him if she got to the boat before him. Whether that would be before or after she hugged him tight she hadn't decided.

Julia helped Aaron into the room and allowed him to sit against the wall where the window was. He held the last glow stick in his lap. The light bathed him in a cool blue that highlighted how he felt. She reached up and grabbed onto the metal guard and shook it. Age had affected its secureness, but she didn't have the strength to push it off, not from the low angle. She had to get higher. Her eyes scoured the room. Fragments of furniture remained including part of what looked to be an old wooden desk. It was badly damaged and didn't look too sturdy, but it was worth a shot.

As she approached it, she looked at the graffiti on the wall. Most of it looked to be Italian but one phrase was in English. It read, *It's all okay.* She dwelt on why someone would write that for longer than she intended and hoped it was. She dragged the broken desk over to the wall and placed it under the window. She climbed on top of it. What came next was tricky. It required a little part of a balancing act on her part but she was able to swing a kick at the metal. BANG. BANG. The guard shuddered but it remained in place. BANG. BANG. As the sound of impact faded, it was replaced by a softer noise. One she recognised instantly, one she hadn't heard before setting foot in the asylum. The Plague Doctor's footsteps. The cadence was unmistakable. She didn't entertain the thought it could have been anyone else.

She kicked at the guard harder. The footsteps got louder. Closer. The metal moved slightly. She wasn't stopping now. Again, and again, she kicked at it. The exertion took more out of her than she expected. She contemplated returning to the corridor and attacking the Plague Doctor in an attempt to slow it down. It worked before, but she didn't want to test fate, not when she was so close.

"How we…how we getting on?" Aaron asked. His voice was groggy, drowsy. Exhausted.

"Almost there," she said. But not there enough. The guard had moved but she was concerned she didn't have enough time. And even if they did, she was worried about getting Aaron through. She didn't have the strength to lift him. He barely had the strength to lift himself. No, they were so close. She couldn't give up.

Aaron agreed. She couldn't give up. Not while there was still a chance, regardless of how slim that chance was. He lay the glow stick on the ground and turned to grab onto the wall. With incredible pain, he managed to raise himself to his feet. They were running out of time. Julia was running out of time. Aaron had already run out of his.

"Hey," she said. "Save your strength. Sit back down. I've almost got it."

"Keep going," he said. "Don't mind me." His voice was dreamlike. He stumbled forward, his balance almost betrayed him. But he stood tall. Bold.

"Aaron!" She turned to see he had made it the door. He didn't look back as he spoke.

"Tell my sister," tell her what? That he hoped she found what she was looking for, that she shouldn't feel guilty about what happened? That he loved her that he blamed her? His mind wouldn't construct the words he wanted to say. "Tell her… make something up. Something nice." He left the room and was gone from her sight.

51

“Aaron,” she screamed. Her voice echoed throughout the room. As it faded she realised there was nothing. No sound. No footsteps. No Aaron.

She returned to the guard and threw herself against it. Again. And again. Her shoulder bled and bruised as she continued to batter it with her body until it finally gave way. The metal fell from its frame and landed into the soft grass below. She wanted to run back. Check on Aaron. To get some sort of closure. Instead, she jumped from the window. Tears streaming down her cheeks.

52

Kirsty stopped running. She wanted to hear if anything was chasing her. The forest gave nothing away. She looked up at the night sky. The stars looked different than they had before. The clouds appeared to avoid the sky above which allowed the force of the full moon to shine its light upon the island. Nothing was familiar. Everything looked the same. She didn't believe she could be lost. The island wasn't big enough, all she had to do was run in a straight line, and she would reach the edge. From there, it'd be easy.

The forest teased her with unknown sounds. The trees rustled as the wind picked up. Animals likely stirred as they found themselves distressed by a stranger. Except that was not all she disturbed. She was able to speak to the little girl, maybe she could bargain with the other thing that chased her. A creature so fierce it even scared a ghost. What sort of monster would find itself in charge of Hell? A monster so reviled in life that even death couldn't stop its evil.

The legends of Poveglia flooded her head. She tried to drown them out but found it easier to embrace them. Perhaps, she could find something of use in what she knew. Something to help her. To aid her escape.

There was nothing. Nothing but half-baked ghost stories

designed to frighten tourists from their cash. Or in her case, something much worse. She didn't want to die, especially on Poveglia. If she did, would she ever really escape? Could she? The island was as much a prison in death as it had been in life. A place where the forgotten were condemned to oblivion. A mass graveyard with a headstone that was meant to warn visitors.

An image flashed into her head. The bell tower. If she could see that, then she could find her way out of the forest easily enough. With purpose, she darted through the forest, her eyes glued to beyond the treeline. She found it. It pierced the black sky with a majestic triumph. She remembered it was once a church. Perhaps it could provide her with salvation.

Aaron felt a floating sensation. His body was still as it cut through the air. Death. It must have been what death felt like. Except he could still feel the pain. The sore on his neck, his fever. His aching muscles and bones. No, he wasn't dead. He tried to open his eyes. It was too much effort. It was easier to keep them closed. He was afraid but no longer scared of what would happen. Whatever was carrying him soothed him. A cooling menthol filled the air. It made it easier for him to breathe.

Still, he had to know. With an incredible effort, he opened his eyes to see what carried him. That faceless mask stared straight ahead. It carried him with apparent ease, he was nothing to it. They approached a bridge and Aaron felt relieved to be leaving the island, or at least, the main part of it. If he had the strength he'd have thanked the Plague Doctor for taking him from the asylum. His death was imminent, to have perished in that awful building would have been an unbearable curse.

To die was nothing to fear. He was concerned about what waited for him on the other side, but to no longer feel the pain that ravaged him was a mercy he longed for. He didn't have the will or the strength to make it to a hospital. He wasn't even convinced that they could help him if he did. And if he was contagious, it was for the best he didn't leave Poveglia.

He hoped that he didn't infect Julia. He had no idea if she was safe. He said a small prayer for her and the others, but deep down he knew they weren't leaving. Kirsty. *My sister. If your time here was as eventful as mine then I'm sure you'll be fulfilled.*

It saddened him to know he would no longer see her in life. The world passed in a dream as he failed to conjure up any strong emotions. His soul was numbed by the Plague Doctor's care as his body surrendered to his sickness.

His carrier stopped. Without warning, Aaron was dropped into a ditch. The dream-like tranquillity was replaced by the harsh reality of falling. His face hit loose soil and dirt found its way into his mouth. The fear within him intensified as the sedative touch of the Plague Doctor faded. He hadn't the strength to turn and look but he could sense the hole he was in was large enough for one. Freshly dug yet stained with the residue of thousands of victims.

Suddenly, a bright flash of light blinded him. As his eyesight returned, he could feel a great heat from below him. Above him. It surrounded him until it became him. His flesh boiled and melted from his bones. A pungent smell filled his lungs. He would have retched if he could. He couldn't even scream as the stench of his own body threatened to choke him. His time in the asylum became a pleasant memory as his fat burned under the watchful gaze of the Plague Doctor. Clumps of his skin fell off the bone, flaked and charred. Aaron watched the ghoulish figure stand over him. He continued to watch until his eyeballs burst, the bubbling liquid covering his ravaged face.

Still, he did not scream. It wasn't for lack of wanting. The pain was the only thing that kept him alive. When that stopped, he hoped he would finally rest. Unless the pain never stopped, and this was to be his eternity. But he knew better. He knew it wouldn't last forever. What came next, he feared, would be much worse.

53

The ground was soft. The thick grass covered the ash and soil which assisted Julia's landing. It didn't prevent her from landing awkwardly and she feared she had sprained her ankle. It hurt to put weight on it but it was no time for slowing down. Aaron's sacrifice had bought her time. How much, she had no idea. What she did know was that the Plague Doctor was nowhere to be seen. She looked up at the window, expecting to see that macabre face look down at her. It was nowhere to be found.

She limped across the grass and looked to the sky for clues on how to get back to the boat. She could see the bell tower high above the trees. Perfect. She could use it as a compass to find her way back to the boat, *if there's even a boat to get back to.* She shook her head as if it would rid her of negative thoughts. There was no point in rehashing her doubts. To escape, Julia knew she would need to stay mentally focused. Her body had been damaged by the fall, if her mind went she knew she was done for.

The forest was sparse enough to cut through as she made her way towards the bell tower. The forest whispered to her, it spoke to her with a hostile edge that should have forced her back. Instead, it spurred her on. The tower loomed over her, the last remnants of a church long since destroyed. Perhaps the only refuge on an island forsaken by God.

Julia wasn't interested in sanctuary. She assessed the best course of action and was ready to make a limped run for the trees when she heard the scream. It was a woman's scream. Distressed and tortured. Coming from inside the bell tower. *Ignore it. Run. Keep going.* It wasn't in her nature. She couldn't. She hobbled over to the door and looked inside. Darkness. She reached into her pocket. Her last glow stick. *Thanks, Aaron.* She squeezed it and threw it into the gloom.

The room lit up with a welcoming orange tint. The walls were grey with green crawling over. A broken staircase spiralled upwards, disappearing past the light into nothing. In the corner, a shadow sat curled up. Sobbing. Julia wasn't afraid. Not anymore. Not of what she had seen and certainly not of what was before her.

"Kirsty," she said.

The shadow crept towards the light. It revealed Kirsty's face, her cheeks stained with tears, dirt and small scratches.

"Julia?" she said. "Please, help me."

A great relief washed over Julia. Someone was still alive. But where were the others? Where was Lawrence? She had so many questions she wanted to ask. *Talk and walk, don't waste time. Keep moving, you're almost at the boat.*

"Kirsty, come with me. I've hurt my ankle but if you help me we can get to the boat a lot quicker." *Where the fuck is my husband?*

Kirsty stood up and shuffled towards her. Was Julia even real or another trick? *Trick,* the word stung her. There were no tricks here, only cruel games. The bell tower was no refuge, it never was. Not for Rossi. Not for Kirsty. Yes, move. Leave.

Get out. Tell her about Lawrence. *She'll kill me,* the shame of abandoning him was a stain on her conscience. The sudden realisation that Julia was also alone hit her.

"Julia…where's my brother?"

At that moment, they were the same. Two lost souls with loved ones gone. Even with what they had both seen, how would the other's story even make any sense?

"Kirsty…I'm sorry."

Grief savaged Kirsty as the words pierced her heart. Sorry? Sorry about what? Her own sins paled as she imagined the horrors that could have befallen her brother. With what she had seen, with what she had experienced, it frightened her to think her brother had been damned.

The same went for Julia. And no matter what the other endured on Poveglia, they would have been unable to comprehend it, even with what they themselves suffered.

"Lawrence?" Julia asked.

Kirsty bowed her head and shook it. A warm fury washed over Julia and took with it her fear. Her anger shot out at everything: the island, Kirsty, Lawrence, Aaron, Rino and finally herself. No targets were missed, there was enough hate to go around.

Use the hate. Let it fuel me. Grieve later. No tears. It's not the time for suffering. The island disagreed. It was born of despair. It thrived on it. Misery flourished on Poveglia as it devoured hope. Julia could sense it circle her as she stood looking at Kirsty. Her ankle burned with pain and it was nothing to her. Just an inconvenience.

"Kirsty," she said. "We're getting out of here. Now." They were both in silent agreement. There'd be time to shout at each other. Blame the other for their own loss. They each saw a chance at redemption if only they could at least save each other. By then they had both accepted Rino was gone. It wasn't feasible that he had survived alone while they endured such loss.

Kirsty moved towards Julia. Her own resolve wasn't as strong. The stench of guilt clung to her. She reeked of remorse. Of sorrow. Sadness dripped from her as she reached out to take Julia's hand. She had almost forgotten she was being chased when the bell tolled.

But what bell? The bell in the tower had long been destroyed. The noise echoed downwards and stunned them both. Julia grabbed Kirsty by the wrist and pulled her towards the door. Despite her injury, she was willing to drag Kirsty across the island if she had to. As Julia turned towards the door, the trees rustled with a violent fervour. It was too concentrated in one area to be the wind. A black mist emerged from the forest. It vaguely resembled a person as its form galvanised into something palpable. It resembled walking tar. A thick and viscous liquid dripped from its core and moulded into the figure of a person. Its faceless features didn't prevent it from oozing sheer malice. It radiated with hate and bitterness. Another victim of the island, although one which garnered no sympathy.

The options were limited. To return inside the bell tower meant the only place to go was up, and with that, only one direction - down. It was unlikely she could outrun the creature with her bad ankle.

Its head pulsated like a rapid heartbeat, twitching violently. It was a vile manifestation. Julia and Kirsty could sense the energy that pulsed from its centre. A move had to be made. Julia went for it. Her adrenaline did its best to mask her pain as she ran towards the trees. The creature extended an oily arm, slick with bile and grabbed her by the back of the neck. The air in her lungs abandoned her as she found herself on her back. The creature twisted its body as it hovered over her.

Kirsty cowered in the bell tower. The echo of its toll still in her heart. It was quickly replaced by Julia's cries for help. Kirsty wanted nothing more than to block them out. The anguish amplified her guilt. Everyone, including her brother, was dead because of her. She was the reason they were all on the island. She was the reason they wouldn't leave. She clasped her hands to her ears. It didn't help. She was unable to drown out the noise. She didn't deserve to. It wasn't right that she was to be absolved of the suffering. The pursuit of fear led her to Poveglia. It separated her from Aaron. It advised her to abandon Lawrence. It forced her to endure Julia's fear, making it her own.

What could she even do? After the thing took care of Julia, it would turn on her. The shame of her actions wouldn't let her run. She was empty. Nothing but remorse masquerading as a person.

It didn't have to be. A fire lit deep within her. What was before her eyes lay in the realm of the fantastical, yet it was real. The rules were gone. Nothing was certain unless she allowed it. Both of them weren't leaving the island. If one could, just one of them, then it would have to count for something.

She looked in the backpack, hoping it was still there. Unsure of what good it would do it was worth a shot. Anything was worth a shot. Her hand clasped around it. The flare. *Use it in case of emergency.* It certainly seemed like that to Kirsty.

Her legs trembled as she left the bell tower. The thing slithered over Julia salaciously, its form was more snake than man. She ignited the flare, a bright flame burst from her hand as the area lit up. The night burned red and Kirsty allowed herself a smile.

The thing stopped its attack on Julia and turned its attention towards Kirsty. It gazed upon her with a confused curiosity. An emotion flickered across it and its body rippled. Fear. It feared the flame in Kirsty's hand. It was frightened. But not undeterred. It wrapped newly formed tentacles of smoke around Julia's body and began to back away into the forest.

No, this wasn't how the story was going to end. Kirsty didn't know if she could hurt the monster, but she was going to give it her best shot. She let out a furious yell and ran towards the creature. The air before her was slashed open with the flare. The red flame cut through the dark as she aimed for the blackest part. She hit it. The flame ripped a tear in its blackened soul. Julia fell to the ground as the creature turned to mist. Kirsty stepped between Julia and her would-be captor. Brandishing the flare defiantly, she taunted the thing. She enjoyed her new-found authority.

"Get up," she said to Julia, "and run. Run as fast as you can." She looked behind her quickly as Julia struggled to her feet. "Go, I'll be right behind you."

Neither of them believed that. As Julia ran towards the trees, Kirsty maintained her threat. The thing swayed in the air as it melted into the night. The air was vilified with a spiteful glee as the surrounding forest encircled her. The creature carefully closed in on her. Looking for weakness. She was done running. She sought out adventure and excitement on Poveglia. She found much more than she could ever have hoped for. She found purpose. She allowed the mist to get closer and she struck. It might have been delirium. The island may have claimed her sanity in the end. Either way, she found herself enjoying the fight. She took pleasure knowing that it could be hurt. That she could make it squirm.

54

With one leg Julia moved as fast as she could. Her ankle was useless, unable to support her weight. She found herself dragging it through the soil. Behind her was the sound of agony. It was an ungodly cry of pain that chilled her. It also acted as a catalyst to keep moving. To not stop. She couldn't give up. She couldn't allow the deaths of anyone to be in vain. *Lawrence could still be alive. Rino even.* The weak optimism did nothing to spur her on. Her desire to escape was fuelled by loss, not by hope.

The cold air bit her as she reached the path. The ocean breeze stung her with an inhospitable welcome. She looked to her left and there it was. The boat. Thank God, it was still there. She dragged herself down the path, her left leg trailed through the dirt. A litany of voices echoed from behind her. They rooted for her, they scorned her. They warned her and pleaded with her not to leave. She didn't look back.

Her feet hit the wood of the dock and she collapsed. She turned, expecting to see the creature chasing her. There was nothing. A faint red glow purified the gloomy tree line. She watched it slowly die as the night claimed it.

Julia grabbed onto the boards and dragged herself across the dock. Her muscles ached and her soul was tired. *Don't give up now. Not now.* She stretched her arm out as far as it could. Her muscles hurt as they stretched out. Her fingers strained against their ligaments as the tips touched the hull.

Almost there. She forced herself to stand up straight and threw herself onto the boat. Landing on her side, she could feel it bruise from the impact. For the first time in what felt like forever, she felt safe. She looked at the island. It appeared wounded. She could feel it. Her eyes were heavy, but she refused to close them. The sudden realisation that she was no longer trapped on the island but trapped on the boat hit her. It was still tethered to the tier and she had no means to start the engine if there was even any fuel left, *unless Rino was tricked like they were*. As she sat herself up, her gaze was drawn to the pathway. Eye-level with the ground, she noticed it move. A dark mist rolled over the ground and towards the boat.

Julia bolted upright. She sat as far back as she could, knowing there was nowhere to go. The mist got nearer, she could swear she saw a face in it. A cruel and hateful grimace that stared right at her. When it approached the dock, it rose to tower above her. Unlike before if kept its vaporous form. It hovered in the air. Taunting her. Mocking her futile attempt at escaping.

She couldn't see eyes but knew it was staring at her and her it. A sinful abomination that knew only how to consume. The choppy water shook the boat. A terrible silence filled the air between her and the mist. Without warning, it lunged at her, its coils wrapped around her face. Its thick smog prevented her from breathing. The lack of oxygen made her panic. Her body spasmed as she failed to get any air into her lungs. All the while she could see its atrocity of a face. A calculating precision flashed across it. There were many voices, gleeful.

Supporting. Encouraging. They faded along with her vision. It was time to rest. For Julia to close her eyes and embrace that final sleep. It was almost peaceful. She felt little regret as the tranquillity dominated her.

As her eyes closed, there was a red flash followed by an animalistic growl. She fell back onto the boat, unaware that she had even been lifted from her position. The mist had dispersed leaving a thin layer floating above the dock. On her knees beyond that veil was Kirsty. A flare in one hand, an old doll in another. Crimson tears ran down her cheeks as her mouth was curled into a smile. She leaned forward and placed the flare against the rope that tethered the boat. It burned so gloriously. The mist returned, a viscid excretion of evil. It attacked Kirsty and dragged her back towards the asylum.

Julia tried to scream, but she could barely breathe. It was a struggle to inhale and her body was limp. The rope snapped and the boat began to leave the dock. Julia looked up to see the mist halt in its path. From the darkness, more shadows emerged. Dark figures circled the thing that attacked her. With a wave of ferocious anger, they swarmed on the mist. A vivid mural of black fought in battle as the creature found itself being torn apart by the shadows.

As a strong current took her from the island, she caught one last glimpse of it. Behind the asylum lay another part of the island. A bridge connected the two parts. On that bridge was a familiar figure, one she'd hoped she had seen the last of. The Plague Doctor stood on the bridge. Hand outstretched, it sprinkled something into the water. Julia lay down on the floor of the boat and looked up at the stars. They looked so beautiful yet so alien. What gratified her the most was how clear the sky was. Not a cloud to be seen. She took one last look, savouring its beauty. And closed her eyes.

Acknowledgements

Writing is a solitary experience but getting a book ready for publication requires all the help you can get.

Jen, thanks for telling me what didn't work and for being understanding and patient as I became more obsessed with Poveglia than any of the characters did. I still think we should take a boat to go see it when we finally get to Venice. Love you.

Ian, if not for you the last book wouldn't have sold as well as it did. With little direction from myself, you're able to capture the tone of the story and give me chills with the art you create.

Vhairi, you continue to know what it is I want to say and are able to word it in ways I didn't think of. Publish your books!

Marc, for offering to proofread and the videos of motivation. That I live in a world where Bret Hart and Sharon Angela know I wrote this book is madness.

Richard, I pestered you with blurb ideas late at night and you helped me craft the right one.

Paul, your nautical knowledge was invaluable. It's one thing being able to Google the correct term but it's another to go straight to the source.

Chris and Mark, you were able to take me on a tour of the island from the comfort of my own living room thanks to your documentary, Island of the Dead.

Last but not least, to all that read and continue to promote my work. The book would be nothing without a reader.

About the author

Thomas Simpson was born in Glasgow, Scotland where he currently resides. He wrote and directed the short film, I, Alive, which premiered at the Glasgow Film Festival in 2011. His debut horror novella, *One of Us*, was published in 2019 and was praised with five-star reviews. He's a massive fan of Metallica and believes *Jaws* to be the greatest film ever made.

You can find him on Twitter @Simmy41

Printed in Great Britain
by Amazon